BY NATURE EQUAL

Josep Maria Espinàs

BY NATURE
EQUAL

Translated from the Catalan
by Anthony Bonner

PANTHEON

Original Catalan edition published by
Aymà S.A. Editora, Barcelona,
under the title of *Tots som iguals*

English translation © 1961 by Pantheon Books, Inc.
333 Sixth Avenue, New York 14, N.Y.
Library of Congress Catalog Card No.: 61-7458
Manufactured in the U.S.A.
by H. Wolff Book Mfg. Co., New York, N.Y.

*Le problème de l'écrivain
revient à rendre compte des
difficultés humaines.*

ROGER IKOR

TRANSLATOR'S NOTE

BECAUSE THE LANGUAGE *in which this novel was written, Catalan, is unfamiliar to most English-speaking readers, a few words of explanation might prove helpful.*

Proper names have for the most part been given in their Catalan rather than Spanish form. Usually this involves only a slightly altered spelling, and only occasionally, as in the case of Lleida for the town of Lérida, is the form not immediately recognizable. Also some ordinary words have been given their Catalan spelling, as for instance Senyor *instead of* Señor *(in this case, the pronunciation is almost identical).*

The only thing which might seem really unusual to the reader, however, is the so-called "personal article," as for example En Pere Jordana, L'Alsina. *In origin it is similar to the Spanish* Don, *but it has lost all connotations of social distinction, and is used before every name (except when someone is being addressed directly, as, for instance, "How are you, Pere?"). With names beginning with consonants, it is* En *in the masculine and* La *in the feminine (En Pere and La Maria); before names beginning with vowels, however, it takes the form* L' *for both genders (L'Alsina and L'Isabel). This personal article has been retained in the translation for the same reason as, from the French,* Monsieur Dupont *would be retained in its original form rather than rendered as Mr. Dupont, and also because this part of speech forms such an essential and characteristic part of the Catalan language that leaving it out would seem like an unnecessary weakening of the flavor of the original.*

ONE

THE ASSISTANT bookkeeper was sitting at his desk. His head was bent forward displaying a bald scalp of a disturbing yellow color. The assistant bookkeeper looked like a wilted sunflower in the late afternoon.

He had, moreover, the ability to ignore any noise or movement that took place in the office. If someone bumped into a chair, or if someone sneezed—and everyone sneezed in that humid subterranean room, for it was the only way occasionally to expel some of the water that entered with every breath—the assistant bookkeeper remained lost in his devotion to his work. He lived at his desk like Robinson Crusoe on his desert island. What went on around him did not exist.

But there would arrive a moment in which the assistant bookkeeper came into contact with the outside world. This happened when the hour of irresistible thirst struck.

The irresistible thirst occurred at midday at ten to one, and again in the afternoon at ten to seven. Then the parade of office boys past his table made him raise his eyes. There would go En Miquel from Sales, L'Artemi from Statistics, En Joan from the Invoice Department, the other Joan from the Accounting Department, and also all the warehouse clerks, one after the other. The thirst was vast, impressive, and very grave. The water jug was way in the back of the office, next to the coat racks. They went to and from their drinking with a majestic slowness, with exemplary dignity, as if they had just taken communion or as if the water were sitting inside their stomachs like a brick.

9

The assistant bookkeeper would watch them pass by stupefied, with his mouth open and the yellow color of his scalp growing paler.

But for anyone who was not an assistant bookkeeper, the secret was easy to penetrate: five yards before arriving at the water jug there was a round clock hanging on the wall. At ten to one and at ten to seven the office boys noticed that their mouths were dry. Boys aren't like grown people. They are full of mystery and strange needs, of weaknesses and peculiarities and exacting secretions.

They would walk in a line down the corridor toward the water jug. With five yards still to go, they would raise their eyes, as if by chance, and look at the clock on the wall. Every one of them. One after the other. It was a strange thing: the longer it was before one o'clock, the longer they would drink at the water jug and the slower and more majestically they would return to their places.

One day, a peculiar thing happened to L'Artemi from Statistics. He had been seized by a diabolical, alarming thirst. As he passed in front of the clock, he raised his eyes as if by chance. It was almost one o'clock. And then the miracle happened: his terrible thirst suddenly disappeared. He did not advance one inch farther toward the water jug. He went back to his corner, but this time in a headlong dash. He had just enough time to slip his books and pencils into his desk drawers and stand there listening, ecstatically, as if waiting for something: then with a sound like nervous laughter the bell for the lunch hour rang.

En Pere Jordana was checking invoices. By then his hand was already tired. He tried to move his little finger without moving the others, but he couldn't. The little finger seemed to drag the others along with it, and set in motion a general, vague trembling.

It was then that he understood his good fortune—that of occupying a relatively independent office, one situated in a corner seldom visited by Senyor Alsina. For the office manager would make sudden raids among the desks of the personnel and, with a

10

peculiar power of penetration, discover, for example, whose hand was tired.

En Pere Jordana rested his hand out flat on the desk for a few seconds and tried to think of nothing. He immediately felt a pinching sensation inside his stomach; he was hungry. Usually it got no worse, but sometimes he would feel two pinching sensations. He told himself that it would perhaps be better to think of something. The place that En Manelet usually occupied—in front of him, on the other side of the big desk—was empty. That is to say, it was slightly more empty than usual, for poor Manelet scarcely filled it at all. He was as thin as a reed on a river bank, and one could tell he was sixteen only by his height. For he had recently devoted himself to growing. So much so that En Pere Jordana was afraid that the boss might possibly notice it. In case this should ever happen, he had suggested to En Manelet a prudent answer he could give: "It's true that I'm growing a lot, Senyor Joaquim, but I assure you that I do it at home. Here I do nothing but devote myself to my job, Senyor Joaquim."

En Manelet entered, drying his lips with a handkerchief rolled up in a ball. He had gone to get a drink of water, obviously, but En Pere still asked him:

"What time is it?"

"Six and a half minutes to one, Senyor Pere."

The office was basically an enormous room twenty-five feet high, divided off by six-foot partitions into ten or twelve smaller offices. In the center there was a larger compartment for the lowlier clerks—the tight-jacket and faded-necktie team. Above was a skylight which let pass a light so gray as to appear to be made of transparent shadow, and this was why each desk had a little lamp which was kept lit all afternoon. One could never tell when it was raining or when the sun was out. But the management had not been able to avoid the thunderclaps' being heard when there was a storm. The management had calculated that there was an average of thirty-eight thunderclaps a year, and that since each man raised his head and took six seconds to lower it again, plus two seconds to readjust to his work, they lost five minutes and four seconds per man per year.

"That jacket's a little small on you, Manelet," observed En Pere Jordana.

"Yes, Senyor Pere."

Perhaps his wife had kept some old one he could give him. En Manelet was now just about the same height as he.

En Manelet looked at En Pere's immobile hands, and En Pere looked at En Manelet's immobile hands. The eyes of the one seemed to say to the hands of the other: "Wait, wait. It's almost lunchtime."

And between their fingers their pencils stood up straight, stiff, and uncontrollable.

Finally the bell rang, and when it stopped there arose an excited buzz of voices—and one of the boys, after getting up momentum, went out at great speed, skidding along with his legs apart and his arms stretched out like an airplane.

En Pere Jordana passed his hands through his hair and went out into the corridor. L'Alsina, the office manager, was looking for him. L'Alsina, the office manager, was a man whose clothes fitted him properly and who was always patting the pockets of his jacket with a certain air of complacency—one might think he did it only to hear the sound of keys, the symbol of his august mission.

"Pere," he said, "Senyor Joaquim wants to see you."

En Pere put his hands on the knot of his tie—that knot that every day became more compressed and more wrinkled, like a dried raisin—and said:

"Senyor Joaquim? Wants me?"

"Yes," affirmed the office manager with that peculiar smile of his which seemed to indicate that he was constantly distributing extraordinary favors.

En Manelet, who felt a great sense of respect toward the office manager, left hugging the wall without looking back, and he managed to make himself thinner than ever.

En Pere Jordana followed Senyor Alsina, the office manager, to Senyor Joaquim's office. En Pere Jordana had been working there for twenty years—he was now thirty-five—and it would never have occurred to him to ask the office manager why Senyor Joaquim wanted to see him. When the boss called in an employee it was always best to immerse oneself immediately in a respectful silence and prepare one's spirit.

En Pere Jordana walked with his eyes fixed on Senyor Alsina's shoes, which squeaked with the insolence of all new shoes. It was a *nyick-nyick* which almost hypnotized him, and just then he would have liked to be far from there, lying in a small, perfumed grove, chewing a blade of grass and listening to the crickets. . . .

"Just a minute," said the office manager.

He knocked on the door. He waited a minute, then pushed it a bit. He went inside the office and, trying to glide along as silently as possible, he went up to Senyor Joaquim's desk. From his timid way of advancing, it looked as if, in order to humble himself properly and acknowledge his total subordination and insignificance, he was trying to walk forward with the same body movements one would normally use walking backward.

After waiting ten minutes for Senyor Joaquim to look up at him, he said:

"En Pere Jordana is waiting for your instructions, Senyor Joaquim."

"Tell him to come in."

The office manager took six steps backward—now giving the impression that he was walking on his knees—and opened the door for En Pere Jordana, the assistant clerk.

It had now been going on for three and a half minutes.

The first fifteen seconds had been the worst. En Pere had been waiting for Senyor Joaquim to question him from one moment to the next.

After a minute his pulse had come back to normal.

Three minutes had already gone by. Now it seemed as if this was what he had come for, as if Senyor Joaquim would never raise his head, or look at him, or say anything to him. The boss must occasionally feel lonely—after all there was only one boss—and surely he must like to have company. "I know how to do that —keep someone company. It's too bad that after standing up for five minutes I always start to tremble." It was a very slight little trembling in the left leg, below the knee.

Senyor Alsina, the office manager, stood between the boss and the employee. That half of his face visible to the boss maintained a rigorous, taut immobility. That half visible to En Pere Jordana had a soft, benevolent quality, as if to say: "Now you will have the opportunity to listen to Senyor Joaquim."

Senyor Joaquim moved the paper he was studying over to the right, placed his silver four-colored pencil delicately on top of it, clasped his hands, and uttered his first word:

"Jordana."

Just that.

He had hardly raised his eyes. En Pere Jordana recognized the dry sound of his voice, the dark line of his eyebrows, the implacable coldness of his mouth, and the humiliating manner of not looking at the person to whom he was talking. With horrifying precision, he thought: "This man's inhuman."

"Jordana," repeated the boss.

"Yes, Senyor Joaquim."

He once again considered the dryness of his voice, the hardness of his eyebrows, the coldness of his mouth, and he made a correction in his thoughts: "Senyor Joaquim is occupied with important problems; Senyor Joaquim doesn't want to offend his inferiors by a false politeness; Senyor Joaquim is perhaps planning some improvement for his employees."

"Jordana," he said, "you know that we have offices in Saragossa and Santander. I've decided . . ."—"He's decided, he's decided something, and now he's going to tell me what he's decided," En

14

Pere realized with great joy.—"I've decided to leave the day after tomorrow, Thursday, to make a quick tour of inspection."

Finally he raised his eyes. En Pere Jordana was about to say: "No, no, don't trouble yourself"; but he had already raised his eyes, and was saying:

"You'll be going with me."

With the tips of two fingers of his left hand he picked up a file card he had placed to one side and said, looking at it distractedly:

"You have a driver's license."

"Yes, Senyor Joaquim."

Ah, those marvellous, incomparably useful file cards!

This piece of paper had had a curious life. The year 1935 contained the first inscriptions: JORDANA FIGUERES, PERE. DOMICILE: *Príncep de Viana, 5, 2nd floor, Apt. 1. Born 18/5/20.* DISEASES: *measles, gastric fever.* VACCINATIONS: *smallpox and diphtheria.* EDUCATION: *Business courses at the Acadèmia Cots. Elementary French.* Announcing his knowledge of French this way had been an understandable vanity on the part of young Jordana. It went on: MARITAL STATUS: *Bachelor,* and where it said CHILDREN he had thought it only proper to put a horizontal line. And where it said PROFESSIONAL CATEGORY: *Apprentice.*

Under the year 1936 the word *partisan* had been written in red ink.

Under the year 1939, after crossing out the red *partisan,* there had been entered in blue ink: *partisan.*

Under the year 1941 there was a new inscription: *Recommended for the position of second-class assistant.*

Under the year 1942 there were two inscriptions: *Typhus* and *Punctual in his work.*

Under the year 1943: *Second-class assistant.*

Four years without annotations. In 1947: *Married to Maria Castelló Andújar.*

In 1948: *Requests for advances on salary.*

In 1949: On the horizontal line next to CHILDREN was written: *One*.

And then in the square next to the year: *Requests for advances*.

In 1950 there were three inscriptions: *Appendix operation, Promoted to first-class assistant*, and *Requests for advances*.

In 1951 two: *Obtained driver's license* and *Requests for advances*.

In 1952 only one: *Requests for advances*.

In 1953 the indication *"Requests for advances"* had been abbreviated to *Req. adv.* The cashier's office had found it too much trouble to write it out on every card.

The year 1954 revealed: *Requests to do overtime* and *Req. adv.*

The year 1955 didn't have an inscription yet. . . .

Senyor Joaquim picked up the silver four-colored pencil he had laid down on his desk and wrote in the still immaculate column under 1955: *Req. adv.*

"Jordana," he said, "besides having your driver's license, are you, in practice, capable of driving an automobile?"

"Yes, Senyor Joaquim."

"Are you accustomed to driving?"

En Pere Jordana did not hesitate.

"Yes, Senyor Joaquim. On my days off I drive a truck for a factory in Poble Nou. . . ."

And immediately he was sorry he'd said it; he felt as if he were accusing Senyor Joaquim of not paying him enough and making it necessary for him to work on Sundays. He was ready to deny it and say that he didn't need to work—that he did it for his own amusement, not for money, for the fact of the matter was that in a whole morning of driving he only made forty pesetas. . . .

"The trip will last ten or twelve days, Jordana. Take along whatever you'll need, naturally, but try to have it all fit into one suitcase, a small suitcase. Remember: the day after tomorrow, Thursday morning. . . ."

16

En Pere Jordana started to retreat. Before he had got too far, Senyor Joaquim, from behind his desk, pointed his silver four-colored pencil at him—a gesture which was a particular proof of confidence—and said:

"Tonight, after closing time, pass by my house and the chauffeur will help you get acquainted with the Stromberg. You'll be doing all the driving, because the chauffeur's staying here with my wife's Fiat."

And suddenly he brought the pencil down again.

Like an energetic baton which imposes silence on the orchestra . . .

Behind En Pere Jordana, L'Alsina, the office manager, was going out, and the farther he got from Senyor Joaquim—that is to say, the farther he went in regaining his independence—the broader and broader grew the office manager's condescending smile.

In the middle of the deserted office he put a hand on En Pere Jordana's arm and murmured, with a kind of make-believe complicity:

"Well done, Jordana! It's part of my job to suggest some name to the head office from time to time. They're so above it all that . . . But now don't let *me* down."

It was a warm, clear afternoon. The light that entered through the overhead window came down full of sunlight. But just as the blood sometimes leaves a man's face, the sun left the light as it passed through the glass, to settle on the desks and the typewriters, on the file cabinets and calendars, and on the heads of two tiny men—gray, sad, and frightened.

"WE'LL ALL go blind in this house."

It was one of En Pere Jordana's habitual prophecies. Another habitual prophecy was: "If we don't send him to a proper school, that kid'll turn out to be a complete idiot."

Just then he was looking for a necktie in the bedroom closet.

"We'll go blind, Maria, blind. I don't understand why we haven't already gone blind."

La Maria folded and refolded a shirt in order to fit it into a little suitcase.

"It's a very gray day today, Pere."

"Even if it were bright red, you tell *me* where the light's going to come in."

There was one small window facing a tiny courtyard which looked like a huge filing cabinet. The iron window gratings were rusted. The walls were eaten by a strange kind of humid measles.

"Turn on the light, will you?"

La Maria turned on the light. This was their best room. It had a *Chippendale* bed. One day their child had broken off a bit of veneer from the foot of the bed, and that night En Pere had dreamed that this had laid bare the words . . . *kling Champagne*. There was a standing closet, a dressing table, two chairs, a glass lamp, a plaster statue of the Virgin Mary, and a framed photograph of a young man with a flower in his buttonhole and a girl with a bouquet in her hand. The photograph was taken on a Sunday and behind the modestly dressed couple one could make out some very elegant gentlemen and determined-looking women going in to hear twelve-o'clock mass.

Every inch of space in the room was therefore occupied. In order to open the closet, one had to sit on the bed, and every time he did this En Pere banged his ankle on a corner of the closet. He felt sure that doing this for eight years had been the cause of the trembling in his knee.

He had found his necktie.

"Here, put this in the suitcase."

He could have sworn that it looked newer, for it had been a long time now since he had worn it.

La Maria turned off the light. In fact, it made little difference. Before, they had used forty-watt bulbs, but La Maria had thought it best to save money and had changed them for fifteen-watt bulbs. This had brought on the following dialogue between husband and wife: "How much did you pay for the fifteen-watt bulbs?" "Twenty-one and a half pesetas." "You call that saving?" "But I managed to sell the forty-watt bulbs." "How much did they give you for them?" "Nine pesetas. I asked for ten and they wanted to give me eight." "So we lost twelve pesetas." "But now we'll be spending less and pretty soon we'll have made it back." When things got to this point, En Pere said no more; he passed his hand over his cheek and decided it was absurd to argue about something that was over and done with.

"How many shirts did you pack, Maria?"

"I can't pack more than you've got."

En Pere was a little vague about such things—like all men, he supposed. La Maria, on the other hand, never thought of "shirts" in general, but concretely of the gray one he'd only just got last Christmas; the beige one with dark stripes whose collar she had already turned and on which she had mended a big hole on the right side, near the second button; and the white one with the thread-bare cuffs.

While En Pere was tying his shoes, the child entered the bedroom. He was six years old, his lower lip protruded a bit—hung out and down like a little balcony—and he walked slightly pigeon-toed. He had clear, sensitive eyes.

"Don't forget your lunch," his mother reminded him.

He pointed to a little package which made a bulge in his pants.

"Come, give Daddy a kiss and hurry off so you won't be late."

When he drew near, En Pere stretched out his arms and lifted him up level with his chest. As he kissed him on the forehead, he thought that it would be eight or ten days before he would again feel his rough hair against his cheek. It would be nice if these eight or ten days with Senyor Joaquim would serve some purpose, bring about some results such as, for example, a raise in salary and the possibility of having another child like this one, who would also place his rough hair against his cheek.

"All right now, be a good boy, huh?"

While his father was holding him up in the air, the boy was looking out of the corner of his eye at the suitcase on the bed. He looked at it with deep curiosity and unconscious pride, and later on, at school, he would explain that his father had left on a trip, one of those important trips that required a suitcase.

"When I come back, your mother'll tell me whether or not you've been a good boy."

He put him down and gave him a whack on the nape of his neck, in a somewhat brusque outburst of affection.

"All right now, don't be late."

From the window La Maria watched him cross the street and enter the National School. En Pere ran a comb through his hair, once, then a second time, and said:

"If we don't send him to a proper school, that kid'll turn out to be a complete idiot."

For he didn't need to give little Pere Jordana a name; he was the "kid." The only possible kid, as things then stood, in the apartment on Príncep de Viana with its fifteen-watt bulbs and its *Chippendale* bed.

It was nine in the morning and the sun had scarcely warmed the air. Joaquim Civit's suburban house, on the heights of Pedral-bes, between the earth and the sky, between the city and the country, seemed to be covered with a fine layer of gold wrapped in silk. The railing, the fruit trees along the driveway, the porch, and the roof were all of the same color—a delicate shade between yellow and rose.

From somewhere came the noise of a dog barking. It was a

happy barking, as if someone were bringing him a plate of steaming potatoes, or as if his master, as he left for work, had scratched him on the head.

En Joaquim Civit could hear the dog from his house and he shut the window. He was sitting behind his desk in his ground-floor office. He had just shaved and there was a faint rose color on his cheeks, as if, in spite of his being seated with his back to the light, the newborn day wanted to place some small part of its joy on his skin.

The office was a large room with a huge bronze lamp and dark red curtains. His desk was covered with a sheet of black glass, and on top of the glass there were an inkwell, a blotter, a little letter file, and a leather portfolio. And there was also a brief case, into which En Joaquim Civit was putting his papers.

When he had finished putting them in, he closed it and looked at the bookcase in front of him, to the rear of the room. There were forty or fifty books bound in greenish leather, which he had inherited from an uncle who had a mania for reading. They took up three shelves. On the bottom shelf there was a *History of Civilization* in twelve volumes, and an encyclopedic dictionary in nine volumes which En Joaquim Civit had bought on his own personal initiative when he had moved into the house. In any case he had no regrets about it, for they were books that would always be of value.

He looked at the books without seeing them. He thought about business matters, whether or not he had forgotten to give some last-minute piece of advice, whether L'Alsina, the office manager, would know how to take care of things.

Someone knocked on the door and opened it. Slowly but forcefully. En Joaquim Civit saw his wife standing in the doorway, and he looked at her. She said:

"Your suitcase is ready."

"Is everything in it?"

It was an absurd question, for since he had no idea of what

should go into it, there was nothing of which he could remind his wife.

"Your breakfast is ready, too."

En Joaquim Civit picked up his brief case, got up, and went into the dining room. His wife waited for him to leave the ground-floor office—slowly revolving her head and thereby always facing him like a soldier when a general is passing. She then went out behind him and closed the door.

La Remedios—with her white hairnet on, and moving in a vague sort of way, as if she were still wrapped in some of the mist from her native Asturias—had put at the senyor's usual place at the table the cup of milk and the four small cakes, the little plate with jam and the half of a toasted roll.

En Joaquim Civit unfolded his napkin and . . .

"Has En Jordana arrived?" he asked.

"Yes. At a quarter to nine."

His wife always followed along behind him at a magic distance —neither so far as no longer to be with him, nor so near that one could say definitely that she was with him—so as to be with him and not with him at the same time, depending on the circumstances.

Of the four small cakes, En Joaquim Civit normally ate three, but he always wanted four in front of him, just in case. He only took a taste of the jam, and that he did on doctor's orders: it was a laxative, and he was a man who suffered a bit from constipation.

"What's that, Lluïsa?"

A shock of fear went through her body. Every time he said "What's that?" it was because something wasn't right and she was to blame for its not being right. When it came to things that weren't right, En Joaquim Civit had keen, unfailing eyesight.

When they were first married, she had always answered: "What?" Now she knew that there was a better solution: immediately to look for the faulty detail, correct it, and keep quiet.

For this reason she went over to the armchair and picked up the

22

package containing the lunch that their child, En Joaquim Maria, had forgotten on his way to school.

"Did he forget his lunch again?" asked En Joaquim Civit, placing a mouthful of cake soaked in milk on his tongue. "Whose is it—En Joaquim Maria's?"

Yes. En Joaquim Maria, the oldest, had lost has appetite ever since he had caught that cold. But in any case, he had never had much appetite. L'Eduard Maria, who was in his second year at college, ate quite a bit more. En Lluís Maria, who had started his commercial studies, had a habit of smacking his lips like a street urchin. Every morning, all three would leave at a quarter to eight when the school bus came by to pick them up. The girls left later, at a quarter to nine: Maria dels Àngels crying and Maria dels Reis laughing.

"What's the weather like, Lluïsa?" asked En Joaquim Civit.

"It's quite a nice day."

"Good," he thought. "Let's see how the car will run and how En Jordana will work out. He seems to be a sensible young man. It's too bad he's got into the habit of writing *Requests for Advances* against his salary. But he isn't the only one who does it; workers nowadays aren't the way they used to be."

"Where will you have lunch, Joaquim?"

"At Saragossa. I'll send you a telegram; don't worry."

He drank the little bit of milk that remained in his cup, dried his lips with his napkin—one, two, three, four times, with an insistence and energy out of all proportion to what he had eaten—and as he got up he said in a slightly lower voice:

"In the strongbox"—he meant the one in the office—"I've left five thousand pesetas in case you need it."

In the course of their married life this situation had come up six or seven times, and his wife had never even touched five céntimos of it. It was well understood that when he returned he would find the money intact, and that he announced the presence of these five thousand pesetas only so that she could rescue them in case the house caught on fire.

23

En Pere Jordana had been sitting in the hallway of the house for half an hour without daring to light a cigarette. He thought that perhaps Senyor Joaquim didn't smoke, and he therefore felt it was wrong to do so in his house.

He had taken the car out of the garage and left his suitcase in the trunk. He had immediately gone up to the house and installed himself in the hall, thinking the boss might need him for bringing down his suitcase, brief case, or something.

In front of him, on the wall, there was a copy of a very famous picture whose title he couldn't remember. Those two men in period costumes about to embrace one another and exchange a key . . . Every time he saw something historical with a key in it, he didn't know why, but it would remind him of Guzmán "the Good."

He didn't dare smoke, nor did he dare get up for fear of seeming impatient. He went on examining all the objects in the hall —a strange little iron chest, plates on the wall with peculiar inscriptions, the two figures embracing one another, one blue- and the other rose-colored, fragile-looking, and a standing lamp more or less in the form of a gilded angel—and he thought that if the entire house were so full of old things, which were the things that were really valuable, this must be a museum, and he should be careful to move with the greatest caution so as not to break anything. But then look how Senyor Joaquim was when it came to practical matters; he really should have been driving around in a carriage, but instead he had decided to buy a Stromberg. And make no mistake about it, En Pere Jordana would have preferred accompanying him in a carriage, for then it would have taken him longer to return to the office and to Senyor Alsina, the office manager, and to En Manelet, who was growing so fast and was so thin. . . .

"Good morning, Jordana."

"Good morning, Senyor Joaquim!"

En Joaquim Civit had said good-by to his wife before stepping out into the hall. She knew that she was to follow him no farther, that from that moment on En Joaquim belonged to another world, and that perhaps Joaquim Civit's authority in that other world could be shattered through an inopportune kiss.

THREE

As HE PRESSED down on the accelerator—gently, so as not to give Senyor Joaquim a jolt—he told himself that he now had only one obligation: to drive as well as possible. For two days now he had been obsessed by this idea.

Upon getting up he had lived through the worst moments of anxiety. He had not experienced such a sensation since the day of his marriage. Then, as now, he had been afraid of falling into some sudden disaster. At noon of that day, when it was all over and he was alone with La Maria in the taxi, the anguish had passed and he discovered that he went on living, and that, when you thought about it, things had turned out much more agreeably than he had expected.

He felt as if his nerves—or something resembling his nerves— were tied in knots, but as he pressed down on the accelerator and turned the steering wheel, slowly and firmly, at the first corner, he suddenly relaxed and realized that it was a matter of doing something very easy.

"What time have you got, Jordana?"

He stretched out his arm a bit on the steering wheel, and his watch appeared.

"Nine thirty-five."

"I've got nine thirty-eight. It would probably be best for us to synchronize our watches."

Taking advantage of a straight stretch, En Jordana set his watch ahead three minutes. He never doubted for a moment that it was his watch that should be synchronized with Senyor Joaquim's.

His thin bony arm remained stretched out on the steering wheel. He had never liked to look at his arms with their sad, grayish skin. Now he was wearing his jacket and the cuffs of his shirt were clean, and his skin was not quite so sad as in the morning when he had washed in the washtub in the hallway and could see the bones sticking out below his neck before he put back on the undershirt that was hanging behind the door.

Without losing sight of the road, he glanced out of the corner of his eye at Senyor Joaquim's hands, resting on his knees. His hands were delicately rounded and hairless, and without knowing why, En Jordana imagined that, like two *brioches,* one could soak them in a glass of milk.

The car was running perfectly. They probably used it hardly at all—it had scarcely any mileage on it.

He heard Senyor Joaquim sigh—he had now moved his hands up to his stomach—and he realized that he had never been so near him, and even less for such a long time. Entire days next to his boss. Basically he didn't find this unpleasant. In the first place, it would mean eight or ten days without being shut up in that office, eight or ten days of seeing the sun and rain, and real sun and rain—not just the shadow of the sun or the shadow of the rain on the gray glass of the skylight. Then there would be meals in restaurants, different cities they would see, and the vermouths they would have . . . but no, it wasn't this that he liked best, it was the business of the sun and rain, which cost nothing but which he had missed for years. He wanted to ask Senyor Joaquim precisely how many days of life he had left: eight, nine, ten, eleven, or twelve. Or perhaps it was better not to know—and keep his eyes open.

"It's a nice day," he said, thinking out loud. He immediately looked more attentively at the stretch of road in front of him.

"Very nice. . . ."

Senyor Joaquim's hands, for just a moment, bounced nervously on his knees.

"We'll be on the highway in a minute, won't we?"

"Yes, Senyor."

"Don't go over fifty. We're in no hurry."

The milk was making a *blup-blup* inside Senyor Joaquim's stomach. It had been just a bit too hot.

He began to think that En Pere Jordana would turn out well. He seemed to have the gift of not being a nuisance. He did not talk unnecessarily, and when one thought about it, he was right about its being a nice day. Toward the right there were long thin clouds, but now the highway made a turn and the clouds slipped around behind and disappeared from the window. A good omen.

The *blup-blup* of the milk reminded him that, in any case, trips had never agreed with him. His partner, En Maurici, would have found this trip more to his liking, but his father's illness had come at an inopportune moment. But let's not think about illness, he said to himself. He reached into his pocket and opened the little silver box his wife had given him five or six years before on his saint's day. These pills were supposed to stave off carsickness. He thought of offering one to En Jordana, but then decided against it. On the one hand, it would be best to see that he didn't get sick during the trip, but if he usually got carsick he undoubtedly would have brought along his own pills. He realized that his desk still remained between the two of them and he shut the little box—with a little click, that scarcely audible click produced by things made of silver.

En Pere Jordana would have loved to know what in the devil it was that Senyor Joaquim had put in his mouth. At first he had thought he was going to smoke, but without looking he knew that he didn't have a cigarette between his lips. Probably a piece of candy. He had heard that rich people had a propensity for sugar, for sweet things. Perhaps this was why his hands were pink and clammy.

It was strange. He had never had such ridiculous thoughts before. In fact, until now, he had never had time to think.

He arranged himself slightly more comfortably in the seat. He looked around. The green of the trees was frankly green, greener

27

than the plane trees on the Ronda. Or at least it would seem so. A couple—the man with his arm around the girl's shoulder—got nearer, nearer . . . now they were behind. He had only noticed that the girl had blond hair and that the man was pushing a bicycle. They seemed possessed by a feeling of complete calm. One might have thought they never intended to arrive anywhere; he could have sworn one of them had been smiling. And undoubtedly things like this went on every day, while he sat in the office like a dead man. Like a dead man. Like a dead man. That was exactly how it was.

He rolled down the window and rested his elbow on the ledge. The wind blew against his elbow; it felt cool. It seemed to go right through his skin and up the bone of his arm. It spread out through his body, like an *anís,* like a new sense of joy. If there was such a thing as a soul, it was now in the tip of his elbow.

En Jordana had lowered his window just as they passed a farmhouse, and a terrible stench of manure reached Senyor Joachim, making a kind of warm knot form in his stomach. "These people" —he was thinking of En Jordana—"never get carsick; they don't have an ounce of sensitivity. But that's the way the world is; it would be ridiculous to try to change it."

The little boy—he must have been six or seven—shot out from the side of the road on a corner and went headlong toward the wheels of the car. At first, it seemed absurd, incomprehensible. It seemed as if the car wheels had acted like a magnet, or like the eye of a hypnotic hunter, to which the child had surrendered himself like some poor, defenseless bird.

En Pere Jordana swung the wheel violently, just in time, and between the car and the child there remained an ever so thin layer of air; it had saved him, but not without knocking the wind out of him as if someone had punched him.

"Goddamn kids!" En Pere shouted, and, bringing the car over to the side of the road, he stopped and stuck his head out of the window.

28

The child was still immobile in the middle of the road with a wild look in his eyes, and then from around the corner there appeared four other urchins, all running with a stone in each hand. When they saw the one they had been chasing, alone and unprotected, they stoned him enthusiastically amid animallike shouts. The lone combatant felt the rocks hit him and took refuge behind a tree. His cheek was beautifully painted with blood. He found his stones still in his pockets, and stretched back his arm, his heart throbbing with joy.

En Pere started up the car, and one could see in his eyes and lips that he was angry.

"What happened, Jordana?" Senyor Joaquim asked—he hadn't turned around to look.

"Nothing. Kids playing."

And now in his voice there was profound pity and also terrible fear. He swore to himself that he would drive through towns at twenty-five kilometers an hour as the signs said.

Yes, kids playing. Grownups playing too. Everybody with his own little game.

"I'd get over this slight nervousness if I could smoke." He had brought along eight packs of cigarettes. Six in his suitcase and two in his coat pocket. He knew that he could smoke and drive at the same time; it didn't bother him a bit. On Sundays, when he drove the truck, he would smoke almost a whole pack. And even when he wasn't smoking, he would leave the butt in his mouth, and the odor of burned tobacco, along with the sensation of touching the little piece of paper with his tongue, used to give him a deep sense of confidence. But Senyor Joaquim hadn't smoked since they left Barcelona. Then he realized that he couldn't remember ever having seen Senyor Joaquim smoke.

He looked at him out of the corner of his eye. He seemed to be half asleep, with his head falling forward. "I'm sure he doesn't smoke." He immediately felt an irresistible desire to smoke. His mouth was dry, and he gripped the steering wheel with his arms out straight. Senyor Joaquim had a placid expression on his face.

His eyes were shut and his lips were moving, as if he were dreaming or thinking of something.

Slowly, En Pere put his left hand inside his pocket, opened the package, and held down the other cigarettes with three fingers while with his two remaining fingers he tried to pull one out by the tip. "You idiot! Either you give up the idea, or you stick one in your mouth and light up without worrying." But it was someone else saying this. Finally he drew his hand out of his pocket and put the cigarette between his lips.

While he was looking for a match, he thought about the fact that no one had ever prohibited smoking in the office. But it was strange that he—and he realized that everyone felt the same—had never dared to roll a cigarette or light one up when the boss was passing near his desk. It was as if each second of their time . . .

"Have we entered the Province of Lleida yet, Jordana?"

He quickly remembered the last town they had passed through. "No, Senyor."

Senyor Joaquim passed a hand over his cheek, thoughtfully, and altered the position of his legs.

En Pere Jordana was deeply annoyed with himself. The yellow cigarette was hanging from his lips, waiting to be lit, in a manner that he found ridiculous. And he was angry with himself for finding it ridiculous, for not having yet made up his mind to do something as simple as lighting a cigarette.

And now Senyor Joaquim was looking at him. He could feel himself being observed. "Damn it!" Every time something made him nervous, his mouth would fill up with saliva. And the more saliva formed, the harder it became to swallow it. At the dentist's they have that gadget to take it away.

The cigarette paper had got soggy, and he could feel little pieces of tobacco on his tongue.

"Stop."

"Excuse me, what did you say?"

"Please stop."

He drew over to the side of the road and stopped.

30

"Give me my brief case, Jordana."

En Pere got out of the car and opened the rear door. The black brief case with its shining lock was on the seat. He picked it up with both hands. He closed the rear door, opened the front door, and placed the brief case in Senyor Joaquim's arms.

For a moment he stood up straight in the middle of the highway, in the strong sunlight. An immense peace reigned outside the car. A strange, powerful force seemed to seize his legs and lift him off the ground; he took a deep breath, and then with an easy, steady motion—and without realizing it—he struck a match and lit his cigarette.

With his eyes he followed the first thick, refreshing mouthful of smoke, and he thought that it would be nice to continue the voyage on foot.

He got into the car and started up.

"One of these Sundays I'll tell them to go find someone else to drive their truck. Forty shitty pesetas! One of these Sundays I'll take the wife and kid and we'll go out to the country."

"Jordana."

"Yes."

"Would you mind closing your window? These papers are about to fly away."

That would be fatal. If one of those pieces of paper filled with figures were to escape out the window, it would unfold its wings, let out a great cry, and never return. For the sky was full of birds.

It was a little black book. At the top of the first page was the heading *Saragossa* written in Gothic-style capital letters. (En Ribes of the Accounting Department, who had an excellent handwriting, had been honored with the task of preparing Senyor Joaquim's little book.) In a column under *Saragossa*, there were three names and addresses, perfectly lined up, and written in brilliant red ink: *Rodrigo Marín. Alfonso I, 14. Francisco Loscertales. Calle del Coso, 9. José Maria Pérez, Alfonso I, 17.*

Senyor Joaquim looked inside his brief case for the three type-written sheets corresponding to the three names. They contained information supplied by the head of the sales department. He looked them over, but he could not help feeling that he was wasting his time. He had them memorized, and the only thing left to do was visit these people.

"How far have we still got to go, Jordana?"

"About a hundred and ninety kilometers, Senyor Joaquim."

He put the papers back into his brief case, closed it, and rested it on his knees. Before giving in a bit to his drowsiness, with his head already leaning forward, he asked:

"Is the weather holding up, Jordana?"

"It seems to be, Senyor Joaquim."

He didn't want to compromise himself too much. Senyor Joaquim might decide to look out the window, and to him good weather might mean something quite different.

When he could make out the high silhouette of the Cathedral of Lleida—which in the sunlight seemed to be made of both mud and gold, the layer of mud that covered the entire plain of Lleida and on top of it a delicate brushstroke of gold—the sun had begun to heat up the windows of the car and Senyor Joaquim woke up.

"We'd better stop here, don't you think?"

He was afraid they'd never stop. En Pere took a deep breath; he was tired. The silence had conquered him.

Sundays were completely different. L'Arnau was going through a difficult period and always talked about money. Sometimes the cab of the truck would seem like a speaker's platform, and L'Arnau would explain things always looking out in front and waving his arms, as if he were trying to convince, or at least make himself heard to, the people crossing the street. And perhaps he himself—this was the first time En Pere realized this—had also given in to a need to talk, and since the child had first gone to school he had had little else on his mind or tongue. But in fact

L'Arnau paid scarcely any attention to him, possibly because he had four children, but in any case it was obvious that it relaxed him to be able to talk with someone.

The first houses of Lleida.

The silence was no longer so oppressive, for as they got farther and farther into the city, the noise increased—a general noise made up of all the little noises of the city.

"Where'll we stop, Senyor Joaquim?"

They crossed a not very large square with three trees in the middle, two benches, and an abandoned-looking fountain.

"Right here."

"Here?" He took a quick look around the square. There was nothing else to do but pull over to the sidewalk.

They stopped. He still hadn't taken his hands off the steering wheel. He was waiting.

Senyor Joaquim let out a deep sigh.

"Fine," he said.

This was where they were going to stop, that much was obvious. En Pere got out of the car and hurried around to open Senyor Joaquim's door. The square was depressing. In the corner, however, there was a sort of café.

Senyor Joaquim walked over to one of the benches, took out his handkerchief and dusted off the stone rather nervously, trying to remove the dust and at the same time make sure that as little as possible stuck to his handkerchief.

After sitting down, he said to En Pere, who had remained standing:

"Do you want to go have something to drink?"

En Pere turned and glanced at the café in the corner. He tried to say: "It won't be necessary," but his tongue stuck to the roof of his mouth. There was a pain in his throat. He made an effort —it seemed as if his neck were breaking in two—and announced:

"Yes, I'll just have a quick cup of coffee."

33

Seated on the bench, Senyor Joaquim had unfolded his hand-kerchief and was immersed in the job of cleaning his glasses. The lenses were full of dust, almost invisible little dots which, at a distance of only one centimeter from the eye, seemed gigantic. Experience had taught him that it was unwise to open the windows while travelling, if one didn't want to get as dirty as a farmer.

He wiped the lenses again and again, and in his blindness, in his temporary defenselessness, he raised his forehead, as if his mother—just as she had forty years earlier—were about to kiss it. . . . A girl crossing the square looked at him and felt an immediate sense of pity for this kind-looking man. If it hadn't been for his being well-dressed—surprisingly well-dressed—she would have stopped and asked if there was anything she could do for him.

The beggar had already approached and was standing in front of him by the time Senyor Joaquim had put his glasses back on and noticed him.

"I'm out of work, Senyor."

It disturbed him immensely not to have seen him coming. Now he was on top of him, disquieting, with his eyes shining with hatred, or fever, or hunger, or perhaps with intense hope.

He fished around nervously in his pockets; his fingers bumped into his keys, the little silver box, and then finally the change. He took out twenty, thirty céntimos.

Twenty or thirty céntimos remained at the bottom of his pocket in anticipation of another event like this, for all the roads in Spain, he thought to himself, were infested with beggars. One should really take along a whole sackful of change.

The beggar gave a slight bow, and then went off without saying a word.

His eyes were still shining, shining with hatred, or fever or hunger.

"He's a good chauffeur, that Jordana," Senyor Joaquim thought. "He doesn't have the elegance of En Marcel, but he's a good chauffeur." En Marcel, who at just this moment had probably appeared at the house in Pedralbes to find out if the Senyora needed the Fiat, was in fact completely different. He always wore a dark blue suit, a starched collar, and a black tie with a small knot; but what really defined him as a first-rate chauffeur was the inexpressiveness of his face, the immobile line of his lips, his lowered eyes, and that gesture of lifting his coattails when he got in behind the wheel, as if to show his complete awareness of the fact that the clothes he had on were not his own.

En Pere Jordana drove less elegantly—with his elbows out, for example, like a dancer in some local dance hall, instead of keeping them discreetly by his side—and his large hands were more like those of a truck driver; but he knew his business. He wasn't the kind of chauffeur one could have in the city, but he had turned out to be very useful on the highway.

"How many more kilometers to Saragossa, Jordana?"

He made a rapid calculation.

"Eighty-six, Senyor Joaquim."

Senyor Joaquim expelled all the air in his lungs; he felt good. Not much farther to go. He looked at his watch: twelve thirty. He couldn't help confiding:

"We'll get there just in time for lunch."

En Pere smiled exaggeratedly, as if to acknowledge the confidence. To him it seemed as if any time was a good time to eat.

The last time he had eaten away from home had been on his brother-in-law's saint's day. At Ca'n Joanet. It was very hot, and they had mixed soda water with the wine. He had the impression that when they had finished, the bill had been bigger than his brother-in-law had expected. The business of the service charge, all the coffees and the cognacs . . . His brother-in-law had asked him for fifteen pesetas to round out the tip.

How much money had Senyor Joaquim taken with him? Until now it hadn't occurred to him that he should be prepared for any

35

eventuality. If he carried it on him, that was his business, but if it was in the brief case, he'd better not be caught napping. . . . No, it was only natural for him to be carrying it on him.

"Pere, you can't go off without any money," La Maria had told him the night before he left. He had wet his lips with the tip of his tongue, which was one of his ways of showing surprise. "You can't tell what'll happen, you know?" He tried not to get too involved in this conversation, and he said to himself that one day he would tell La Maria not to end all her sentences with that "you know?" which was so annoying.

Then La Maria had opened the closet door and rummaged about in some mysterious corner. He watched her from the bed—he had been reading the paper while she put the finishing touches on the day's work—and when La Maria had turned around with a piece of paper in her hand and a strange look in her eyes, a vivacious look he had not seen for years, he thought that she suddenly looked much younger, almost like a child.

"Here are a hundred pesetas, Pere." He folded his paper. "I kept them just in case."

He gave her a deep look. Faith and illusion are sometimes tangible and concrete, like a shimmering light in one's eyes or a tentative smile. "The time's come, Pere—yes, the time's come."

But people who experience faith and illusion only one day a year can't show it openly; there is a painful shyness. His wife's voice changed. "And now you can go and spend it on cognacs—I didn't have to kill myself getting it."

He had folded the bill and put it in the inside compartment of his wallet, underneath the picture of his child.

Without moving his hands from the steering wheel, he now tried to feel the weight of the wallet against his chest. Out of the corner of his eye, he could see Senyor Joaquim once again occupied with his papers. As the car went around a corner, their knees touched.

If La Maria had made up her mind to give him the hundred pesetas, it must be that the time had really come.

36

He had been in doubt for a long time, before choosing the restaurant. In fact, since they left Barcelona, he had been unconsciously turning this little problem over in his mind. And he would have had no doubts if En Maurici, his partner, had not insisted on giving him advice. En Maurici had said: "There's no good place to eat in Saragossa, Joaquim. If you go to a restaurant, you'll have to limit yourself to eating a couple of napkins and washing them down with some mineral water." And then, laughing: "A pretty miserable combination, eh what?"

"If your job permits it, it would be worth while going on to Alagón. It's only a few kilometers farther on. There's a sort of tavern . . ." He stopped, undoubtedly thinking over an idea that had just occurred to him. En Joaquim was looking at him with admiration—the admiration of a man who does not understand how a certain thing can be as it is—which his partner aroused in him. Even before he had been his partner, when they were no more than friends, En Maurici was always the sort of person who knew where in Barcelona you could get the best codfish, kidneys, or beans. And what place had just changed chefs, and if their cooking was better or worse than the year before.

Finally, En Maurici had proclaimed: "I've got it, Joaquim, I've got it! Go up the Calle Alfonso, and at the first corner on the right, on the far side, there's a little low door next to a barbershop. . . . Go there, if it hasn't changed. It's called 'The Farm.' Just go on in, don't worry." He nodded assent, but he immediately realized that he would not go there.

But in some respects, En Maurici's ascendancy over him was still so great that he had not managed to forget the advice. Nor the name. The name of the place materially prevented him from going there: "The Farm." No. It was the kind of name you'd see over a saloon—it was a vulgar, ambiguous name. En Maurici would have burst out laughing, but he didn't feel the same way about things.

At the last minute, when they had finally arrived at the center of the city, he made up his mind. He decided on The Metropole

37

—a name recommended to him over the telephone by the Tourist Bureau.

As they entered The Metropole, En Pere Jordana realized that each step and each gesture could be fatal. That he could be led to a prohibited terrain where it would be easy to fall, for if on the one hand it was obvious that his prohibited terrain must actually exist, it was also obvious that he had not formed a concrete image of what it must be like. Senyor Joaquim went unhesitatingly over to a table. En Pere remained standing by the door. It was absurd that at that moment he should think of the phrase they always used in circuses: "The slightest error in judgment might be fatal to the performer."

"Where's the bathroom?" he asked a waiter.

Upon returning, he looked at the table in the corner. Senyor Joaquim was examining the menu, and in front of his own plate there was another plate with its own glasses, knives, forks, and spoons.

This was exactly what he had wanted to know. It had occurred to him that he might be sent to eat in the kitchen or—he had admitted to himself—in some tavern next door.

He drew back the chair in a natural way and sat down. On his plate, there was also a copy of the menu.

And then he suddenly and powerfully bumped up against a world that wasn't his own. He realized that he could react to it in either of two ways.

"Have you thought over what you'd like?" Senyor Joaquim inquired immediately.

He had not even given him time to finish reading the fish course. Had he possessed a bit more malice, he would have realized that Senyor Joaquim had already chosen for him.

He could not have said why, but En Pere had already chosen one of the two possible reactions. That of a man who was seemingly inept, not very intelligent, and less fortunate—that of the assistant clerk that he was. He knew that a clever man wanting to get ahead would have said: *Côte Dubarry*, for example, and risked everything. In the same way, an ambitious man, one conscious of his position with respect to the boss, would, whenever possible, talk about a *bath*—even though he washed himself in a laundry tub—and the price of *taxis,* of which the only thing he knew was that they were yellow. For it is a fact that the majority of rich people feel a certain sense of confidence in poor people who are ashamed of being poor.

But he didn't say: *Côte Dubarry.* He said, with a little smile that did not leave his lips:

"To tell the truth, I wouldn't know what to choose. What's more, I don't know what half of these things are."

If L'Alsina, the office manager, had heard him, after offering En Pere Jordana this job—and after twenty years of faithful service to the firm—he would have been disappointed. L'Alsina had arrived at the position of office manager as a result of killing, little by little, day by day, word by word, lie by lie, the poor man that he was.

Without realizing it, En Pere Jordana was proud of the poor man that he was, and he had an unconscious desire to communicate this fact to others. He had no idea to what degree this could seem violent to others—and even less idea to what point this was compromising, damning, and important.

He was lucky that the following day turned out as it did.

And the fact of having now said: "I'm a simple man, Senyor Joaquim, who usually just eats bacon and vegetables," seemed to vest him with new interest in the eyes of Senyor Joaquim.

"En Maurici always exaggerates." He felt satisfied as he paid the check; he had eaten well. And in order to put the finishing touches on his conviction, he once more noted the silent discipline of the three waiters who had served them, the green carpeting, the discretion of those eating at other tables, and the good quality of the napkins—which he could appreciate—and which, according to En Maurici, would be the best thing on the menu.

He usually had little appetite, and after the three *canelones,* he had done little but sculpt a bit, with his knife, on the drumstick of a chicken.

He had, thank God, an iron constitution.

"Will you have some coffee?"

En Pere said he would. Fine idea, a cup of coffee. He placed the pack of Ideales on the tablecloth and lit one of them.

"They're very cheap cigarettes," he apologized.

Senyor Joaquim nodded as if to say: "I understand," or possibly: "No cigarettes are much good, are they?"

"Do you smoke a great deal?"

En Jordana smiled.

"A fair amount."

He didn't know how to tell Senyor Joaquim what a peculiar sense of satisfaction it gave him to do something merely for the sake of doing it, something that was not strictly necessary. He imagined that this was what it must be like to be rich—to live as if living were smoking.

"I haven't got the vaguest idea of what a pack of cigarettes like that might cost," Senyor Joaquim thought to himself. "They're cheap, so let's say one peseta, or maybe two—but over the course of a month, that can add up to fifty or seventy-five pesetas. . . . Ten per cent of a clerk's wages." Terrible; he had never thought about things like this before. And then they went to the cashier and asked for a week's wages in advance in order to finish out the month . . . smoking.

"Did you ever try to stop smoking?"

"Yes. Every year, at Christmastime."

Senyor Joaquim maintained a silence which seemed to say: "And then what?" En Pere Jordana drained off the last drop of coffee and confessed:

"Then every evening I start a fight with my wife, and begin to think that my kid, who asks me questions about what he's studying, is an idiot and will never be anything but an idiot."

He had spoken slowly, watching the Ideal burn between his

40

fingers. It seemed to have difficulty burning, as if it were suffering, or sacrificing itself for someone.

"On the other hand," En Pere went on, "economically it doesn't cost as much as you'd think, just adding it up. It's maybe just thinking about it that makes you hungrier, but if I don't smoke I spend the two pesetas on bread."

He then noticed a roll that hadn't been touched, Senyor Joaquim's.

"You neither smoke nor eat bread," he added with deep, genuine admiration.

En Pere Jordana finally became completely convinced that Senyor Joaquim was an exceptional person when, after lunch, he accompanied him on his visits to his clients. They were so attentive about opening doors for him, they were so thorough in the way they had him enter the various offices, and they pronounced his name with such respect that En Pere was afraid of not having treated him with enough consideration. And he realized to what degree he worked for a solid firm and that his wife was right, when he came home in the evening at his wits' end, in telling him to be patient.

Perhaps one day he would have a precise idea of who Senyor Joaquim was and what he had done—something which these people in Saragossa undoubtedly knew.

In addition, he had never believed that the company's woollen goods were of exceptional quality. He himself, on opening the sample book, would have said that they differed little from ordinary cloth, and that they were more or less the same as the cloth turned out by other companies in Catalonia. And he still thought so. But then the miracle took place when he opened the suitcase and Senyor Joaquim made a little gesture with his hand over the samples, as if he were letting fall some invisible substance; it was then that the Aragonese had exclaimed admiringly and that in En Pere's eyes the pieces of cloth had acquired a unique beauty he had never seen before.

41

Before leaving Barcelona they had reserved two rooms in the Hotel Excelsior. Senyor Joaquim's was on the second floor, with bath, telephone, and radio, three things he would not use. (The previous Tuesday, at midnight, a young German had used the telephone in a final, all-out assault on a girl who had already decided to give in. On Thursday a notary from Bilbao had turned on the radio with an extraordinary sense of satisfaction, trying to find the Saragossa station—for he had read in the newspaper that at eleven twenty they would broadcast Mozart's *Don Giovanni*.) It was just past ten when Senyor Joaquim got into bed, and he went to sleep instantly, as if the top fold of the sheet were impregnated with ether. "Tomorrow morning at eight, we'll meet downstairs for breakfast," had been his last urgent message.

En Pere Jordana's room on the fifth floor had no bath, telephone, or radio. But these were details one noticed only in the daytime or with the light on, and in fact hotel rooms are exclusively for sleeping in the dark.

As soon as En Pere had shut the door and become conscious of being alone, he realized that he wasn't there of his own free will, even though it was he who had turned the key in the lock with his own hands. The door, as it closed, had interrupted the flow of some kind of fluid which governed him; it had cut, after an entire day, the thread which bound him to Senyor Joaquim.

At first he thought that this situation was enviable and that he should keep the door closed. He breathed deeply and ran his hands through his hair with a lazy, free gesture, as if almost relishing his independence.

But, when the gesture was over and his hands fell down alongside his legs, like a soldier, a guilty man, or a subordinate, he felt a terrible fear of being irremissibly destined to sleep. He imagined the next day, even though it was in fact still far off, as being a treacherous adversary hiding in the next minute on his watch. He looked at the dial: ten eighteen. Eight in the morning was more than nine hours away. But he was afraid of being deceived by numbers. One had only to close one's eyes for a moment—that was all, just a moment—and the world of numbers would vanish.

He turned the key in the lock and went out into the corridor. There wasn't a sound on the entire floor. He closed the door from the outside and began to go slowly downstairs.

It was unjust that he should have the feeling he was fleeing, that he was breaking some rule of conduct.

As he went past the second floor, he instinctively listened with redoubled attention, as if he could hear Senyor Joaquim moving about in his room, dropping his shoes on the floor or turning out the light with a clicking noise.

He crossed the lobby—the clerk behind the reception desk was already beginning to turn stiff, to stretch the muscles in his face and hands, turning pale and opening his mouth; he was nodding off to sleep.

Immediately beyond the revolving doors there was the street.

He turned to the right and walked a short way to the first corner. He looked up the street: there was almost total darkness.

As he retraced his steps, he slowly tried to make out the doors of the houses and shops around the hotel. It wasn't until another minute had passed that he realized that the street had deceived him, that when he had been alone in the room he had imagined something quite different. He had felt a vague but deep conviction that out in the street he would find some kind of celebration, an outburst of music and lights, a happy irresponsible world. That he could drink *anís*.

He was once again in front of the hotel door. He went on walking, and after he had gone several meters to the left, he found a café. It was a small café, ill-lit and empty.

The proprietor watched him enter with a certain look of surprise, as if he had been sure that no one would enter all that night.

Once he was seated at a table, the silence became more intense, for he had given up making any kind of noise. It felt ridiculous, absurd to be alone in the midst of such silence. It would have been much better to have slept, to have waited until his watch

43

said eight and once again to have been with Senyor Joaquim in the lobby. His intent in escaping had been to have a casual look around, but instead he had only succeeded in looking within himself. More than ever, for here he was without his house, or his wife, or even the familiar noises of his neighborhood. It was he alone, with no one else.

The silence in the café made him drowsy, and the proprietor himself, leaning on the bar, seemed made of stone.

The change from the *anís* was on the table. He had begun to spend the hundred pesetas Maria had saved "just in case." While he put the bills away in his wallet—very carefully: the one-peseta bills in the first compartment, those of five pesetas in the second, and those of twenty-five and fifty in the back—he thought that his wife was probably sitting at the dining-room table sewing buttons on shirts. This was a job La Maria did in secret, certain that he knew nothing about it. He had no idea who gave her this work, or how much she was paid for it, but he had noticed that on the top shelf of the kitchen closet, behind some empty bottles, there was always a pile of new shirts without buttons, and next to it a tin can full of shirt buttons. Moreover, four or five times he had caught a glimpse of her doing this work, but he had always instinctively pretended not to notice a thing.

La Maria, today, was probably still working. But he wasn't there beside her, reading the paper or listening to the radio. Perhaps his absence allowed La Maria to make five pesetas without worrying. If it weren't for the child, he would have tossed those stupid buttons and shirts out the window long ago.

In the oppressive silence of the café, thinking of the child made him feel the same anguish he always felt when he thought of him, but possibly more sharply and painfully. He lived with a secret fear that something unpleasant would happen to the child. He didn't think specifically about death, but about possibilities that seemed still worse: a paralytic stroke, or some accident in the street that would leave him crippled for life.

He would tell himself that having only one child was like having only one peseta. The one time he had confided this to La Maria, she had reprimanded him. She hadn't understood him. Undoubtedly one child, each child—each human life—had its own intrinsic value. But one could understand losing a child if one had others. This was the way he felt, and he didn't think of himself as having a heart of stone. It was that then the loss would be bearable. It occurred to him that what men really wanted—as in chess—was to protect the king until the end, even at the price of sacrificing pawns.

But he told himself that he must surely be wrong in what he was thinking. If he really did have another child, or several others, he would see everything in a different light.

A little warm wave crept up the walls of his chest. For the first time in five years he could reasonably entertain such an idea—the idea of another child. A second, marvellous opportunity to create a little amiable creature. This time it would be a girl, for La Maria.

And the man capable of making this decision, the man who had possibly already made it without anyone's knowing it, was sleeping up there alone, in a silence similar to the one in the bar. He listened for a moment, respectfully, as if something were putting the two silences into contact with one another.

He imagined Senyor Joaquim doubled up between the sheets, with his legs up against his stomach—his round, childlike stomach and hands—and once again a warm wave crept up his chest.

He drained off the last drop of *anís*, went quickly out into the street, and entered the hotel. The stone statue of the clerk tried, in vain, to open one eye.

He went up the stairs with increasing satisfaction, and when he got to Senyor Joaquim's floor, he stopped to listen to his inaudible breathing.

When he had shut himself in his room and turned the key once again, his feeling of being accompanied was as intense as his previous loneliness.

45

(He had felt it without knowing it: Senyor Joaquim provided him with hope in return for denying him independence. From that day on rebellion had a bitter, salty taste. The boss had turned out to be an irresistible force, like sticky honey. For twenty years he had known nothing of this force and this honey.

Today they had eaten at the same table, and the least the dog could do was to refrain from barking.)

While Senyor Joaquim, at nine in the morning, was paying the hotel bill, En Pere Jordana went to send the telegram. It was a classic telegram, one which Senyor Joaquim had written before breakfast: "Leaving Saragossa. Operation successful. Letter follows."

The letter had also been written, and En Pere dropped it in the first letter box.

While he was writing out the telegram, on the desk full of bumps, holes, and splinters, it occurred to him that he might also send one to La Maria.

He would not have decided to do it, however, if Senyor Joaquim's message had not spurred him on. The beginning was easy. He just copied: "Leaving Saragossa." But it would have been absurd to add: "Operation successful." He couldn't make up his mind. "All well." Or "Am well." No, "All well" was better. He reread the telegram carefully: "Leaving Saragossa. All well." Was something missing? "Leaving Saragossa. All well." Fine—now for a closing. But he couldn't think of the proper formula—perhaps such a formula didn't exist. He couldn't decide between "Love" and "Yours," and he finally just signed "Pere." There were five words, without the signature. Surely this would get under the maximum number of words.

When he handed over the form and the man behind the window made a rapid, incomprehensible calculation, Jordana still had time to read the text upside down. "Leaving Saragossa. All well. Pere."

46

In any case he would have liked to have thought of some closing formula.

"All set, Jordana?"

He let out the brake and started up with a feeling of assurance. He had taken another look at the road map, and he had a pretty good idea of what they might run up against.

Until they had passed the last houses, he did not notice that the sky was cloudy. And a minute later it began to rain.

En Pere felt an immediate and deep sense of comfort. In spring, rain is for people to get wet in. In autumn, however, rain is pleasant when it falls around the sheltered onlooker. And the car offered a pleasant shelter. His own sensibility was extended out through the car, which seemed like a solid, inexplicable prolongation of his own body.

Senyor Joaquim was in an excellent mood. A mood which was made evident by occasional whistlings of short sections of melodies, by a greater attention paid to the countryside than the day before, and by drumming his fingers on his knees. The cause of all this was subtle, but certain: his finger movements were no longer the result of nervousness, but of euphoria.

He had not yet said a word, but he often leaned over and his intent was clear: "What a day!" Maybe even: "What a day, eh, Jordana?"

En Pere was glad that all this had happened before he reached forty. He remembered clearly when he was thirty-one, and he felt as if the last four years had not existed. But he felt that when he turned forty, each succeeding year would fall on him like a stone.

He looked in the rear-view mirror, and once more verified the fact that he didn't have a single gray hair. La Maria, however, had half a dozen in the middle of her forehead.

"Leaving Saragossa. All well," he remembered. He drove with ease, and gave himself over to sending other telegrams in his mind. It was extraordinarily easy—he didn't even have to give the matter a thought. "Raining." "All well." "Maria." He repeated the telegram: "Maria." "Best regards from Senyor Joaquim," he thought. It rang true. "Rain continuing." "All well."

"What rain!" Senyor Joaquim said suddenly.

It was as if he had joined the game.

"What rain!" En Pere said mechanically. "Leaving Saragossa."

They came to a corner; he put his foot on the brake.

The air inside the car had turned cold.

Another corner. En Pere turned the wheel, quicker and quicker, for the car was skidding out of control.

"There's ice on the road," he thought, and the phrase kept on repeating itself a thousand times "there's ice" per second "there's ice" within his mind "there's ice" like a mad heap of telegrams.

But Senyor Joaquim couldn't understand any of them.

The car crossed the road sideways, slowly, but in fact it crossed it, and it fell down the embankment, almost as if it didn't want to fall, but it fell.

The wail of useless brakes pierced the air like the cry of a frightened bird. It was a lovely corner of the world, and the rain immediately laid down its magnificent silence.

FOUR

THE GLASS of the skylight was of an intense blue color. En Ferran looked up and thought: "The sun's out."

His sister-in-law was getting married on Sunday. What an idea, to get married on a Sunday! In fact, what an idea to get married! She was marrying an assistant photoengraver, or something like that, a profession with a big name and a small salary.

Filing correspondence was a job that tired him. Not so much because of the work, but because it lacked interest. It was a job that he did more and more slowly every day. And in addition,

48

ever since En Pere Jordana had left, he had felt completely discouraged. Every day at lunchtime they would take the No. 29 trolley together, and today, when he had gotten into it alone, he had felt more miserable than ever. He had no one to talk with, and he realized that there were twenty other men like him on the platform, all disguising deep interior fatigue by means of the usual sarcastic joking one hears on trolleys.

The only ones he envied were three boys standing in the corner. Three boys giving each other friendly punches in the stomach and filling each others' ears with laughter. He realized that rich people have to be alone in order to be powerful—the company of others might endanger them—but the poor have to stick together—for them the company of others is a remedy.

The company of others is a remedy. For company is a forgetting of oneself.

It had been a strange experience to resemble oneself, to feel alone, tired and impotent, a man on a platform, the tolerated twenty-third man on a platform legally intended for fifteen. To be aware of life as an uncomfortable condition.

He now understood why En Vila was an old man in a perpetual state of irritation, why he suffered from stomach trouble, and why the management accused him of being an "anarchist." He was an extremely intelligent man who, before the war, had started a magazine in Poble Nou. He was a man who, every day upon arising, realized what he himself realized only once a year: that he was irrevocably such and such a man, with such and such a face and such and such a life.

Senyor Alsina's hand dropped a bundle of papers on En Ferran's desk. They were held together by a paper clip, and on top was a note saying: "To file."

Senyor Alsina was surely not a man, En Ferran thought, but a hand, a hand that goes around to all the offices like a trained dog, like those dogs that can carry newspapers in their mouths and never make a mistake.

En Manelet missed En Jordana. He was not unaware, after six months of working there, of the fact that En Jordana looked at him across the table with constant affection. He did not know the reason for this affection, nor did he care to know. He did not know that, just as he would have liked this man to be his father, En Jordana would have liked this boy to be his son.

En Manelet made people uneasy, as do all intelligent children.

"Don't you think you'd better finish that today? There'll be more work to do tomorrow."

It made him unhappy that En Jordana's place, in front of him, should be occupied by En Vila, and not necessarily because it was En Vila, but because he would have preferred it to remain vacant until En Jordana's return.

"If you'd been concentrating, you'd be through already."

It wasn't an accusation. En Vila had said it simply, without any bitterness in his voice.

And moreover, En Manelet knew that he was right, that he hadn't been concentrating, just as En Vila said.

And it wasn't that he had been preoccupied with anything specific; he hadn't been thinking of his mother or brothers. His mother and brothers were an inevitable obsession when he went home, but here, in the office, he thought about nothing, his mind far from any problems, jobs, or reality. He functioned in a manner that was unconscious, and undoubtedly defective. His psychic attitude was that of a person who had resigned himself to hoping.

And he did hope. He had placed immense confidence in the fact that time would pass, that he would grow and become a man. One day En Pere Jordana had given him an old pair of trousers, for the only pair he had were almost transparent. At that time— it was the third or fourth time En Jordana had done something for him—En Manelet had confided in him, almost as if excusing himself: "When I'm older, Senyor Pere, I'll earn a lot of money and I'll be able to buy everything we need at home."

His salary was his family's only fixed income. When he had first started working for the company, he had made four hundred pesetas a month, which had finally been raised to four hundred and eighty a month. Even the boss, when he was fifteen, hadn't earned that much, they told him.

But En Manelet wasn't talented. He was no more than a sensible boy, with a serious look in his eyes and a perpetual cold.

Even En Pere Jordana didn't understand him, didn't understand the practical limitations of every human destiny, when he advised him: "You should make use of your evenings, Manelet, to study accounting and a little French."

If, through some miracle, everyone could make use of his evenings by studying accounting and French, the obvious uselessness of the effort would tragically destroy mankind's last hopes.

L'Ignasi was one of the most punctual men in the office. Every day L'Ignasi arrived at exactly three minutes to nine. His house was six minutes from the trolley stop and the trolley stop half an hour from the office. He would go from his house to the trolley stop and back again along narrow paths which bordered on fields, and when it rained they turned into thin tongues—humid, viscous, and slippery. In the summer, the sun hardened them and they became incandescent: then it was like walking along a knife blade.

And in spite of this he was one of the most punctual men in the office. One day he was late because the trolley had stopped at the Plaza Maragall. The current had gone off. That day he wondered if there was some way to avoid a repetition of this misfortune, but he couldn't think of any, except that of staying in the office and sleeping every night on top of his desk.

For the management had said: "Punctuality is a worker's prime virtue."

With a pillow for his head, and his legs a bit bent, he felt he could sleep there, on top of his desk.

On this particular day, L'Ignasi had not yet arrived, and it was already nine thirty. And it wasn't on account of the trolley, for all the others who lived on the Horta line had already arrived.

Now when he would enter, he wouldn't go immediately to his desk. Everyone knew he would knock on the door of Senyor Alsina, the office manager, and recount, in the simplest possible way and with the fewest possible words, the fact of his being late and give his excuse. He would undoubtedly be pardoned, for those who work in offices do not easily alter their norms, their theories, and their judgments; and L'Ignasi was, by definition, one of the most punctual men they had.

Senyor Alsina, the office manager, alone in his office with the door shut and a little electric heater pointed toward his feet, was looking at his fingernails. Those of his right hand were longer, because he had to cut them with his left hand and he had never been able to develop the necessary technique. He looked at his fingernails and they looked strong and of noble lineage. It was too bad that the tip of the little finger on his left hand was missing. He always kept it bent, so that no one would notice that it was shorter.

This was why the office manager, Senyor Alsina, did not look at his hands the way most people do. He liked to do it only when he was alone, as he was now. Then he would touch his fingernails, check their polished surface, their delicate pointed shape, and their distinguished, pale rose color. Then he would straighten out his little finger, which had been bent inward, and look at the stitched-up part on the end. It was a sure testimonial to the fact that, thirty years before, a packing case had smashed it against the ground; that in those days he used to unload packing cases; that, in short, he had been a warehouse clerk.

With peculiar pleasure he touched, for a second, the deformed tip of his little finger, and then immediately went back to contemplating the delicacy of his nails, which he had stubbornly pampered for thirty years in a spirit of revenge, with a deep-seated realization that they were a visible symbol of his progress.

He looked at the door, which was still shut, and at the heater, which protected his feet. For a moment he listened to the silence of his office, and then he closed his eyes.

En Maurici Danès, Senyor Joaquim's partner, was also known in the office as "Senyor Maurici." It was an old firm which preserved these more familiar forms of address. But just the forms. Maurici was incapable of working for four hours at a stretch. The work which he had at first assigned himself, he had little by little handed over almost completely to his partner, Senyor Joaquim, and L'Alsina, the office manager. En Maurici always had four or five French novels in the drawers of his desk, the latest best sellers that were causing a stir, and then later he would discuss them with the group of friends he met every Thursday. He did not play bridge, but he never missed one of these weekly reunions. He would take the most comfortable armchair—a privilege which nobody would have dared deny him—stretch out his legs, drink more cognac than was considered proper to drink, set down a pack of Abdullah cigarettes on a nearby table with a certain amount of ostentation, talk about what he had read, look at the cardplayers out of the corner of his eye, and be unable to get rid of his boredom. But he never missed one of these Thursdays. He and his wife, La Marta Vallador—of the Vallador family from Girona, who were in the cork business—kept the pact they had made. He would accompany her on Thursdays, and she would let him go out alone on Saturdays.

Just then L'Alsina, the office manager, brought him a telegram. "Thank you."

To the office manager, "Thank you" was not an obvious formula for leave-taking, but strictly an obligatory phrase. This was why he waited, smiling with a very discreet air of complicity. He felt certain that in this small matter he had the upper hand.

"Leaving Saragossa. Operation successful. Letter follows." In this little bit of blue paper, in these thin, sticklike letters—all in all like a caricature of a letter—En Maurici could see his partner's entire soul. It was as if he now held it between his fingers, reduced and condensed. He imagined that, when he died, En Joaquim would leave nothing but a similar message: "Leaving this world. Operation successful. Children follow."

L'Alsina, the office manager, was still waiting, sure of himself. And in fact—

"Senyor Joaquim, Alsina, has just left Saragossa and everything's fine."

"Very good."

When someone knocked at the door of his office, L'Alsina, the office manager, always waited five seconds before saying: "Come in."

It was L'Ignasi, one of the warehouse clerks.

The tip of a beret was sticking out of his coat pocket. The top button of his shirt was buttoned, but he wasn't wearing a tie. He hadn't shaved, and the hairs of his mustache covered the wart under his nose.

L'Alsina, the office manager, looked at him without taking any interest in these details. This was why, like all people who pay no attention to details, nuances, or the little elements that go to make up reality, he had a cold look. One day someone will invent an electric machine which will look at things this way, and classify them the way the office manager was now classifying: "A warehouse clerk."

On very rare occasions Senyor Alsina's eyes would light up with profound passion: when he remembered that he too, a long time ago, had been the same thing—a warehouse clerk. This memory made him feel uncomfortable; he would tell himself that it prevented him from thinking and acting with freedom or with completely independent judgment. He felt that in a certain sense there was still a small bit of him in every one of the clerks now working in the warehouse. But he knew that in any case it was impossible that he had really, in those days, been a warehouse clerk like one of these nowadays. And he was right. If he had been like these warehouse clerks, he would still be one, just as

54

idiots are always idiots and clever men always clever. Nor, in reality, was he now office manager—what did it mean to be an office manager? He was a strange cog in the machinery of the firm; he had the imprecise and complex attributes of supervisor of the cashier, confidential agent of the directors, and inspector of personnel. He was obviously much more important than any of the workers, but he lacked the sense of reality (the simple joy, the pathetic strength, the pitiful illusion, the painful humanity), the precise and inimitable profile of an authentic warehouse clerk.

"What is it, Ignasi?"

L'Ignasi, on this particular day, had small wrinkles around his eyes, as if the act of seeing required great effort and caused him terrible pain.

"My son . . ." he said, "my son's got typhus."

L'Alsina, the office manager, had four children. Two boys and two girls: the ideal combination. They were eleven, nine, seven, and five years old. They had all had whooping cough, and three years ago the oldest had got jaundice. But it hadn't been serious. The second child didn't like fish, but he would get to like it. The youngest, according to the music teacher, had an exceptional gift for dancing. People said that the best age to begin a ballerina's training was at seven or eight.

L'Ignasi looked at the man sitting in front of him, Senyor Alsina, the office manager, whose head was bent over his desk, and he knew that everything depended on how well he could make his words circle around this man's head.

"It's very serious. The doctor says we have to act immediately."

"What doctor?" the office manager inquired, in order to reduce L'Ignasi to a concrete, exacting conversation, a conversation with a hierarchy of values.

"Doctor Roura."

It was a fairly usual name. There could easily have been twenty Doctor Rouras.

"Is he a pediatrician?"

"A what?"

"A children's specialist?"

L'Ignasi hesitated. "I don't know, Senyor Alsina. He lives on the corner, in the same building as the café."

"Oh!"

In any case, nowadays, typhus isn't something that gives doctors much of a chance to fool around.

"Are they giving him chloromycetin?"

"Yes, they gave him the first shot at eight. He says they have to be given one after the other. . . ."

There was a fairly long pause. L'Alsina, the office manager, shook his head and felt a sense of pity, less for L'Ignasi's son than for sick children in general.

"I wondered . . ." the clerk started to say.

The office manager got up, walked around from behind his desk as if from behind a barricade, and L'Ignasi realized that he had been at least partly successful.

"You don't even have to say anything, just do whatever you have to do."

He put a hand on his shoulder for a moment and walked him toward the door.

"Go back home. Don't worry. Everything will be all right, and we'll fix things up around here so they'll go smoothly without you."

The wrinkles around L'Ignasi's eyes increased nervously.

"I wondered," he said, "if I could borrow some money for chloromycetin. It's a question of life or death, and . . ."

Senyor Alsina, the office manager, became totally immobile, with an impressive air of solemnity about him.

"For God's sake, Ignasi! Didn't I tell you to go ahead and do whatever had to be done? Ask for whatever you need; we're not going to scrimp on a thing like this. You yourself can go to Senyor Riera and tell him from me to give you whatever you need. And don't give it another thought."

L'Ignasi suddenly unwound inside; he was overcome. He couldn't say a word. He left the office and the little wrinkles around his eyes could finally fulfill their destiny of sheltering tears. For one should not forget that behind the always plastic ballet, behind the artistic counterpoint that makes up all conversations or situations between men, there is occasionally a truth, something elemental and magnificent. Like a child in danger of dying.

It made little difference that five minutes later Senyor Alsina, the office manager, got inside-line No. 6 on the telephone and asked Senyor Riera, the cashier: "How much did L'Ignasi ask for?" and wrote in a voucher: "Two thousand pesetas."

The man said:

"He an old character who's gone back to work to help his girl."

Without raising her eyes from the typewriter, the woman said:

"What's her name?"

The man said:

"I don't remember. But she's a good worker."

Without raising her eyes from the typewriter, the woman said:

"Better than him?"

The man said:

"No, not better than him."

Without raising her eyes from the typewriter, the woman said:

"I love Charlie Chaplin."

The man said:

"So make sure you see it."

Without raising her eyes from the typewriter, the woman said:

"I don't know if they're going to show it at the Vergara or at the Cataluña. I always go to one of those two theaters."

The man said:

"They're always too crowded. I like the Lido better; it's a big theater and you can always get in without standing in line. And the sound track comes through nice and clear."

Without raising her eyes from the typewriter, the woman said:

"Is the Lido the one in the Paseo de Sant Joan?"

The man said:

"That's right. On the left as you're going up."

Without raising her eyes from the typewriter, the woman said:

"I always get it confused with the Niza."

The section chief entered and left a stack of duplicate purchase lists on her desk. He asked, in a worried tone of voice:

"Do you think you'll be finished with the invoices by one o'clock, Enriqueta?"

Without raising her eyes from the typewriter, the woman said:

"Yes, Senyor."

It was a quarter to one.

The moment of thirst.

The boys began their parade down the corridor, toward the water jug.

They passed in front of the clock.

They looked at it and winked happily.

They drank slowly. They dried their chins with their hands. They dried their hands on their trousers.

Three of them formed a group and began to talk, nervously and in continually louder voices. Then they said "shhh" and one by one they went back, each to his place.

It was ten to one.

In his pocket En Gregori was carrying a folded piece of paper and protecting it with his hot hand.

En Gregori waited, with all the caution of a hunter, in the corner with the washbasins.

En Ramon passed by and he let him pass by.

En Joanet passed by and he let him pass by.

L'Andreu passed by, and En Gregori, from his corner, stretched out his hand like a semaphore.

L'Andreu could see a mysterious invitation in En Gregori's eyes.

And suddenly a piece of paper unfolded in his hand.

It was a photograph from a newspaper, which En Gregori had

gone over with a red pencil, exaggerating its traits with a prime-val, brutal voluptuousness.

"This one's for you—I'll get some others."

The piece of paper was folded up again. This was its fate, to be rapidly folded and unfolded, day after day, night after night, until it would finally fall apart in four sections.

L'Andreu went off with one hand in his pocket.

En Gregori, in the semidarkness, lifted up the water jug and took a long drink, with a feeling of satisfaction. It was a good thing, he thought, that L'Andreu was two years younger than he.

As soon as the bell rang, En Graugés took the newspaper out of the drawer and spread it out on his desk. He found the noise of everybody leaving extraordinarily pleasant, a delightful ac-companiment to the glance he gave the front page.

He knew that Senyor Joaquim was away, that Senyor Maurici would never take the trouble of making a tour of the office, and that Senyor Alsina, the office manager, had before him the only ten minutes in the entire day when he had some work to do. Had someone been able to see him, he would not have done it, for he didn't want them to think he spent all morning reading the news-paper.

One more person said "Good-by." He didn't answer, for from the moment the bell rang he considered himself alone.

He read with incomprehensible concentration and joy, as if the paper really contained something fascinating. This satisfaction seemed to be less the result of what the paper might or might not say, than of the simple fact of reading it. The result of ostenta-tiously spreading out this bit of the street—yes, that was what it was—on his office desk.

He once again told himself that Senyor Joaquim was away; that Senyor Maurici had probably left by now, somewhat fur-tively so the office manager wouldn't see him, to take his glass of vermouth at the Heidelberg; and that Senyor Alsina, the office manager, was now engaged in his ten minutes of work: entering the payments made by Senyor Riera, the cashier, and putting the vouchers in order.

It felt nice, then, to turn over a page and hear the noise of the paper amidst the silence of the office. To lean back a bit and stretch out one's legs. To think he didn't have to catch any trolley, that he lived on the corner, and that his wife was setting the table. The table next to the open balcony, for today the sun seemed to be out. And the stew—for it was Thursday—covering the sensual form of the soup plates.

The next page. Local news.

At home he couldn't think about all this. He would be living it. That was why he liked to be alone, with the newspaper.

And the radio, and the cigarette, and the feeling of being a bit sleepy. Occasionally, far off, a boat whistle, or inside him the sonorous vibration of a vein. Identical sensations.

The next page.

He looked at the desks his companions had abandoned, but only for a moment, for without people behind them they gave him a strange feeling of uneasiness. Being accustomed to seeing his friends there gave him the feeling that they were now exposing themselves to some danger—as if each one in leaving his desk would no longer have anything to justify his existence, as if he might dissolve in the outside air.

He waited a moment longer, to intensify the pleasure of going out into the street.

He folded the newspaper and put it back in the drawer. That evening he would finish leafing through it.

He went slowly down the corridor. He passed in front of the door of Senyor Alsina, the office manager.

Senyor Alsina saw him pass. "En Graugés is the only one," he thought, "who knows enough to stay ten more minutes. Those stupid young kids leave as soon as the bell rings."

There was a confused noise from far off, which indicated that En Graugés had opened the street door.

Now that Senyor Alsina was alone, he looked at his nails,

60

closed his eyes, and began growing larger and larger—he could feel himself present in every corner of the office—and a little bit larger, and yet larger, and if someone had now opened his office door, they would have punctured his skin.

FIVE

The silence in which rain envelops the earth is more important than the silence of night, of solitude, or of death. The silence of rain is deeply alive. It does not smother the voices of things—as does the silence of night, of solitude, or of death—but rather purifies them and imbues them with a new vigor. The silence of rain brings order.

The river in the valley had a river smell; the dry grove gave off the precise, penetrating odor of a dry grove.

And there were the voices, diverse yet compatible, which were accentuated by the water falling with infinite wisdom and sensitivity, moving a thousand small, stimulating hands.

On the embankment, on the rotten shoot of a plant, on a green leaf, or on a dazed insect, it rained. It rained actively on the same rainwater that already lay on the ground.

En Pere Jordana opened his door. The car was embedded in a tree on the sloping embankment. Several ribbons of dirty water came trickling down from the road and went past his feet, running together and then apart again as if playing some game. Some inexplicable instinct had made him get out of the car. He stood up straight with his legs stiff, and for a few extremely intense seconds prolonged the sensation of being all in one piece.

A little blood was flowing from somewhere on his head. Then he thought of Senyor Joaquim. He was ashamed of his initial need to find out if his legs were all right. Senyor Joaquim was slumped into a corner of the seat, and his hands had forgotten their rapid drumming motion on his knees.

First of all, he had to get Senyor Joaquim out of the car. The obstacle presented by the steering wheel made it difficult. He held the door open with his shoulder, and with the slow, even smoothness of a machine passed his arms under the unconscious body. Slowly he brought the weight toward his chest. Suddenly the injured man was no longer in the seat, but lying entirely in his arms. Near his right elbow he felt a painful pulling sensation which spread to his shoulder, and he felt something warm sticking to his skin and shirt. Until then he hadn't realized that he had a cut in his arm.

He sustained the weight of Senyor Joaquim with his good arm and pulled him out. It was raining, still raining—but perhaps more gently, as if the rain felt a little respect for Senyor Joaquim, that man who was so powerful and at the same time so fragile, and who had just been forcibly taken from the car as from a protecting shell. In the moment of decision, standing up straight in the midst of that solitude, En Pere Jordana realized that what he was actually carrying was Senyor Joaquim. At first it was an unpleasant sensation. He felt as if he had committed a serious blunder in taking him out of the car, because until now he had never laid hands on his boss, either physically or morally. By relegating to himself the right to decide, to impose his will, he had reversed the fundamental relationship between Senyor Joaquim and himself. And even though this new situation had been brought about by a chance occurrence, he could not accept it without a strong sense of guilt.

Very slowly the rain started to let up, as if it had already accomplished its purpose. The curtain of water became thinner, and the landscape began to stretch out before En Pere's eyes. New rolling hills came into view, each one farther off than the last, and the various shades of green became progressively more intense.

Suddenly En Pere no longer thought of his responsibility with anguish, but with pleasure. His face was now completely relaxed, but with an unprecedented expression of energy. He put the wounded man on the ground; it didn't matter if he got dirty. Then he took care of his own injuries, bandaging his head in two handkerchiefs to stop the flow of blood, and clumsily wrapping his jacket and shirt around his arm. Without effort, he picked up the body again and began to walk. About twenty yards away he had seen a road running off the highway, and he imagined it would lead to some inhabited spot. They were far from any town.

Before starting down the smaller road, he turned around. The car was lost among the foliage like a badly wounded beetle. At the third bend it disappeared. The road obviously led to an invisible farmhouse, through fields of old olive trees. Soon his whole body began to hurt, and he put Senyor Joaquim on his shoulder. It was as though suddenly, and increasingly with each moment, his muscles were becoming soft, as though he were turning into a cloth puppet. "I must have got pretty banged up," he thought. He went on walking, but with a great fear that at a certain moment his eyes would close like Senyor Joaquim's.

He had a vague feeling that he was in a compromising situation, that serious problems were arising which he would understand only later on. His conscious mind was preoccupied with only one thing: walking. At the end of the road there would be a house, and his arms and legs would hold out before giving in completely.

A rainbow took shape in an uncertain sky. He wondered if it was some false image inside his eyes. How many years had it been since he had seen a rainbow?

How many years had it been since he had worked in the office, since he had left home, since La Maria's last kiss, since the glass of *anís* in Saragossa? At each bend in the road, painfully left behind, he felt more and more isolated in space and time, and he could find nothing in the past to justify his present situation. He had to admit that this was a new man who was trying to save another man in a place he'd never seen before.

At that moment, what he needed more than anything else was to stop at the side of the road, watch his own blood flow, and have someone put his hand on his forehead and say a familiar word—or to have Senyor Joaquim open his eyes and look at him the way he had always looked at En Pere Jordana.

Two magnificent olive trees in the prime of life formed a natural gateway leading into the farm. As he passed beneath the arched branches with the injured man in his arms, En Pere Jordana also had the majesty of a tree.

He stopped and gazed at the open, deserted doorway of the house, and then at an upstairs window. There was a woman's face in the window, and she seemed to be looking at him—or rather at them—unhurriedly, or perhaps with profound surprise. En Pere walked up to the door and entered.

Inside there was a large entrance hall with farm tools hanging on the walls. En Pere had to find a bed at once. He was about to open the first door on the left when a girl came down a wooden staircase. The face in the window turned out to be a girl with astonished eyes, with an air of irrepressible surprise visible in the line of her lips and eyebrows, in the rigidity of her arm.

"A bed—he's had an accident," En Pere explained.

She looked at him without saying a word, and motioned him to follow her down a corridor.

The room looked as if it had been closed for twenty years. En Pere deposited the wounded man on a high bed. His arms immediately relaxed, and he felt an unbearable pain in the right one. "It must be broken," he thought.

The girl opened the shutters. Sunlight fell on a monstrous chest of drawers, on a *prie-dieu,* on an iron cross, on a jar and washbasin, on the headboard of the bed made of worm-eaten wood with gilt edges, but this light lacked the strength or transparency it had out of doors. It looked as if it had been preserved for twenty years inside the window—it might even have been as old

64

as the furniture. It was dense and a bit rancid—the dregs of light.

The girl looked at him openmouthed, and En Jordana felt himself getting faint. If nothing happened, if he didn't make up his . . .

"Go get your father or mother, will you."

"They're not here. They're in Tesera."

"What's Tesera?"

The girl gave him a look of surprise, as if it were impossible that En Pere didn't know what Tesera was.

"It's the nearest town—half an hour away by cart."

He went up to the bed, placed Senyor Joaquim's head on the pillow, and was about to take off his shoes when, without knowing why, he stopped short. His eyes met the girl's, and he became nervous.

"I've been waiting for them; I don't suppose it'll be long before they come."

She was referring to her parents.

"My mother knows how to treat wounds," and she pointed to a dark spot near one of Senyor Joaquim's knees.

En Pere turned pale. He hadn't seen the blood. He quickly rolled up the trousers.

It was strange how he tried to alter as little as possible Senyor Joaquim's normal appearance. He held off as long as he could before taking off his trousers, and it didn't occur to him to loosen his necktie. Senyor Joaquim always wore a perfectly starched collar, and En Pere would have died rather than touch it.

The wound didn't seem deep; blood was oozing slowly from it.

He asked for some rags.

The girl went out.

He followed her with his eyes, then turned his head and suddenly saw himself in the mirror over the bureau. He felt increasingly queasy, his head began to turn, and in his mind the vision of a man with a bloodstained handkerchief around his head kept on repeating itself, more and more feebly. He swayed next to the bed

65

occupied by Senyor Joaquim, and anticipated his fall by stretching out on the ground with the fitful movements of a drunken dog, a submissive dog at his master's side.

He woke up in bed. He wasn't too comfortable; the mattress was thin and full of peculiar lumps. Five or ten marvellous seconds elapsed before he reached complete consciousness. His legs, which had turned into a kind of fountain of pleasure, were infused with an extraordinary sense of well-being, and he had the idea that he shouldn't move, that this happiness was brittle.

Then he remembered that the bed wasn't his own; he remembered the accident and the girl with the astonished eyes. He made an effort and sat up a little; in the back of the room, partly hidden by the foot of the bed, he noticed the girl sitting on a low chair.

He could tell by her eyes that this was her room, and that she had brought him here as if he had been a sack, or a sheep. (He didn't know why, but he felt sure that this girl often carried sheep in her arms.) There was something direct about the way her eyes told him this, like a child who didn't know what it was to lie. Then En Pere Jordana let himself fall back and rest on the pillow again, with no other desire but to feel once more that sense of well-being in his legs and that drowsiness, the vaguest yet most intense of pleasures.

"What about Senyor Joaquim?" he thought.

With one powerful contraction he managed to sit up in bed. His dizziness lasted scarcely more than a second. He stood up and walked slowly toward the door. She went up to him and took his arm—which somebody had bandaged—and accompanied him without taking her eyes off him, as if she anticipated his every move.

En Pere Jordana looked at his watch; he had slept only an hour. This calmed him a bit.

Whenever he hesitated, the girl would help him. They crossed the entrance hall and opened a door.

66

Inside there was a little woman, inexplicably little, dressed in black and leaning over Senyor Joaquim's body with the fluttering motions of a bird. She was not only moving her arms and hands, but also the tip of her nose, her ears, her lips, and the wrinkles on her forehead, as if she were a puppet controlled by invisible strings. It was strange how such excitement, such an abuse of expressive resources, produced in the end the most complete lack of expression. It became impossible to know what she was thinking, or guess whether she had a favorable or pessimistic opinion about what was going on. It was even difficult to tell whether she was trying to cure him or kill him.

But En Pere Jordana did not stop to examine the woman, for the impossible had taken place—something that was perhaps even disastrous: Senyor Joaquim was stretched out on the bed, naked.

He immediately thought that Senyor Joaquim was dead. Only total annihilation could justify this nakedness, the nakedness of a body that was no longer Senyor Joaquim's. The old woman continued her movements, with her black dress constantly quivering; it was as if she had put on some extraordinarily complicated costume for this solemnity. On the night table there was a casserole containing an oily, wine-colored paste which she spread on the patient's forehead, chest, and stomach.

Senyor Joaquim was obviously still unconscious.

This scene went on for an hour. En Pere Jordana stayed inside the room watching, without daring to interrupt the old woman's activities. He left only once. "I've got to piss," he thought. There was no way of finding out where to do it, so he decided to go out in the patio. There was a corner with a pile of cane in it; each piece had a sharpened point and was ready to be stuck in the ground to support the first crop of kidney beans. There were thirty-six; he had time to count them. As he returned to the house, he became aware of a man sitting on a stone bench looking at him. He was tall, thickset, and a bit stoop-shouldered, and he seemed even bigger, possibly because the image of that tiny woman who had taken possession of Senyor Joaquim was still engraved on his retina.

It was the husband.

En Pere drew nearer to him. He was a man who gave one a certain sense of fear, but of fear that was the result of anguish. For he was so tall, so thickset, so immobile, and kept staring at him so shamelessly.

While the old woman gesticulated and flitted about over the invalid, this man remained outside with an air of cruel indifference. En Pere was afraid, but at the same time he wanted to say something normal and cheerful. But he passed by. He entered the house, and in the darkness of the entrance hall he stopped, overwhelmed by the secret he had just discovered: the man was an idiot.

After an hour Senyor Joaquim woke up.

A slower rate of breathing, an almost imperceptible tremor on his lips and around his eyes announced the change, which the old woman accepted with more respect than joy. It was as if the favorable outcome, which she gave to understand was the result of her work, were less a piece of good news than proof of a powerful superhuman intervention.

En Pere Jordana had a moment of energy. When he realized that this naked body with its undeniably exaggerated potbelly was about to turn into Senyor Joaquim, or at least into an approximation of him, he performed his own kind of exorcism by throwing the old woman and the girl out of the room. It was impossible to have Senyor Joaquim revive under such circumstances.

He watched over his boss's reappearance with peculiar impatience. He nodded affirmatively even before Senyor Joaquim had opened his eyes, asked for anything, or passed any kind of judgment. This was the purest and most disinterested form of collaboration, a form that had continued unchanged for twenty years.

68

At the last moment, he thought of covering Senyor Joaquim's stomach and chest with the blanket that was rolled up at the foot of the bed.

The first sensation Senyor Joaquim experienced upon awakening was that of something irritating, of an unbearable itch on his chest and stomach produced by a woollen blanket of incomprehensibly poor quality.

And there was En Pere Jordana bending over him and smiling. He didn't understand why he was smiling. He didn't understand why the blanket was so coarse. He didn't understand why he was lying down.

He immediately relapsed into unconsciousness.

But En Pere, for an instant, a very brief instant, had seen Senyor Joaquim open his round eyes. And when their glances had met, a sort of alarm bell had gone off inside him; some switch within had been turned on and he was flooded with a strong interior light. He went out into the hall to shout—why hadn't it occurred to him before?

"Go get a doctor!"

It was raining. Beneath this falling water the mare and cart stood immobile in the middle of the patio. Puddles had formed around the animal's feet and around the cart wheels, and they seemed to be slowly melting.

The idiot climbed into the cart. He covered himself with a sack and picked up the reins. The reins were wet, the wood was wet. The cart started off. The idiot's mouth hung open. The water fell and landed on his protruding lip, and from time to time he blew and spat it out.

An immense peace reigned on the highway. Now he was happy; he opened his mouth wider and wider. Standing on top of the cart, he let the reins hang loose and paid attention only to the trees. This was his favorite game, his greatest pleasure. Travelling as near as he could to the edge of the road, he would wait for an oncoming branch, duck down, and then stand up again. He wouldn't duck until the last moment, when the branch had already brushed against his face—that was what made it fun. Then he would suddenly shout victoriously "Yo-aye!"

It was also raining three hundred kilometers away in the city.
There the rain had given birth to those rare black flowers—men's umbrellas—and to those even rarer yellow, blue, gray, and green flowers of transparent, fragile girls' umbrellas.

He saw a branch, ducked, and shouted "Yo-aye!" and the shout spread out into the valley of pure silence.

The Capitolio store took advantage of every situation. They now took advantage of the rain and installed in the entrance, which was on the most crowded street in the city, a stand full of low-priced umbrellas. The clerk, who had been selling neckties an hour before, was no longer shouting "They never wrinkle—only fifteen pesetas," but had taken up a new line: "Anyone who gets wet does it of his own free will!"
Fifty city-dwellers had taken refuge in the vestibule. Fifty city-dwellers looked ill-humoredly at the sky and worried about their shoes' getting wet; they protected their wallets so they wouldn't be robbed, looked at the sky again, and calculated what it would cost to take a taxi. . . .

He saw another branch, ducked, and shouted "Yo-aye!" and he missed it so narrowly that, in his joy, he let out a terrible, magnificent burst of laughter, a burst of laughter that made a rabbit in his hole on the other side of the lonely valley lift up his ears.

A notary's assistant, after looking absent-mindedly out the window, picked up a piece of white paper and put it under a pile

70

of papers on his desk. He then pulled out a corner of it and wrote, shielding the words with the palm of his hand:

> *When it rains, girls'*
> *eyes are green*
> *beneath umbrellas.*

It was going to be a lovely poem.

All the stores had turned on their lights, for no one could see a thing.

The notary's assistant went on looking fixedly out the window, trying to find a fresh, new stimulus, new ideas, new lines of poetry.

It was tragic. Nothing more came to him.

To cheer himself up a bit, he reread:

> *When it rains, girls'*
> *eyes are green*
> *beneath umbrellas.*

It was lovely.

Branches and more branches passed—now he was going through a forest—and the man scarcely had time to breathe between each shout. The sack, now sopping wet, slid off his shoulder.

The mare's breath remained suspended in mid-air for a moment, and then quickly disappeared, absorbed by the powerful respiration of the entire valley.

After each of the idiot's resounding shouts, one could hear the sustained *ssst* of the rain, as if in admonition.

His voice perhaps lacked its usual resonance.

"Pere."

And then quickly, in order to be more specific:

"Pere Jordana."

"Yes, Senyor Joaquim."

Senyor Joaquim, from the depths of his pillow, announced:

"I'm all right," and he waved his hand as if to cut off any possible discussion. "Don't make any decisions without consulting me first."

But then something happened inside him, a sense of pain or perhaps a memory, and he spoiled the ritual phrase by stating the contrary:

"Do whatever you think best, Pere." And then after a pause: "Thanks."

For Senyor Joaquim had had a dream. He had dreamed that the car was at the bottom of a gully, that he was seriously injured, that an unshaven man with a mended shirt and dirty forehead—a man who turned out to be En Pere Jordana, even though he didn't look like him—a miserable wretch of a man, picked him up in his arms and put him over his shoulder. In the dream there was a blurred area, as if a long rain had turned it soggy. Or maybe nothing had happened, except that a miserable wretch of a man had carried him over his shoulder for hours and hours, jumping agilely over huge precipices and dodging black, rabid dogs that wanted to bite him (he had never liked dogs). They left a little trail of blood on the ground, but it was the blood of the man carrying him, while he slept and felt brave, as he had when he was a child.

He knew now that he was out of danger, and this was why, when he had opened his eyes and seen En Pere's real face, he had said: "Thanks."

The doctor who arrived from Tesera was a short man with bumps on his head, wearing a red scarf inside his coat.

Senyor Joaquim suspected that he wasn't wearing a necktie, and he had no desire at all to let this man examine him.

The doctor, who had been told about the accident by the head of the family, suspected that the patient was a man of importance and had no desire at all to examine him. But he couldn't refuse.

He examined him slowly, in order to have time to think about what he should do and say. Without realizing it, he was carrying out the best examination of his career.

Nor had Senyor Joaquim ever been so patient. He answered, although briefly, all the doctor's questions. The doctor looked at his head again and again, and, what was worse, felt it on both sides, on top and behind.

Before finishing his examination, the doctor pointed to a kind of oil staining Senyor's Joaquim's chest and stomach.

"What's that?" and he glanced at En Pere.

Even though they were alone, En Pere lowered his voice a bit: "The old woman."

When he made a face with his mouth stretching out into an arc, the doctor's bulbous head was transformed into a grotesque piggy bank.

Finally he stood at the foot of the bed, took a handkerchief out of his pocket, and wiped off the oil that had got on his hands. Then Senyor Joaquim questioned him.

"What do we do now?"

He had cut short the sentence. Something had prevented him from saying, as would have been usual: "What do we do now, Doctor?"

The doctor explained:

"I don't know if you realize that a miracle has taken place. You're all right. You're lucky, you're practically unscathed. You came through the trauma"—trauma, trauma, in Tesera it had been twenty years since he had used that word, and perhaps he no longer knew its correct application—"without any lesions to speak of. If only I had a portable X-ray machine . . ." and he glanced accusingly around the room.

Senyor Joaquim was also looking at the room, but through different eyes. Through unexpectedly benevolent, almost affectionate eyes. If En Pere Jordana had been able to understand this look, he would have been surprised, for Senyor Joaquim could not possibly feel comfortable here.

But he did feel comfortable, with an inexplicably deep-seated feeling of well-being.

"In any case," the doctor said, "anyone who, like you, has been in a coma for a considerable *lapsus* of time"—*lapsus, lapsus,* like ictus, angina pectoris, gastralgia, cephalalgia, forgotten words; in Tesera they say heart attack, migraine, stomach cramps—"has to remain quiet and under observatian for several days. In all good conscience I can't advise you to return home or go to a hospital. Remain here three days if it's possible. Sometimes unforeseen reactions set in."

En Pere Jordana was sure what the answer would be: "I can't." In spite of this, Senyor Joaquim, in a completely unfaltering voice, said:

"Fine; that's fine with me."

He felt such a strange sense of satisfaction that this time he did not cut short his sentence.

"What do I owe you, *Doctor?*"

By means of a gesture he told En Pere to pay.

When they were alone, he said:

"Come to some understanding with these people, Pere. Find out if they can do something to make this bedroom a bit more cheerful, and what kind of meals they can give us. Whatever happens, come to some understanding."

En Pere Jordana had many problems he wanted to discuss. He hesitatingly mentioned the first:

"We should notify the office, Senyor Joaquim."

"Why?"

"They'll get worried when they don't receive the telegrams they're expecting from Pamplona, Vitoria, and Bilbao."

Senyor Joaquim took a deep breath and closed his eyes for a moment.

"There's only one thing that matters, Pere, and don't forget it. I don't want to be bothered with anything for three days. Absolutely nothing. Do you understand?"

"Your wife . . ."

74

Senyor Joaquim looked at him.

"What? Was the doctor lying to me? Am I going to die?" And before En Jordana could answer, he added: "It's best to dissimulate in a situation like this. If they found out about it at the office, everything would get in a terrible mess, and I have a feeling that several days alone would do me a lot . . ."

He nervously folded the top of the sheet with his fingers. He waited a minute before asking:

"I'd appreciate it, if it isn't absolutely necessary for you to notify your wife. . . ."

The light coming through the window was growing weaker by the minute.

En Pere Jordana's face suddenly looked as if it had been painted gray.

"You don't look well, Jordana. Are you all right?"

"I'm fine, Senyor."

There was a long silence.

En Pere went over to the window and announced:

"It isn't raining any more."

He turned around. Senyor Joaquim had gone to sleep.

SIX

She climbed into the bus.

Four had already passed, four busses that ate the line in little nibbles, for they were already full.

Once she was inside with her bundle, she couldn't make up her mind whether or not to go down the aisle and see if some passenger would give her his seat.

"You can't stand here," shouted the conductor, giving the signal for the bus to move on.

An old man got up.

"I'm getting off at the next stop," he explained, as if excusing himself in front of everyone, so they wouldn't find his gallantry ridiculous.

"Go ahead, sit down," the conductor told her, with rural familiarity. There were thousands like him, who had lived for forty years without ever having even seen a train, lost in some corner of Andalusia, and who now—after travelling for three days and installing themselves in some shanty near the old cemetery, without electricity, without water, without a bed—had miraculously found a steady job in the great city. They not only formed part of its rhythm, but many had come to believe that it was actually they who had produced it. They treated everyone (like this woman with the package) either with an authoritarian wave of the hand or with benevolent condescension. If there is such a thing as the newly rich, then this type of man—this conductor, that garbage collector, that waiter, that mason's assistant—after forty years of mortal obscurity, is surely *newly alive.*

La Maria, En Pere Jordana's wife, put the package of shirts on her lap and crossed her arms over it. The bus moved and jumped frenetically, in spite of which she remained inexplicably immobile, with that sculpted look which lends dignity—a dignity midway between tragedy and comedy—to poverty.

She had just delivered thirty shirts.

"Now that En Pere's away, I can get more done." She thought of the dining-room table all covered wtih shirts. Now they could stay there all day without En Pere noticing them. "If he doesn't come back for two more days, I could finish a hundred and eighty shirts."

The scarf she used for wrapping the shirts was in her hand, folded to an improbable size, and inside the scarf there was a tiny purse with a twenty-five-peseta bill in it.

While she waited for the bus to return, she went over to look at a shop window full of leather goods.

It was full of luxury items; what they were and what they were

76

for she would never know. Little boxes, minute cases for mysterious objects and accessories that were impossible to identify. They were like the currency of another world.

But there was an enormous, shining, butter-colored brief case. She would have liked to touch it with her fingers, sinking them into its surface which seemed compact and yet soft.

Should En Pere need a brief case when he returned, she would come and buy this one. She was sure that someday En Pere would need a brief case.

Fortunately, the bus came around the corner and left this problem up in the air.

Those busses that bring people home in the evening, those busses that are so noisy without and so silent within, that cross wide, brightly lighted avenues like startled animals, for their flanks still contain shadows of the suburbs—those are the busses that carry resignation.

The tips of shirt collars have wilted, and there is a deep, static wrinkle in the middle of each forehead, an ancient woundlike wrinkle, through which flows no blood; it is through this dark wrinkle that resignation flows.

The men's beards have grown, and their fingers are turned in toward the palms of their hands. The men . . . who look at each other with blank eyes, and none of them know whether the person in front is another man or himself. There is dust—in the summer—or mud—in the winter—on the sides of their shoes and on the bottoms of their trousers. In their mouths or between their fingers they have a cigarette butt, like a symbol of the butt-end of the day remaining for each man. The women sit with their heads bent and their hands on their stomachs, as if they wanted to prevent the last bit of life's force escaping from their bodies.

An old man about to get off covered his face with his scarf up to his eyes. He was carrying a lunch basket wrapped in a blue and white napkin, and his fly wasn't completely buttoned.

The policeman didn't sit down. He stood near the door, hanging on to a pole. He took off his hat and scratched his black hair for a moment. His uniform had turned a lighter shade of gray, faded by the sun. He yawned. The conductor said "Hello" because he saw him every day. The conductor had an Ideal behind his ear, and from time to time he struck the metal poles of the bus with a *clink, clink,* and it seemed like the only remaining recourse, the only way to make the sound of this kind of music carry to the other end of this immense bear, this bus of resignation.

En Maurici Danès had decided either to sell the Panhard or to get a chauffeur like his partner Joaquim. For two hundred yards now he had struggled with this terrible bus, and his nerves were frayed. A chauffeur would be the ideal solution.

He put on the radio. Something cheerful:

> *Tu es ma p'tite folie,*
> *oh, ma p'tite folie.*

"How much," he wondered, "do you suppose En Joaquim's already sold in Aragon and Navarre?"

When they returned, he must talk with En Joaquim: he wanted to persuade him to let him have En Jordana. If he had turned out to be a good chauffeur, he would take him.

> *Oh, ma p'tite folie!*

He'd heard that song somewhere before. Perhaps at En Toni's house.

In a moment he would be able to ask him if he remembered it.

Before they sat down at the bridge table, for it would be hopeless afterward.

The child, seated at the dining-room table, had fallen asleep with his head on his arms. The light bulb gave forth a pale light, as if it too were asleep.

La Maria, when she entered the apartment, found him like

this. She stopped for a moment on the threshold to contemplate her son.

He was blond. Every afternoon he played with his friends after school and came home with his hair all mussed up. At first his father, En Pere, had scolded him and tried to get him to neaten up, but she had never understood why it was better to have his hair combed than uncombed. One day En Pere must have thought about this and he undoubtedly didn't understand it either, for from then on he stopped scolding the boy.

He was asleep. It was lovely to watch him sleeping. Next to his bony elbow there was a notebook, and a little farther away some picture cards and some comics. In order to read the comics, he had pushed aside and piled up in a corner of the table all the shirts on which his mother had to sew buttons.

The woman smiled.

And she kept on looking at him.

And she felt it was sad that the child had been alone.

She imagined that in the middle of the table there was a mirror, and that another child was on the other side—another child which through some inexplicable law was the same and yet a girl.

It seemed as if someone—En Pere—was climbing the stairs and was about to knock on the apartment door. She listened: from the patio came the sound of a radio:

Oh, ma p'tite folie!

"Good evening, Toni."

"Hello, Marta."

They shook hands under the Venetian-glass chandelier in the hall.

"Where's En Maurici?"

En Maurici had stopped in the garden to take a look at the Juliàs' black dog, but without getting too near.

"I don't understand. He's never taken any notice of Barbut before."

79

They went out into the garden. There was a cool breeze and a smell of jasmine.

"Why the sudden interest?"

En Maurici suddenly turned his back to the dog and, taking En Toni's arm, entered the house.

"I was offered one the other day. I didn't want it, of course, but it made me feel as if I should have a closer look at a dog. I didn't even have any idea of what one was like."

"I could lend you a book."

They stopped to let En Maurici's wife enter the living room first.

"After you," said En Toni in English. He smiled, showing flawless teeth.

What unshakable peace and tranquillity reigned in the hall-way of this house! With a glasslike sound the hours were struck by the wall clock made in Paris.

"Hello, Marta."

"Hello, Maurici."

"Hello."

La Isabel Julià gave En Maurici a drink.

Someone reading the paper got up from his armchair, stretched out his arms, and welcomed them.

"Sensational news, Maurici, sensational. Hoad's reached the finals. Six-four, six-one, six-three against Seixas."

The heating had been turned way up. On top of the radio-phonograph the roses picked from the garden an hour before were fading. Three men were now looking at the newspaper, veri-fying Hoad's sensational victory. Their instincts concerning their own social status obliged them to be interested in tennis.

"Come, sit down," said Isabel Julià. She was holding their latest photographs of Puigcerdà.

In the hallway, the clock struck the hour again. It always seemed to strike the same hour.

La Maria Jordana finally picked up her son and carried him in her arms to his bed. He was heavy. He was getting heavier day by day. It was nice having heavy things close to you. The effort increased one's love.

The boy's mouth was half open. The doctor said he had to have his tonsils taken out. In the old days they would already have been out, but now you had to be a bit more careful. They must be in there for a reason.

La Maria Jordana looked at her son stretched out on the bed. He had the same slightly underslung jaw as his father. She started to untie his shoes, and then his pants. The child rubbed his eyes and cheeks with his fists, without really waking up. "What time is it?" he asked. She sat him up on the bed in order to take off his shirt: "Time to go to sleep." Little Pere always wanted to know what time it was and it always made him unhappy to have to go to sleep so early. He would have liked never to be sleepy. Occasionally, from time to time, when he had a fever in the night, he could hear the magic striking of the clock in the dining room, and in the darkness, in that moment, he was surrounded by a world of different shapes, sounds, and odors.

La Maria Jordana left him asleep. She washed his socks in the washbasin, for En Peret had to put them on again the next day. She went out onto the balcony and hung them up. The breeze made the water that had remained on her hands seem colder.

"Maria!"

It was La Ramona calling from the floor above.

La Ramona, seen from the floor below, was nothing more than a head guillotined by the railing of the balcony, a head which nothing seemed to prevent from falling into the street.

"Did you pay your gas bill?"

"Yes."

"Have the rates gone up or what? I had to pay eighteen pesetas more than last month."

"Me, too, almost twenty-five pesetas, but En Peret had the grippe and I had to keep the gas on all day."

She talked without looking up, because it hurt to twist her body around.

"I asked him, the man who came to collect, if the rates had gone up, and he said no he didn't think so, and in any case he didn't have anything to do with it."

"They think they're different from us just because they've got a uniform on. You'd think they didn't have gas in their own house."

"Maybe they don't pay for it."

"Maybe."

La Maria Jordana listened for a moment. Total silence reigned in her apartment. The child was asleep.

"Is En Pere still away?"

"Yes."

There was a pause. They could hear the noise of a trolley car, at the Ronda. La Maria Jordana knew perfectly well what La Ramona of the fourth floor was thinking. La Ramona was jealous.

"Let's see what he brings you," she said, for she was sure he wouldn't bring her anything.

"As long as everything's all right . . ." La Jordana counter-attacked.

What did "all right" mean? What did it refer to? Why had they got the idea that something was to come of this trip, something good?

"Hello, Maria."

La Ramona's husband had come out onto the balcony. La Maria looked up. The man's head was also sticking over the railing, but more than his wife's: his neck and part of his chest, like a statue.

Just then La Maria Jordana would have liked to go back in. She found it cruel that this man should be on the balcony with his arms crossed on the railing, that these people living on the fourth floor had nothing else to do but wait for the moment to go to sleep. That their heads should be bowed, because great unhappiness is like a sickle around one's neck.

But then the husband shifted his arm and put it around his wife's shoulders.

And suddenly La Maria Jordana felt terribly alone.

En Maurici Danès speared a piece of *gruyère*—he preferred *brie*—smelled it meticulously, put it back on the plate, took a slice of sweet ham, wrapped it around the cheese, and put it all in his mouth at once.

"When are you going to Rome, Toni?"

En Toni, who had been talking about architecture, saying that the finest architects were the Swedes, and that the Finns would be even better if their style were not so *glacial* (a word that was frequently on his lips and that always gave people a slight feeling of admiration), seemed to grow pale, and he made nervous motions with his feet.

"I've had to put it off for a while. Something's come up."

He put his glass down on the table. He leaned over toward En Maurici and lowered his voice a bit.

"Do you know that I have an engraving studio?"

Yes, he knew it. En Maurici knew five or six things of this sort about him, businesses of all sorts that would be laughable with someone who did not have the immense textile machinery company that he had. But it was amusing the way he had got it into his head to run a bookstore, a flower shop, an engraving studio, and goodness only knew what else.

"There are certain types of personnel you can't deal with, Maurici. I've never had a bit of trouble at the factory. And what's more, there'll never be any. I have a hundred and eighteen workmen. I'm the boss and they're the workmen—that much is clear. The accountants, the office manager, the engineer—all those people—they've also got their place. And to tell the truth, I have very little to do with them."

En Maurici believed it. He had always considered En Toni an adventurer in the field of business—that was why he enjoyed his company more than that of the others. Every day he wanted to start up something new and let the textile machinery factory run itself—he wasn't so foolish as to want to shut it down.

"I have little to do with them, and everything runs along smoothly. On the other hand, I set up the engraving studio in a completely different way. All my life I've had a passion for engraving. I'm just an amateur, if you will, but I managed to take some lessons in Lyons and Rome. Three years ago I decided to make use of a specific engraving process, and I started looking around for personnel. The cleverest of the lot, the one who's in charge, is a man called Costa; I got him from a printing shop."

He poured himself a little gin and tossed an ice cube into the glass. The ice floated around in the gin and hit the side of the glass with a derisive tinkling noise.

"Fine. A month ago we finally perfected this process of mine. I had just come back from Rome with the finishing touches on it. Fine. After having spent three years teaching Costa not only his job, but also *my* method, the son of a bitch waits for me to return from Rome and give him his last lesson before telling me: 'If you don't give me two thousand pesetas more a month, I'm taking off tomorrow. And I warn you: I've rented a place up the street, and I'll take three of your engravers with me, and all your clients.' "

En Maurici took a second slice of ham and wrapped it around another piece of cheese. He didn't know why, but he was sorry he had been told this story. But En Toni couldn't stop:

"You understand that this business of the two thousand pesetas was just a disgusting pose to maintain his dignity, a pretext that even he didn't have any desire to maintain."

"How much was he making?"

"Four thousand."

He still found this whole story unpleasant.

"He really has rented a place and made off with my workers. And he'll do good work too; he's a good engraver." His lips were trembling. "Do you want me to tell you how much money I lost?"

But it wasn't the money he'd lost that made his lips tremble.

84

En Maurici knew he should work up an interest in the problem, for the other man was asking him to sympathize. That was why he asked:

"What do you plan to do?"

"I've already done it: folded shop. I told them all to go to hell."

Isabel Julià drew up with a swirling motion and sat down next to him on the sofa.

"Have you seen the photographs of Puigcerdà, Maurici?"

"No."

En Maurici looked at them slowly with his head bent forward.

"They're good photographs. Did you take them with a Retina?"

"Yes. Look at the clouds there. But . . . you haven't got anything to drink. Do you want more ice? That's Sam, Cardellach's dog. See the reflection from the glasses. . . . Not bad, eh?"

"Isabel!"

She went off. The servants were awaiting her instructions.

En Toni recovered the photographs from the sofa and said to En Maurici:

"And let me tell you, when I told them to go to hell, that took the wind out of their sails. I've decided that it's impossible to have a small business." And as if it had something to do with what he'd been saying, he asked: "What have you heard from En Joaquim?"

"Not a thing."

He turned around, and shouted over the back of the armchair:

"Lluïsa! Have you heard anything from En Joaquim?"

They were playing poker. Four red-stained cigarettes were burning in four gold-painted ashtrays on the green table. En Joaquim Civit's wife answered, screwing up one side of her face, because the smoke was making her eye tear.

"No, not a thing. And you?"

"Not a word."

En Toni looked inside his glass—the ice, almost melted, was still tinkling against the edge as it floated around—and he swore to himself that when it was all melted he would forever stop thinking about the mess with the engraving studio.

Then the chimes in the hall spread forth into every corner the irresistible hour for smiling, and called the entire ballet company to order.

The people on the fourth floor said "Good night" and went inside. La Maria Jordana remained a few minutes longer on the balcony. She heard some noise issuing from the bar up the street, and at night it seemed much closer. It was a noise that was always the same, yet always different, like the water boiling in a kettle.

Her mind wandered off without her realizing it. She thought about nothing.

But in spite of this, her mind was working, feeling happiness, sadness, hope and fear, going over a thousand sensations and ideas which are never consciously felt.

She listened and looked at the bar. It was as if she were listening and looking at her own life—always different, yet always the same.

When she was about to go in, she heard someone whistle.

"Maria!"

It was La Ramona again.

"Maria!"

She was talking in a low, conspiratorial voice.

"I couldn't talk to you about it before, because En Tomàs was around. It'll probably take him a couple of minutes to realize I'm out here."

"What's wrong?"

"Maria!" It was like an invocation. She always called to people as if she were asking for help. "He's out of work."

"En Tomàs?"

"Yes. They fired him—fired everybody."

She immediately thought of En Pere. She would have liked to see what En Pere was doing now. She would have liked to be sure that everything was all right, that he was at his boss's side.

86

Once again his absence gave her a sense of happiness and—she could not help it—anguish. She knew she should feel happy, but she felt lonely.

"He doesn't know what to do, Maria. Oh, good God!"

If she had gone in a minute sooner, La Maria thought, this wouldn't have happened. But there she was, and she had to say:

"How did it happen?"

"What's going to happen to the kids," La Ramona went on, "and who's going to make sure . . . You know, Maria, that En Tomàs was sick. I have to feed him steak, and . . ."

Now she would start in on her usual kind of chaos. She thought about ten or twenty things at a time, and couldn't manage to confine herself to one of them. But La Maria knew all this by heart. She also knew every detail of that fourth-floor apartment—the two tiles missing from the hallway, the purplish-blue wallpaper, the old woman's room in front, the old woman who was as decrepit as La Ramona would soon be; the old woman whose only occupation was chasing beetles—and above all she knew the air in that apartment, and she felt that everything that happened to this family was on account of that humid air which should have been scooped out by the shovelful.

And little Tereseta with her blond hair and her thin arms as white as lilies. La Maria liked this fragile child, whom they didn't deserve—she didn't know why, but she was sure they didn't deserve her.

"Just imagine, Maria: my mother who costs us more money than . . . and then all of a sudden you find yourself high and dry. . . . En Tomàs is so sore I can't even . . ."

"How did it happen?"

In the silence of the night, the bar with its noise suddenly seemed extraordinarily far away. La Maria Jordana heard only the voice coming from above.

"Some of the men wanted to leave the shop to go work somewhere else. I don't know too much about it. And the boss fired them all. He must have had some kind of stroke, and he closed the shop."

The voice stopped, and then it immediately started up again, but this time more conspiratorial than ever:

"Maria! I was thinking . . . If En Pere could help us out . . . When he comes back from his trip, maybe he could find En Tomàs a job, and . . ."

"What does he do?"

"He's an engraver, but if he had to he'd take on other work— you know what I mean. . . ."

Little Tereseta, with the lily-white arms, was probably sleeping now with her mouth open. . . . She felt like saying: "En Pere'll help you if you give me the little girl."

When En Pere got back from his trip, a lot would happen. She suddenly felt the chill of the iron railing against her stomach and drew back a bit.

"Isn't it about time to go to sleep?" a thick voice inquired.

En Tomàs had come out onto the balcony. She did not dare look up.

The wind did not dare stir up anything in this quarter. It had gone and hidden like a coward.

The night did not like to kill everything. It allowed all the griefs, all the injustices, all the insecurities, and all the doubts to last until the following day.

Time passed like a slow fever.

SEVEN

"DON'T MOVE," the doctor told him.

He knew that he was being observed, as if he were a dog. He imagined that people were looking at him out of the corners of their eyes, and that even when they said something simple and straightforward, there were unspoken thoughts behind it: "We must keep an eye on him in case he does something peculiar, like suddenly turning pale, closing his eyes, or letting his head fall on his chest."

From the moment he had waked up that morning, he had had the impression that he was an object of general curiosity, and that he had something to hide. In fact, however, only En Pere Jordana and the old woman entered his room. En Pere sat down in a low chair made of reeds which time had dried out and almost caused to flower, bringing out their perfume. He stretched out his legs— they always seemed longer when he sat in a low chair. For a moment he looked at Senyor Joaquim's face. For a moment, no more, because Senyor Joaquim was looking fixedly at him. Afterward he turned away and looked at the countryside out the window—bathed in a dusty light in the morning, in an ashen light in the late afternoon.

Senyor Joaquim would have liked En Pere not to move so much. He didn't stop moving. One arm was bandaged and immobilized in a piece of cloth, but the other only increased its activity. He would never have thought it necessary that, in order to exist, a man should indulge in such continual motion, in such small motions. He himself could not move, not a bit. En Pere's one remaining arm was therefore working for four arms. His arm became an obsession, and he instinctively respected it as if it had greater strength and freedom than he.

Even the old woman of the house had been forced to give in before the energy of this arm. Around the bed it had traced an invisible, private circle: there the cups of broth changed hands. And moreover, after a few hours, the farm family understood that the two strangers governed their lives by different laws, and that in each of their words, silences, and gestures there was a closed world, which was only his, and into which they could never succeed in entering, even through the most violent physical coercion.

"Jordana."

En Pere Jordana turned around.

"Don't talk. You should rest."

Senyor Joaquim was silent for a few seconds, and then he said: "My head's buzzing in the strangest way, Jordana."

"Try to relax. It's only your nerves."

It was buzzing in a really very strange way, as if in a state of repressed excitement. He would think about something and then the idea would rapidly become blurred; he would bring it back obsessively and then lose it again; then it would reappear absurdly tied in with subsequent ideas, and it was impossible to bring order and tranquillity into his thoughts.

One of his obsessions was En Pere Jordana's face. He couldn't erase it from his mind. He could call to mind the car ride, the office, and his wife; he could play a game of reciting in alphabetical order, forward and backward, the names of his children, but En Pere Jordana's face was always present, with greater or less clarity of outline, with greater or less reality, in the recesses of his memory.

It was a dominating face, perhaps because he was lying down and had become accustomed to looking up at it from a lower level. His jaw seemed enormous.

"Would you do me a favor, Pere?"

En Pere Jordana leaned over still more.

"Sit here next to me."

En Pere felt nervous.

"I said sit down here. Sit down."

He watched carefully how En Pere bent down, bent down until he was seated in the reed chair. He was no longer looking up at him. The old bed was higher than the chair.

"You must be very tired, Pere. You should rest."

He closed his eyes, but he continued to see a precise image of En Pere's head looking down at him, and suddenly he had the impression he was participating in a trial, that his hands and feet were tied, and that he was in an immense, dark room, in which the only illuminated object was En Pere Jordana's face; but he couldn't make out if that face was there as a judge, a witness, or a prosecutor. It did not open its mouth or speak, but in his

90

entire field of vision there was nothing which so held his interest.

En Pere had gone to sleep in the half-light of the corner, when he heard Senyor Joaquim's voice.

"Who are you really, Pere Jordana?"

At first he didn't know who had asked him this question. Senyor Joaquim was looking at him with his head leaning on the pillow, and his eyes were shining, reflecting the last rays of the afternoon light. But Senyor Joaquim had never asked him such a personal question.

"What kind of witness are you?"

En Pere turned around and said, attentively and stupidly:

"Can I do something for you, Senyor Joaquim?"

And his eyes kept on shining, staring fixedly. Then En Pere felt afraid, *and he placed a hand on Senyor Joaquim's forehead.*

En Pere himself did not realize that with this gesture he had answered Senyor Joaquim's question. He did not realize that the element of truth within every man—which cannot be perfectly explained in words—is often conveyed by the pressure of a hand, by the warmth of blood, with a fleeting contact that becomes total. There are men who in moments of anguish need a hand to open up the paths inside their foreheads, clearing away the cobwebs. This hand brought with it a strong light which suddenly lit up the immense room, and Senyor Joaquim knew what kind of witness En Pere Jordana was, and to what he was testifying. And he saw himself perfectly reflected in the light, and he realized that not only he but all men testify to an indestructible truth.

"It'd be awful if he died. How could I, in front of everyone in the office, justify the fact that Senyor Joaquim died here?" He had not yet taken his hand off his forehead; he wanted to transmit to him his warmth, his desire to live. "It'd be awful if he died." Right now, in this house, on this trip, now that he, En Pere Jordana, was beside him and receiving strength and hope from his presence. Had he died a week earlier, En Pere would not have given it a thought. Not a one. He would have had a day off.

Along with everybody else, he would have contributed five pesetas for the wreath. He imagined L'Alsina, the office manager, saying: "He was an exemplary man," and making his keys clink together in his pocket. He would not have been able to say yes or no, for it had been impossible to know anything about Senyor Joaquim, who had seemed like a being invented by L'Alsina, the office manager.

The forehead now felt feverish, and it calmed him to realize that the temperature was not subsiding, for that meant that he would continue to live. His eyes filled with tears: "O Lord, I've got a wife and child, and this man can't die! It means nine hundred pesetas a month, and soon I'll be forty, and I want to have a daughter! Let him live a year, enough time to find out what I'm like, and say something favorable about me!"

Once the prayer was over, the hand withdrew from Senyor Joaquim's forehead.

It had calmed the buzzing inside his head. Images came into focus, and thoughts became precise. He looked at En Pere Jordana, the pressure of whose will he had felt. The hand had not seemed indifferent, but rather trembling with desire. It was the first time that an underling had revealed a desire—a human desire.

Then suddenly he remembered the man. Perhaps he had in fact not forgotten him for a single day, even though he would have sworn to the contrary. He remembered with incomprehensible precision, considering he was making an effort not to visualize him, to have him before him as little as possible.

L'Alsina, the office manager, had properly *expedited* the matter, as he put it. Three serious offenses had been noted against this man in the book. (He couldn't remember his name; he had forgotten it, even though he had repeated it a hundred times. It was a common name. On the other hand, he had tried not to notice the face, and now he had it before him. The face was also common, like En Pere Jordana's. Perhaps if En Pere Jordana had not got

92

so close to him, he wouldn't have remembered the other face. And he began to wonder if it wasn't the same face, if everyone he had ever seen in the office and in the factory had not now become distilled in this face of En Pere Jordana, which therefore seemed so vigorous and terrible.)

He had committed three serious offenses, all of an identical nature: three times he had been found asleep in the warehouse when he should have been wrapping packages. L'Alsina had presented the case to him in clear, outline form, in order to save him trouble. There was proof of these three offenses—there were possibly fifty others which had not been noticed. The man entered his office with a frown and remained absolutely mute. He seemed to have reconciled himself to his fate. He would have to sign the book. He signed. He remembered—he didn't understand how he could remember, for he thought he hadn't even noticed it—a capital F that was large and complicated and—that was it!—he was called Fernández, Joan Fernández. He himself signed on the right-hand side: Joaquim Civit. (He mentally weighed the two names, and tried to make his own stand out; it was useless. They were obviously two minute, precise names.)

"In a case like this, there is no pay," he was informed by L'Alsina, the office manager.

And he was right.

"There are three serious offenses, according to company regulations."

And he was right.

"You have the right to place counterclaims, within the fixed period of time, before the magistracy."

And once again he was right.

It was strange that this man had such a frown on his face.

A few minutes later, L'Alsina, the office manager, left with him.

Before closing time, he came and explained:

"This fellow works at night too, as a watchman somewhere. With the result that he does both jobs badly."

Suddenly Senyor Joaquim felt a doubt:

"Has he been paid his portion of the bonuses and vacations?"

L'Alsina, the office manager, smiled:

"Of course, Senyor Joaquim. His portion was twenty-nine per-cent of his salary." He rapidly handed him a document. Salary of warehouse attendant: six hundred eighty; twenty-nine per cent; a hundred and ninety-seven and twenty céntimos. He had signed the receipt.

Before leaving, he accentuated his smile and explained:

"Everything's been taken care of; you needn't trouble yourself a bit."

L'Alsina, the office manager, was far away now. Something deep within him that had been buried for years was now coming to the surface in the cashier's absence. It was a general, distress-ing, and as yet uncertain preoccupation—like the beginning of an illness.

He went off to sleep. En Pere took his pulse; he perhaps still had a little fever. He was sleeping deeply, and his cheeks trem-bled with each breath like two rose-colored meringues.

He felt slight misgivings about leaving him, but he wanted to go out into the fresh air. He crossed the kitchen and looked for a glass in order to get a drink of water. The old couple were in bed. He was somewhat surprised to notice the girl with the astonished eyes sitting in the corner; she got up and took a wine-skin off a hook for him. She moved with a strange silence, as if she were propelled by an invisible wind coming down the chim-ney.

He took a long drink and seemed not to notice the harshness of the wine.

He put the wineskin back in its place, trying to avoid those eyes with their look of wonder he could not fathom.

Outside the night was misty. The trees, the well, the cart, the stone—everything was sleeping, dreaming sluggishly within the mist. En Pere Jordana advanced several paces into the courtyard, turned to the left, and then looked back over his shoulder. Each step required an extraordinary effort, for his brain was not sending out the proper commands, as if it too was full of the night mist. He tried to keep on moving, to find a path for his steps, and for his thoughts. But he noticed that the night was immobilizing him, and that the air was becoming dense, and was about to turn into a tree or a stone.

All alone, he shuddered with cold. He wanted to know if somewhere there was someone who remembered him and the things that were familiar to him.

He woke up lucid, with a feeling of innermost animation. Senyor Joaquim felt as if his skin were a warm covering layer, and he avariciously maintained his immobility as he watched the light slowly gain ground on the wall.

Perhaps what had wakened him was the sound of a cart getting under way. The master of the house had left for Tesera to sell wood.

When he entered the room at about nine o'clock, En Pere Jordana noticed that Senyor Joaquim's eyes were no longer feverish, and that his entire face seemed to have been re-formed and strengthened.

"Did you have a good night?"

"I don't know; I don't remember a thing."

He turned his head toward the wall, which the light now covered from one end to the other.

"But it looks as if it's going to be a nice day. What do you think, Jordana?"

"It looks that way, Senyor Joaquim."

He put the cup of milk down on the night table.

"Do these people have cows?"

"No. They've got four or five goats."

Senyor Joaquim raised his eyebrows.

"I've never had goat's milk before."

95

The light grew stronger.

"Have you already had breakfast?"

"Yes, Senyor Joaquim."

En Pere Jordana felt doubtful. Were they really in some forgotten place in the mountains, surrounded by strange people, and so little interested in their own situation that Senyor Joaquim could hold such a conversation?

Senyor Joaquim took his arms out from under the covers and crossed them over the top of the sheet. His hands seemed to flutter about in the air like featherless doves.

"Perhaps your family's worried, Jordana. And I asked you not to say a word, not to put anyone on the scent. . . ."

"No. I sent a telegram from Saragossa. And actually, not much time's passed since then."

"Oh!"

While he sat up in bed to drink his milk, Senyor Joaquim thought that this chauffeur named Pere Jordana was already, at that moment, something more than a chauffeur; he was a man capable of sending a telegram on his own account, a man who had unsuspected thoughts.

"Why are you getting up, Senyor Joaquim?"

He felt like sitting. En Pere went to get his overcoat, and he put it around his shoulders.

"Do you still have some of those, some of those cigarettes . . . some of those cheap cigarettes you said you smoked?"

He was about to say exactly what he was thinking: "Do whatever you usually do; please feel free to be yourself."

En Pere lit an Ideal and sat down on the low chair at the foot of the bed.

There was a prolonged silence. It seemed as if each of them were situated in a predestined place. This seemed to be where they should wait for a sign, for some unknown occurrence. The cigarette smoke rose in the air as if it were the only thing alive—as if it were a materialization of time.

Suddenly there was a finger of sunlight on the wall.

Senyor Joaquim did not know what there was about this tenuous yet magical presence that stirred him to continue the stimulating, arduous adventure of their dialogue.

"Whom did you send the telegram to, Jordana?"

He felt hesitant. What he had really meant by this question was: "What sort of family do you have?" It was strange; he was being initiated into the virtue of knowing, of participating, and of understanding, with the same kind of pleasure and dissimulation one feels upon being initiated into a vice.

"To the missus."

He himself would have said: "To my wife." But he shouldn't think of such things now.

He had finished his milk. En Pere took the cup away, put it on the night table, and lit his cigarette, which had gone out.

"The doctor's coming this afternoon, Senyor Joaquim."

Senyor Joaquim smiled and put his arms back under the sheets.

"I don't care about the doctor, Jordana."

"We have to know when he'll let you get up. . . ."

"I'll get up when I want to. Tomorrow. There won't be any complications."

En Pere remained silent. He thought: "And once he's up . . ."

"Are you all right, Jordana? When you're completely well, we'll get in the car and return to Barcelona."

It did not occur to him to argue, comment, or make any suggestions.

"But there's no hurry."

He turned toward the wall and looked at the spot of sunlight, as if to return to the world of the present. There was no longer merely a finger of light; it had spread out like a banner.

And Senyor Joaquim with great tranquillity, facing this cordial and profoundly alive banner, said the inconceivable:

"Jordana, you remind me of my grandfather," and then he looked at him. "My grandfather was a man who lived in a little house in Terrassa, a house built alongside the wall of a factory and that we tore down when he died. He was old when he died"

97

—he wiggled his feet under the covers. "He was thin like you and smoked black things that gave off a horrible stench. He had been a workman's assistant in the Jou Company. In the winter he wore a beret that came down to his eyebrows."

His cheeks puffed out; he had belched. Would the goat's milk harm him?

"At the age of forty he began to make some money on his own. When he was fifty he went to England, with that beret of his, and when he came back he set up the factory for his son. The workmen called him Senyor Pepet. I know he was a fine person, but I could never accept the fact that he didn't buy himself a decent hat and that he never gave up smoking those black things that gave off such a stink."

He looked fixedly at En Pere, who had just tossed away what remained of his Ideal, and went on:

"Now I can accept it."

En Pere Jordana repeated: "At the age of forty he began to make some money. . . ."

"You remind me of him, Jordana."

The sun was now covering the bed like another blanket, and Senyor Joaquim could not resist the sensation of floating in a honeyed dream.

En Pere Jordana, implacably outlined in the icy shade, thought: "At the age of forty he began to make some money."

It seemed as if the air in the room were getting warmer. Senyor Joaquim closed his eyes for a moment: the milk had settled well.

And he didn't dare say what he was thinking: "My grandfather and you, Jordana, are both a kind of man I've underestimated. A man of deficient quality, below the norm of what is today expected of a civilized being. Consciously or unconsciously, I have always tried to ignore this type of man."

Something inside him, however, made him resist accepting this basic resemblance. It disconcerted him to think that the blood of

98

one of these men had been charged with enough energy and sensibility for his sons and grandsons, for this thought prevented him from being disinterested in the copy sitting before him. And then suddenly everything was clear—but grotesque: "I could be the grandson of this Jordana."

This revelation was less disturbing than he would have imagined. This revelation seemed to heal an interior wound; it seemed like a pacifying, definitive answer.

If someday he had to be the grandson of this Jordana, of this rough head of hair, of this sad, gray skin, of this vulgar mouth, everything would have greater significance. Above all, every thought and desire of the man now looking out the window would influence his own future desires and thoughts. No man has ever been able to contemplate his own remote birth through the gestures and reactions of his forebears. But he realized that, to a certain extent, he could do this.

For the first time he realized that there was no other way to regard—and love—the world except in terms of the blood running through his veins.

"It's ridiculous that, just because of the chance fact that this man is not my grandfather, I should look at him—and feel disdain for him—as if he were a stranger, a man who had nothing, absolutely nothing to do with me."

(And he had carried him on his shoulders, protected him from the wolves that were lying in wait for him at every turn of the road, he had watched over him and put his warm hand on his forehead—in a transfusion that was at the same time vague and profound.)

The vision of En Jordana's face came back to him, lit up like a mask in a huge room, and he began to realize more and more clearly of what he was bearing witness. A week before, he would have unthinkingly admitted to the saying: "All men are brothers." The Church said it. Now he had learned to go beneath the surface, and he was suddenly no longer pleased with his first thought.

His final conclusion was less symbolic, and he shied away from invoking a spiritual relationship. His idea was simple and yet terrible, for it contained no gloss on reality: "All men are men."

And then he closed his eyes, as if to preserve his own impartiality.

From the window, En Pere Jordana could see the cart returning from Tesera.

The idiot was coming down the sun-baked road, and the sun was shining with an inexplicable, glorious intensity on his forehead.

EIGHT

THE DOCTOR had given him permission to get up and sit in an armchair.

"To all intents and purposes," he said, "there's no reason to fear any further complications."

He seemed to be apologizing for having kept him in bed. He was undoubtedly accustomed not to being obeyed by the local people, and to a certain extent he was impressed by the fact that the big shot from the city had been so easily manageable.

The cuts were healing almost completely by themselves. He did little else but act as an attentive spectator. Today he found that his two accident cases had recovered physically, and above all psychically. When he had finished making the necessary movements, when the technical part of his job was done, he could not immediately bring his hands to a standstill; it was as if they were draining off his impetus in a vague, magic activity.

Senyor Joaquim said to him:

"It's been three days now since the car was put back on the road. Do you know how to drive?"

"Yes, Senyor."

He had worked his way through medical school—how long ago that was!—driving the municipal ambulance.

"The fellow who lives here"—Senyor Joaquim was referring to the idiot—"put the car back on the road with the help of four or five others like him." He looked admiringly at En Pere. "That's quite something, isn't it?"

The doctor pontificated timidly:

"The mentally weak often display physical strength. . . ."

"The motor may still work. Give him the keys, Jordana. Take it to the nearest garage and have them fix it. You don't have to bring it back till the day after tomorrow, but make sure they do a good job."

"What if it doesn't start . . . ?"

Senyor Joaquim felt sorry for the doctor. He was a man who no longer believed in life.

"Why shouldn't it start?"

"The car will probably start," thought the doctor, "just because it's owned by a big shot."

"You can bring it back when it's ready. Then you can make your final visit."

After the doctor had left, Senyor Joaquim asked En Pere:

"Did you see to it that we got the brief case back, Jordana? And the luggage?"

"The man brought it back, Senyor Joaquim."

Must remember to give "the man" a tip.

The idiot, ever since he had brought the doctor, had remained seated on the stone bench. His hands, hanging between his legs, were turning bluer by the minute. He looked at the wheel of the cart, intently, as if hypnotized. He was waiting for the doctor to reappear so he could take him back to Tesera. Finally, as a result of looking at it so long, the cart wheel started moving: the spokes began to tremble and swing back and forth, and then suddenly they became indistinct and jumbled: the wheel was turning. After five minutes, a sharp pain between his eyebrows made him close his eyes, and when he opened them again, the wheel had stopped turning and was completely immobile.

The doctor came out. He waved to the idiot: "So long!"

He got up and put his hand on the horse's neck.

"I've got to try to start the car!" the doctor, who by now was far away, explained.

"Start the car, thecar, theca . . ." The words went around and around in his head, just as the spokes of the wheel had done before. When the pain between his eyebrows returned, he closed his eyes and stopped thinking. When he opened them again, the doctor had already disappeared around the bend in the road, behind the oak trees, and there were the trees standing straight as always, and the immobile neck of the mare beneath his hand.

Late in the afternoon, Senyor Joaquim pulled aside the sheets and got out of bed. It was like a chrysalis opening, like a transformation.

During these last hours something in fact had been transformed within Senyor Joaquim.

En Pere Jordana helped him put on his overcoat.

"I'd like to get out of this room, but I don't want to go into that kitchen. Where could we go, Jordana, where we wouldn't be too cold?"

"They could bring us a pot of coals wherever you'd like."

They went out into the entrance hall. It was the first time Senyor Joaquim had got some idea of what the house was like, of what sort of world he had chanced upon. The hall, which was perhaps the largest and emptiest room in the house, did not look very inviting.

"There's the kitchen," En Pere pointed out.

In front was the door leading out onto the patio. To the right there was a staircase and to the left another door.

"How about over there?"

The floor was covered with hazelnuts. In a corner there was a pile of empty sacks. A little window gave out onto the back of the house, onto the fields.

"Is there something to sit on?"

En Pere looked in every corner of the house. He found an uncomfortable but usable armchair, and an ordinary chair for himself. The old woman prepared the brazier. The girl with the astonished eyes was not around. She had probably gone out into the fields with her father.

The room they had chosen was full of the dry scent of the hazelnuts. While putting Senyor Joaquim's chair in place, En Pere squashed three or four, and the scent seemed to increase in intensity.

On the other side of the main room they could see the kitchen. It was strange: they seemed to have chosen a place opposite that of the family, separated from them by the broken-down vestibule, which was like a strip of neutral territory.

Minute by minute the light coming in through the window grew feebler, and simultaneously the red of the coals grew more intense. En Pere Jordana bent over and picked up a hazelnut. He split it open with his teeth. With the tip of his tongue he could feel the wrinkled skin and instantly his tooth was covered with something acid.

"They're green!" he said.

And he spat.

Senyor Joaquim closed his eyes a moment. He could not bear to have someone spit in his presence.

(He was a corpulent man with powerful shoulders. He had a large nose and a black mustache which spread out into an irregular shape like an ink-blot.

That day at noon the radio had announced that the army in Africa had revolted.

He himself had been standing in the doorway, watching the people walking up and down, as always, and the women going into the bakery across the street and buying cake, and the blind man on the corner playing the same piece he always played on his violin. It gave one a sense of tranquillity. Then the man with the hump on his back passed by with his head down and his feet dragging, as if he were deliberately ruining his rope-soled shoes, or as if he were treading angrily on the city.

Senyor Joaquim felt his hard, cold look, and the palpitation of something menacing underneath the enormous mustache.

The man stopped for a second and spat vehemently.

The way he spat was deliberate and insulting, and a glob of warm saliva paralyzed the pulse in Senyor Joaquim's cheek.)

His stupor had lasted twenty years. Once again he felt the same genuine pinprick, in this corner filled with the scent of hazelnuts, in front of a man who had carried him in his arms. He rubbed his cheek, as if to take away the old glob of saliva.

Once again, with deep concentration, he looked at En Pere Jordana's face. His low forehead, his somewhat excessively large nose, his wrinkled lips. He could picture him perfectly with an enormous black mustache, with a hump on his back, and with huge rope-soled shoes ruined with rage. He could also picture him spitting at a man.

But he could not imagine him spitting at a man *without* a motive. That was important, the motive. He realized that perhaps for twenty years he had thought that in the world there were things which appeared to be men, but in reality were spitting machines.

And it was terrible—he once again rubbed his cheek—to think that a man always had some reason to spit: because the fruit was green or because a thick, bitter acid sometimes rose from his heart to his mouth.

En Pere Jordana bent over and offered him a handful of hazelnuts.

"You want to try them?"

He looked at the extended hand.

A week ago he would have refused.

104

But now he took them with his own rosy hand, and made up his mind to put one in his mouth. He pressed down with his teeth, nervously; he was afraid of breaking them.

He had never known how to break things with his teeth. He had always worried about his teeth. Poor people had enormous, sharp teeth.

Crack!

There was no doubt about it, the hazelnut was green, and the acid sent a chill through one of his molars.

He felt as if a glob of saliva were forming in his mouth; he waited a bit and then spat. He had never spat in front of anyone else.

He had spat without anger, in order to understand the life of people who spat.

NINE

Senyor ALSINA, the office manager, had called Senyor Llobet to his office. Senyor Llobet was a kind of head of the lower ranks of personnel; he kept a record of the hirings and firings, took care of the administrative situation, and kept an eye on the warehouse clerks, the apprentices, and the second-class assistant bookkeepers, boys who did not yet have jobs that were of much importance in the office.

Senyor Alsina, the office manager—who, in the same way that he acted like an office manager when Senyor Joaquim was present, now acted like Senyor Joaquim—had called for Senyor Llobet as being the one responsible for the conduct of the younger men.

It was a serious matter:

"Senyor Llobet, I've found an impolite inscription in the bathroom."

"An . . . inscription?"

"Yes, an inscription. And a most indecent one." He rattled his keys, master of the situation. "You must look into who did it."

Senyor Llobet lowered his head in meditation. As far as he was concerned, it could have been anybody. Forty years ago it could have been himself.

"Check the handwriting; it could give you some proof." His eyebrows came down over his eyes, gravely. "Perhaps it's that new boy, what's his name. . . ."

"Palau."

"He looks as if he has no principles."

Principles. What does Senyor Alsina mean by having principles? Keeping in your urine until closing time, so you won't have to get up in the middle of a job; not catching cold on workdays; not knowing how to whistle; and above all informing the management of those who have no principles.

"It would seem that these boys have enough spare time to be able to write on walls."

Senyor Llobet decided that first of all he must see the deleterious inscription.

He found it on the frosted glass of the door. He felt certain that he could have passed it a hundred times without noticing it. And in fact, he must have passed it, for who could tell how long it had been there.

It said: *Shit*.

Senyor Alsina, the office manager, had a peculiar ability to notice instantly the smallest defect. If twenty-four chairs had been dusted and the twenty-fifth left undone, he would run his fingers only over the back of this last one.

Senyor Llobet reread it: *Shit*. There was nothing at all unusual about the handwriting. It did not occur to him, however, that this could be the end of it all. There were no precedents for someone stopping the mechanism voluntarily. And the mechanism began working.

He called for En Palau, the boy without principles. "Did you write *shit* on the bathroom door?" "Me? No, Senyor." "Do you know who did it?" "Me? No, Senyor." He called En Joan. "Did you write *shit* on the bathroom door?" "No, Senyor, no." "Do you know who did it?" "No, I don't." He called the other Joan, the one in the Invoice Department. It was strange, but it took some effort to articulate once again: "Did you write *shit* on the bathroom door?" "Me? . . ." And then En Manelet, the boy who missed En Jordana, even though he had already grown too much to be able to wear his old trousers. "Did you write *shit* on the bathroom . . . ? Do you know who . . . ?"

Half an hour later he entered the office of Senyor Alsina, the office manager, on whose desk was a graph of the 1940–1950 production and a folder marked: *Pending Business.* He went in to tell him that he had not been able to find out who had written *shit* on the bathroom door.

(Just then, in the warehouse, four men were loading a truck and sweating, and they would have liked, once they had finished, to drink a glass of hot wine, and they thought about the fact that it cost one peseta and that they would have to sneak across the street. They finally decided on the jug in the corner, with its water that would have the taste of poverty and the weight of life.)

"Make sure that such a disagreeable thing doesn't happen again," warned L'Alsina, the office manager, with an expression of disgust, "and have it erased at once."

While going over the accounts, L'Orfila let his mind wander back over the discussion he had had on Sunday with his brother-in-law.

"I'd be happy if I could get three hundred more pesetas every payday," he had said.

His brother-in-law looked at him with curiosity.

"Why exactly three hundred?"

"I've calculated it. You know how I like to make calculations. It's like a mania of mine."

L'Orfila's child was crawling across the floor on all fours; he found a sock that was waiting to be mended and had fallen off a chair, bit it, and then left it; he bumped against the leg of the table and began to lick it; his mother passed and stepped on his hand. . . .

"Take him away!" L'Orfila could not bear to hear the child cry. His wife took him off, and next to the stove she found the crust of bread she had given him half an hour earlier. The child mashed it up a bit more, but then got bored again.

"Three hundred would suit me to a T. Have a cigarette?"

"Don't expect too much."

"No, that isn't too much. For me it would be really great. Sometimes"—he lit a match and passed it to his brother-in-law—"I wonder why it should be so difficult."

Then the brother-in-law smiled mysteriously, as if he were in possession of some secret.

"It isn't that it would be difficult," he said, "but just plain impossible."

"Don't make me laugh! You know where I work, don't you?"

Yes, he knew. It was one of the biggest companies in the region.

"I said three hundred, but I might just as well have said thirty thousand."

The brother-in-law let out a thick cloud of cigarette smoke, and with his eyes half closed he watched it rise, as if he were watching something new.

"You're wrong," he insisted. "They couldn't give you three hundred more pesetas a month."

"They couldn't? Baloney. . . ."

"No, this is no baloney." The brother-in-law seemed possessed by a profound seriousness, and he moved his hands gravely. "I can't believe that anyone who likes figures the way you do could say such a thing."

"Listen: if there's one thing I know, it's the figures concerning the company."

The brother-in-law looked up at the smoke.

"What's their monthly net profit?"

L'Orfila thought for two seconds.

"Let's say a hundred and forty thousand."

"Aren't you exaggerating a bit?"

"Let's say a hundred and forty thousand," he insisted.

"All right," and without changing his facial expression: "How many people have they got on the payroll?"

L'Orfila knew that too:

"Twenty-five or thirty in the office, and four hundred and fifty in the factory."

"Let's say five hundred, all right?"

There was a silence. From the kitchen came a cry from the mother and a cry from the child. The brother-in-law threw his cigarette on the floor.

"Now figure it out. You want three hundred pesetas, and you're sure that what you're asking for is nothing, and you can't imagine why they wouldn't give it to you. Well, listen: at least admit that there are five hundred men who need three hundred more miserable pesetas." They could hear a neighbor's radio. "Multiply it. If the company gives each worker a raise of three hundred pesetas . . . Multiply five hundred by three hundred—they'll pay out a hundred and fifty thousand pesetas more at the end of every month." He looked at him. "How much did you say the bosses made?"

"A hundred and forty thousand."

So look: if they wanted to make you all happy and give you a raise of three hundred pesetas, they'd have to close down the company: they'd be losing ten thousand pesetas a month."

L'Orfila kept on looking at him.

"So you see, it's impossible. No baloney. *Im*possible."

He was so preoccupied that now, after making sure there was no trace of L'Alsina, the office manager, he placed a sheet of paper under the stack of expenditure slips, and for the fourth time did the multiplication suggested to him the previous Sunday by his brother-in-law.

It was so simple that it made his hair stand on end.

They couldn't pay out three hundred more pesetas. It was *impossible*.

But there must be some mistake. He began from the beginning. From his papers he could verify the fact that there was a net profit of a hundred and forty thousand pesetas. . . . He wrote the word *verified* and underlined it four, five, six times, and suddenly the whole matter completely ceased to interest him.

Dining early always put En Maurici, Senyor Joaquim's partner, in a bad mood. Because dining early meant that one was in a hurry, and there was nothing he hated more than having to do something immediately after eating.

It was Thursday, the day for the opera.

He got up from the table, lit a cigarette, and went to put on his tie in front of the bathroom mirror. In point of fact, he didn't really have to rush out after dinner. It took La Marta almost an hour to get ready, and he wasn't one of those husbands who got nervous, paced up and down, and opened the door every five minutes to shout: "Not ready yet?" He was thankful to La Marta for this traditional delay, and accepted it as a touch of delicacy on her part.

Until it was time to leave, En Maurici sat down in an armchair and read the latest best seller, holding a glass of cognac which he sniffed rather than drank.

He was very impressed by this book on robots, electronic brains, and automatic factories. How was it that people didn't know about these things' being invented every day? In ten minutes a machine can make a calculation it would take a scientist a hundred years to do. . . . If he remembered to, he would explain to La Marta about these kitchens that work by themselves. . . . It wouldn't be a bad idea for somebody to invent a husband-go-to-the-opera robot. . . .

He hadn't put on his shoes yet. He delightedly wiggled his toes inside his warm slippers.

In fact, he thought, there is no such thing as a real man. Men are always robot-men, who function completely automatically. Soon he would have to get up, and from that moment on all his movements would follow in a fixed course, as if dictated by some tiny engineer.

The odor of the cognac reached his nostrils and awoke a thousand minute nerves. It was a strange and yet pleasant sensation, and he felt that if it went on much longer, he would take off and start flying.

La Marta's voice rang out as if from behind a pane of glass, and suddenly the pane of glass was shattered, and En Maurici once again became completely part of a world in progress.

When he got behind the wheel of the Opel, he said to his wife:

"This morning I signed a paper asking for a Seat. This one's too old-fashioned."

She threw her overcoat back on the seat.

"One like En Joaquim's?"

"No, he has a Stromberg."

"The one you asked for—is it better or worse?"

"You can't compare them. . . ."

It was a pity you couldn't compare them.

"Nobody's heard a thing from En Joaquim. We received a telegram and a letter from Saragossa, and since then nothing. This silence is very unlike him."

They turned into the Rambla. He crossed his arms on the steering wheel and put on the brakes. The same traffic jam as always.

"En Joaquim is a man who's always tied to the office by a string. Come what may. Now it looks as if that string's been cut."

The din of car horns. The useless, exacerbating, childish din of car horns. En Maurici hadn't moved.

"The idiots!" he said. "As if we didn't all want to move. Those dimwits making all the racket—do they think that someone's stopped on purpose?"

"What do they say at the office?" La Marta asked.

"L'Alsina, the office manager, is baffled"—they were starting up; En Maurici laughed. "I got the impression, I don't know why, that L'Alsina was peculiarly disgusted with 'Senyor Joaquim' for not keeping him posted as he had promised. He finds it very bad form."

There was something that amused En Maurici. Surely it was the thought of L'Alsina, the office manager, who, in front of the workers, ostentatiously clinked his keys in his pocket and from time to time coughed authoritatively, who had passed from assurance to total conviction that a person's best fate was to rise from a warehouse clerk to being the boss's right-hand man.

"Today, when he brought around the papers for me to sign, he couldn't resist telling me: 'No news from Senyor Joaquim.' But I decided not to continue the conversation. He knows I don't take much interest in the company. It's obvious that, as far as he's concerned, I'm a signing machine that you plug in every morning from eleven to twelve and every afternoon from six to seven."

He put on the brake, violently. When would they take these trolleys off the Rambla?

La Marta threw her overcoat back on the seat again and asked: "What do you think's happened to En Joaquim?"

"It would be a miracle if something has happened to him. Nothing ever happens to him"—he accelerated. "If you're so curious about it, you could call up La Lluïsa. Maybe she knows something. No, but you're right"—he smiled—"L'Alsina, the office manager, has inquired into traffic accidents. Not a sign of En Joaquim."

Suddenly he felt with one hand for his wallet. Sometimes when he changed and put on his dinner jacket he forgot it. He felt calmer; he was carrying three or four thousand pesetas, in case the Giralts or the Bardellas afterward suggested winding up the evening in one of their habitual and unbelievably boring *dives*.

TEN

It was a strange drink, a strong liqueur prepared by the old woman according to some vague recipe. It was thick and violent, and Senyor Joaquim's palate rejected it convulsively.

En Pere Jordana had gone to the kitchen to ask for it, and he had returned to the room where the hazelnuts were stored with a little jug in his hands. The old woman had been happy to give him the liqueur, for she interpreted his desire to drink her preparation as undeniable proof of trust, as a possibility for contact.

The brazier immediately revived with the fresh coals.

It was an unusual night, starting off as it did illuminated by the brazier, perfumed by the hazelnuts, and stirred by the drink. There finally arrived a moment when Senyor Joaquim and En Pere Jordana lost all sense of time.

Senyor Joaquim put the glass down: there were tears in his eyes. En Maurici would have liked this diabolical drink. En Maurici would have said that it had such and such a body, such and such a bouquet, and that it wasn't sufficiently distilled or properly aged, but that these country brews had great charm.

He dried his eyes and slowly folded his handkerchief into eight folds.

"Are you feeling all right, Senyor Joaquim?"

En Pere, holding his glass in his hand, looked at him fixedly. "Fine."

From somewhere came a noise of ducks quacking. And afterward silence.

En Pere brought the glass to his lips. He would have liked this strange vigil to last eternally. The liquid burned his tongue, and suddenly it burst between his eyes like a sweet, heavy bubble. He wanted the sun never to rise. He was afraid that the doctor would return with the car all repaired, and that they would have to go back to Barcelona.

And everything would have ended there.

La Maria, who had given him the hundred pesetas "just in case"; La Maria, who had said good-by to him with a disguised yet strong hope; La Maria, who had thought that for the first time she could stop to think, without a sense of pain, about being forty, about the child and his next day's homework; La Maria, whom he now imagined with her hand suspended in mid-air, waiting, before sewing on the next button, for a voice to come and set her free . . . In reality, La Maria was doomed to the never ending dust, discouragement, and fatigue beyond the sweet, thick wall that was now rising within his forehead. He drank.

"Are you really feeling all right, Senyor Joaquim?" he insisted.

Senyor Joaquim's cheeks and lips were red in the light from the coals. His eyes were in shadow.

En Pere looked for them anxiously, and for a moment he was afraid that Senyor Joaquim had no more eyes, and would never again be able to see what he, En Pere Jordana, chauffeur and martyr, was doing. He liked that: "Chauffeur and martyr." He repeated chauffeur and martyr, chauffeur and martyr, chauffeur and martyr, until the outlines of the words became blurred and a new, absurd, and inexpressive word was created: "chauffeurand-martyr."

"I don't see how you can drink that stuff," said Senyor Joaquim; "it burns everything it touches."

"It doesn't burn," he answered; "on the contrary. Alcohol's an anesthetic. Everything sensitive and painful inside gets clouded over, and put inside a soft wad of cotton. Excuse me."

He took a drink. He excused himself because of what he had said or because of the noise he had let out. . . . He was sweating. It was hot inside this den.

"What is it that makes you unhappy, Jordana?"

En Pere hesitated. He looked at the glass. Then he closed his eyes.

"What makes me unhappy . . . everything."

He didn't know if he'd done the right thing in saying this, he

114

didn't know if what he'd said had any meaning. He pulled his head back into the shadows and lifted his glass. One more swig and that would be enough.

Senyor Joaquim's voice was muted.

"What do you mean, Jordana?"

And he immediately thought: "Why do I ask? Why do I want to know? Wasn't that a grotesque thing to say: 'What makes me unhappy . . . everything'? Isn't it obvious that this fellow's had a bit too much? I should send him to bed."

"Everything makes me unhappy," En Jordana repeated, and he tried to remember what he had thought before, but he couldn't remember that it was "chauffeur and martyr."—"What makes me unhappy is my wife, and my house, and this"—he pointed to where his shirt had been darned under the collar—"and what makes me unhappy are the years I've lived, soon it'll be forty, and those I have yet to live, and what makes me unhappy is the son I have and the sons I don't have—I have sons I don't have, you understand? And what makes me unhappy, what makes me unhappy, what makes me unhappy . . ."—his eyes looked paralyzed, and he slowly stretched out his arms, and he looked as if he couldn't say another word, and yet he did say: ". . . so you see . . ."

"I should send him to bed," Senyor Joaquim thought. But he couldn't move, he was rooted to the spot. He had the feeling that he had never seen a man from so close. He could not understand why this didn't give him a feeling of anguish: possibly because the man was practically unconscious and didn't realize that he was listening to him with such interest.

"And not only me, but everybody, everybody . . . Open your eyes and you'll see En Manelet on the other side of the desk . . . You only have to open your eyes"—he frowned. "Why should I have En Manelet in front of me?"

Now he was looking for Senyor Joaquim's eyes.

"En Manelet? Who?"

En Jordana looked at him in astonishment.

"You don't see En Manelet?"

And he looked for Senyor Joaquim's eyes in the shadows yet more avidly. Maybe he was sticking his foot in it, maybe Senyor Joaquim never had eyes.

"I gave En Manelet an old overcoat"—and he opened his eyes extraordinarily wide, with a sense of satisfaction. "Haven't you ever noticed it? It's beige with thin stripes. . . ."

One more swig, and that's all.

"But now he can't wear it any more. He's grown too much. The more he grows, the sorrier you feel for him, you see. But really sorry—so sorry that you'd give anything not to see him make that face."

He began to suspect that he was talking too much, and so he politely handed the conversation over to Senyor Joaquim.

"How are your children, Senyor Joaquim?"

He vaguely remembered some children with tiny neckties and white socks. . . .

Senyor Joaquim tried to remember who En Manelet was.

"How are your children?" En Pere insisted metallically.

There must be a personnel card on En Manelet, but he couldn't remember. It wasn't customary to write on these cards: "His face makes you feel sorry for him."

En Pere had the feeling that he'd slept for a minute. He rediscovered Senyor Joaquim's presence, and out loud he continued a train of thought that until then had been advancing underground.

". . . and she put fifteen-watt bulbs all through the house to save money. Isn't that a riot?"

". . . bulbs . . . ?"

"Yes, my wife. Fifteen-watt bulbs, fiiifteen"—he stretched out the *i,* amused at the idea—"to save money. Isn't that a riot?"

Senyor Joaquim rubbed his hands together, and he could feel En Pere Jordana's penetrating gaze fixed on him.

116

"Yes, it's a riot," he confessed.

En Pere's lips trembled with joy.

"You think it's a riot too!" And then as if to an accomplice: "But a man can't tell this to his wife, can he? Would you?"

A strange feeling of heat spread out through Senyor Joaquim's chest, and he could have sworn he was sweating. It was hot in this den.

"You wouldn't tell your wife either," affirmed En Pere.

He looked at him, raised his glass, and drank a toast to him. He closed his eyes a moment. Another sweet, heavy bubble burst within his forehead. He leaned forward a bit, and said in a confidential tone:

"I forgot to tell you before: what makes me unhappy is also the fifteen-watt bulbs, and what makes me unhappy is also you—you're always inside your office and you only see Senyor Alsina, the office manager, and he's a son of a bitch. Excuse me, but then we're not having a bad time here, are we?"

He let himself be taken to the bedroom. Senyor Joaquim pushed him gently as they went. It was the first time he had taken his arm, it was the first time he had touched En Jordana— En Jordana—with his greedy fingers. He led him to bed with the realization that he was protecting him.

En Pere tried to maintain a thread of lucidity till the very end. The moment he lay down he gave up. It was as if he had suddenly been mineralized.

Senyor Joaquim watched him with exceptional attention. His forehead was wrinkled as if it were old and worn. A vein protruding from his neck trembled compassionately: it looked like a worm or something alive. But above all he was fascinated by the skin around his mouth. It was worn-out, tired skin, and bloodless. He was impressed by the fact that this could be the head of a man.

He then gave way to a strange desire. He was tempted to see

117

En Pere Jordana's long, thin arm, which was floating on the sheet like flotsam, like an object with its own, independent existence. The naked, pale skin gave him a simultaneous sensation of anguish and pity.

It was then that he rolled up the sleeve of his jacket, leaned over the bed, and placed his arm next to En Pere Jordana's.

He looked at them both for five minutes, obsessed.

They were the same. En Pere Jordana's arm was exactly like his. The same naked, pale skin which made one feel both anguish and pity.

It was strange, but he found himself unable to remove his arm from the bed. It was as if both arms belonged to the same person. It was a new and surprising sensation to find oneself bound in some mysterious yet indestructible manner to another man.

ELEVEN

SHE FOUND A SEAT in the lower part of the bus. It was the bus of resignation. The bus that brought workers back to their houses, when the city was already dark. The men wearing berets dirty with plaster, their hands stained with acid, their cheeks spotted with paint or grease from machines. With extinguished cigarette butts in their mouths and with their socks falling down.

La Maria, who had gone to deliver the shirts with their buttons on them, now let her hands rest on her lap. She calculated that before En Pere returned, she could finish two hundred and forty more. Her fingers danced with excitement and joy.

At the La Carme dairy store she would buy herself a *croissant*. She couldn't remember how long it had been since she had felt like eating a *croissant*.

The bus crossed the Paseo de la Gracia. She looked at the lights, at the cars, and down at the end, at the illuminated fountain, which from the Calle Provença seemed small, very small. The bus passed by rapidly, as if embarrassed at having incrusted in its flanks the dust and shadows of the suburbs.

"Tickets please . . ."

The ticket taker advanced down the aisle, agilely, knocking against the metal bars with his ticket box. He approached a girl, gave her a ticket, took the money, and gave her the change without taking his eyes off her neckline. He was a man with a flat nose, as if he had lost the tip of it one day through an excess of rash curiosity.

"Tickets please . . ."

From pockets, from wallets that were coming apart, from the warmth of chests, from defensively clenched fists came the bills, the hidden, softened, honest, and untiring one-peseta bills, that seemed worn out of all proportion to their modest worth. Sometimes these dark bills leave the hands of poor people as if they were a layer or a slice of worn skin. . . .

La Maria looked at the street, which, because the bus was now travelling at top speed, seemed to be blinking with colored lights. She looked, but she could see only the bewitching and ever changing play of the city lights. This was why she didn't realize there was going to be a collision, and she banged her head against the metal bar.

"It's pure worsted, Senyora. Feel the weight. Very light. I could show you cloths of different quality, but it would be no use trying to deceive you. That goes without saying."

He lifted up the piece of cloth a bit more.

"And the design—it's exclusive, of course. This shade has vigor and yet it's delicate. We also have it in olive green and pale yellow."

Senyora Civit, En Joaquim Civit's wife, touched it, examined it, and put it down with a certain regret. If she had felt like buying something, she would have bought this.

"It's lovely," she admitted, and with these words of praise paid for the time she had taken up.

An errand boy opened the door of the shop for her. The chauffeur opened the car door for her. It did not seem as if the air in the street opened a path for her as she walked, but rather as if the air around her was always the same and always moved along gently with her to keep her from any rude shocks or violent contacts.

Parking was a problem. The chauffeur's life was one great obsession with the parking problem. Had it been possible to advise the Senyora, now that they had found a space in front of Martí i Martí, he would not have given it up. Trying to get near Can Pellicer meant running the risk of not finding a place until they reached the Calle Mallorca.

But this was a suggestion he would never dare make.

While they were stopped at a red light, a hand waved just outside the window. A pair of black eyes were staring intently, and before the light changed Bel Terrades got into the car and filled it with the scent of her perfume.

("Why is she wearing a fur piece?" La Civit thought with a frown. "It isn't in fashion any more, except for maids." She couldn't understand it. "And it's new; she just bought it.")

"How are you, all right?"

("It would be a fine thing, after everybody wearing them, and now nobody wearing them—if fur pieces once again became something the upper classes wore.")

"I haven't had any news from En Joaquim—he's taken a trip —but you know how these things are. . . ."

("Fifteen or twenty thousand pesetas . . . Oh, but she just had her saint's day. It must have been a present from En Terrades.")

"Wherever you'd like, the Salon Rosa sounds fine."

(She identified the perfume: Femme by Rochas. "It isn't too long since poor Rochas died. La Terrades probably doesn't even know about it. I'd like to hear her pronounce Femme.")

120

"Yes, I know. It's been so long since we've seen each other. . . ."

It was the hour of satisfaction. In the tearooms with large, gilded mirrors, rose-colored tablecloths, waiters in well-pressed tails, indigestible pastry and excessive steam heat, it was the hour of densest satisfaction.

The women artificially kept their eyebrows at a height one centimeter above normal. Each one was listening, expectantly, for the moment of greatest collective satisfaction; each one was aware—while they talked, while they smoked, while they ate—of the useless, empty, and glorious satisfaction of being there, in a place whose only reason for existence lay in one single fact: that they were there.

Lluïsa Civit put her tiny silver cigarette lighter on the table.

"You can't imagine," she said, "how happily they go off to the German School. I'm astonished at the two older children. I never remember going off to school so calmly."

She didn't have time to light her cigarette. The waiter quickly came over and lit it for her.

"And it's so amusing to hear them reciting the Paternoster, saying *Vater unser* or something like that, all so seriously!"

"The boy of a friend of mine, La Mascort—do you know her? —goes to the Italian School. They don't overwork them there: they spend their time cutting out colored paper. Can you imagine, they make them fold paper all different kinds of ways—but nicely, you know—and glue all the pieces together and sew them. They say that manual exercise helps form sensitivity or . . ."

"What nonsense. . . ."

"En Josep thinks it's pretty ridiculous; he says that it's all nonsense and that men shouldn't be made to sew . . . but what I tell him is that with children you have to try a bit of everything . . . so they won't ask you one day why they aren't better than they are."

"Every Sunday we give En Joaquim Maria twenty-five pesetas. As a gift, you understand—with complete freedom to do what he wants with the money: buy candy, put it in his piggy bank, or give it to a beggar or . . . whatever he wants! En Joaquim's forever telling him: 'You can do whatever you want with the money, Joaquim Maria!' That kind of responsibility is what forms them."

Bel Terrades blew a bit of smoke out through her nose and said tearfully:

"There's nothing so complicated as educating children. . . ."

This thing which was so complicated was followed by learning how to blow smoke out through one's nose.

They went up through Balmes, and the car stopped in front of a red light, next to the sidewalk. The line waiting for the bus looked like a frieze, a bas-relief, beneath the street light. But now none of these figures moved, no hand came forward to knock on the car window, as Bel Terrades had done. All the eyes of this frieze looked at the car window with the same purpose and respect with which they would have looked at a movie screen. For them it was a small but very interesting screen.

In the line a woman carrying a child changed it to her other arm, but the frieze immediately regained its immobility. La Lluïsa Civit glanced at it for a moment, but without realizing how complete and terrible this immobility was.

"I'll give you a ring one of these days and . . ."

"You always say you will and then you never . . ."

"But I can never catch you when you're in. . . ."

"We have a lot of things to discuss. . . ."

"You could also try giving me a ring. . . ."

They were thrown forward, bent over at the waist across the back of the driver's seat, and the car, as it collided, dirtied its silver-plated headlights in the dust and shadows of the suburbs the bus carried in its flanks.

"It's nothing."

She didn't hear him.

"My boy, my little boy! Poor child!" she sobbed.

"Nothing's happened to your little boy! Calm down!"

The druggist, as he went from one person to another, stopped in front of this woman with a little blue purse and a folded scarf clutched in her hand, and asked the doctor:

"Is it serious?"

"Not at all. She's recovered from the shock all right. Now it's nerves."

"My boy, my boy—what'll En Pere say!"

The doctor left her in the hands of a clerk in the drugstore, who patted her affectionately.

"Everything's all right! Don't worry."

"Now that En Pere's away . . ."

"Don't worry about En Pere. Who's En Pere?"

But she didn't hear him.

"My child, you need me, don't you? I could give you anything, I didn't think I'd . . . Maybe the sacrifice . . . I'd just returned twenty-four shirts, you saw me working." Suddenly her tongue was paralyzed and the words exploded inside her head. "We couldn't do any more, my boy, we couldn't . . . Your father . . ."

Then the familiar name reawakened her voice and her first cry came out broken: "Pere! Where are you? Come—there's the child. . . ."

The clerk, exasperated, fumbled nervously for her pulse. Perfect. He brusquely let her arm fall back down.

"I got your telegram. *All well.* Do you hear me, my child? All well. Your father says all's well. We did what we could. Poor boy! I've got three hundred and fifty pesetas in a tin box on the top shelf of the closet. Three hundred and fifty after nine years! Even your father doesn't know about it. I never touched this money, even when you had the scarlet fever, or when you, Pere, lost your wallet. . . . We couldn't do more for you, my boy. . . ."

"Is she unconscious?" someone asked, taking interest.

The door of the drugstore was continually opening and closing, letting in repeated bursts of cold air.

"Your father would have liked to do more, but he couldn't—they wouldn't let him . . . for the moment. . . ."

Her hand relaxed, the scarf for wrapping bundles fell to the floor, and she took three deep breaths, as if she were asleep. Then she came to.

Finally her turn at the telephone came.

"Don't be alarmed. La Bel's strong: shaken up a bit; at worst a broken rib . . . no, it's the truth, come and see for yourself. . . ." "What's the address, please?" she asked the druggist. "I'll wait for you, fine . . . No the children weren't with us . . . They're safe at home. . . ."

As soon as his mother had gone out to deliver the shirts, little Peret had closed his notebook and put his hand in his pocket. He took out two clothespins he had stolen from his mother. He tried to get the metal spring off the wooden part; he had chosen the two oldest and weakest clothespins. He tried as hard as he could, and the metal left a white mark on the end of his fingers.

They had taught him how to do this at the National School.

He had already got one apart. The spot on his thumb from the indelible lead pencil had almost completely rubbed off onto the porous wood of the clothespin. It was a shame. He thought he would scrape it off with a razor blade. Where did his father keep them?

He spent half an hour going from one end of the apartment to another, opening closets and bureaus, getting up on chairs, sometimes forgetting what he was looking for and touching with expectant fingers the thousand small, strange objects he found along the way.

Little Pere, the Jordana boy, didn't know that that afternoon he could have lost his mother. He didn't know that he could lose her at any moment, any day, any time. Had he understood this, he would no longer have been a child.

You can make a pistol out of a clothespin. That was what he knew. And that is what men do not know.

A chicken, a dog, and a rabbit were painted on the door of the toy closet in red, yellow, and blue. It was a cheerful, well-lighted, and stimulating playroom. On the table there was a crane made with a Number 4 Meccano set. On a shelf there was a little theater with the stage set for *The Merchant of Venice* and all the paper actors piled up on the stage. Open school notebooks, and a litter of colored pencils, compasses, rulers, erasers, and pencil trays, and for each child a sharpener in the form of an airplane, a telephone, or a car.

The mother was out; she had left with the chauffeur.

Every now and then a maid with a starched apron stuck her head in the door, said something, and then went back to sitting on the bed and reading the novel they lent her on Thursdays.

On the table there was also a strange electrically operated game that was extraordinarily instructive, which consisted in guessing which flag was the Italian flag and which of the animals on Plate III was a puma.

In one corner L'Eduard Maria and En Lluïs Maria were sitting on the floor trying to take apart a clothespin in order to make a pistol, the way they had learned at the German School.

They also didn't realize that their mother could have died, that she could die any day.

They also didn't realize that it was a pity that the parents of all children had already forgotten that a clothespin could be made into a pistol, and that they had all become accustomed to enjoying life as if it were a personal, unsharable game.

TWELVE

HE STRETCHED OUT cautiously under the covers. Bit by bit his slowly moving toes came into contact with the coldness of the sheet. He was lying completely flat, with his hands folded over his chest.

The silence besieged him, disquieted him, and kept him awake. He had never before drunk a drop of homemade liquor, and his forehead felt cool and as if illuminated from within. He tried to remain as immobile as he could; he tried to blend into the night, to blot himself out into the shadows. En Pere Jordana was probably sleeping soundly, and he realized that he envied him.

The minutes passed and he could not forget the dry scent of the hazelnuts.

At first he had thought that it was this strange, delicate, and yet penetrating odor that wasn't permitting him to sleep. But it didn't take him long to realize that something was giving him a feeling of awe and making him breathe silently. He had the impression that En Pere Jordana's arms were still stretched out alongside of him.

At one point he took his right arm out from under the covers to make sure that there was nothing there but the cold surface of the sheet.

Uneasiness was a sensation he had never known before. He now realized that his life had always been easy and assured. The fact of the matter was that until now he had never stopped to think. He had always gone to sleep the moment his head touched the pillow, every night for fifty years.

And now he thought that there had been times in his life when he might have felt uneasy and suffered. At school, at the office, in his family life. And in spite of this, he had overcome every difficult moment with unbelievably natural ease.

"Good work, Joaquim," his father had said one day, congratu-

126

lating him. "But you've studied enough. Now the factory's waiting for you."

The factory then was something relatively new. His father had just given it its almost definitive dimensions, but every day there were still surprises, situations that required initiative or improvisation. The words "Now the factory's waiting for you" really meant: "The time's come to do something, and to make something out of yourself."

There were eighty men in the factory, and he entered as a weaver's helper. That was the local custom. The director's son spent two years under the orders of an experienced worker, who used no formality in speaking to him and called him Pepet or Quimet or Joanet. That is why, in older firms, the director is still called by his first name. (At that moment, Senyor Joaquim became aware of the illogical distance that had grown up between his own familiar name and the life of the office.)

He was slow in learning his job. His first teacher was only relatively patient: it annoyed him that the boy's progress was not more rapid. At times he seemed to ignore him, and did the work by himself. Years later, Senyor Joaquim had explained to his friends: "I started at the bottom. I was a worker too." Until now, in the silence of this soundless night, he had not realized that his old teacher's annoyance had never bothered him—that he had never really been a worker. He earned only twenty pesetas a week, with no more days off than was normal, he wore overalls and got his hands dirty; he acted like a worker but he was not a worker. Because when the left the job he went to the director's house to have supper and he sat in the place of the director's son.

He had vivid memories of that place. The chair made out of dark wood with a high, straight back, the iron lamp and the glass-top table, and in a corner a grandfather clock that struck the hours with a sonorous, unhurried solemnity, and which his grandfather said had been made by the best clockmaker in Zürich. This unknown Zürich clockmaker had been one of the men he had most admired during his childhood.

One day, as if at a single stroke, he had learned all he had to know and had escaped from the old worker's hands like a bird. For four years he went from one job to another within the factory, and he earned twenty, and then twenty-five, and then thirty pesetas. One afternoon he ruined eighteen yards of cloth, but that hadn't bothered him either. At the time he thought it had, but now he could see clearly that it hadn't bothered him a bit. That one second after the disaster, while the blood was flowing back from his face to his heart, he had thought in order to calm himself: "At dinnertime, as always, I'll sit at my place at the table." In the place of the son of Senyor Joaquim, the director.

Now, in a night of insomnia, in a strange bed, in a strange house, he felt disturbed for the first time in his life.

He had been a boy without problems. When the time had come—when he was a bit older—he had married with a great sense of satisfaction and peaceful pride. La Lluïsa had fitted into his life automatically. They had moved into an apartment on the Calle de Balmes, and after five years they had bought a suburban house in Pedralbes.

"We've got a chauffeur starting tomorrow," he announced one day. "Driving tires me." His wife, a month later, announced: "Monday we'll have another maid: it's a big house to take care of." On St. John's Day they had their third child.

His father had a stroke which paralyzed his right arm, and after that he could walk only with difficulty. He took his place effortlessly, and there were several years in which he made money almost without realizing it. L'Alsina, who had been cashier, was made office manager. He knew the business and the employees, and with him around there was no useless wasting of time.

Not even En Maurici had ever become a problem. His job didn't interest him, and in fact nothing interested him, but he was cautious enough not to make any blunders. Two hours at the office at the end of the day was all he could take. And En Joaquim never asked more of him.

Then came the fourth child, and two years later, the fifth.

In the silence of the night he thought he could hear a slow, heavy tread. He listened carefully: the tread neither approached nor receded. Always the same. It could be the branch of a tree against a wall, or a door.

He closed his eyes and tried to go to sleep to the sound of this measured tread. There was something that made him feel vigilant, that was keeping him company and not letting him sleep. En Pere Jordana. Now he wasn't dreaming him—the man was there in his thoughts; and his mind was as clear as his vision, for he could now make out in the darkness the outline of the chest, the rectangular picture frames, and the empty chair at the foot of the bed.

It had calmed him, and at the same time had been a disappointment for him, that En Pere Jordana, after starting in on his monologue next to the brazier, had suddenly been conquered by the alcohol and grown silent. This was not the Jordana he had known, the gray Jordana without voice or blood, the Jordana who had been reduced to a file card. He was a new, frightening man, a man illuminated and naked like a flame; there was a warmth emanating from this man's skin, and at a certain moment he had felt his presence as something burning hot. It had been awesome to realize that an obscure man like that could be so pathetic; En Jordana's explosion had not offended him. It had surprised him and inundated him with an unfamiliar confusion. Now he could see things clearly: it was this intimate confusion that was making him restless, a confusion that was struggling to acquire a specific outline, to convert a hundred memories and shadowy doubts into a precise point of light.

And it should have been so easy to understand what was happening to him, and to understand En Pere Jordana! But he was struggling against his lack of experience; it was an effort for him to spend even a half a minute thinking about En Pere Jordana. Thinking about him as something different from a chauffeur; thinking about En Jordana as if this man were himself.

He wanted to imagine himself with a shirt mended under the

tips of the collar, but he could only see En Jordana's shirt. He wanted to take En Jordana's wife and child upon himself, but his thoughts became entirely occupied with his own wife and his own children. He tried repeatedly to erase these familiar images, but they kept on reappearing. He saw that he was incapable of knowing what another person was like, and that what was torturing him was the realization that this other person's existence was deep and authentic—perhaps as real as his own.

For a moment he thought of getting up and going to drink a glass of that thick liqueur, to find out what his reaction would be, and if deep down the mainsprings of his actions would be the same as En Jordana's. The liqueur would bring him to a sudden knowledge of himself and of others—of what was common to all people.

". . . L'Alsina, the office manager, is a son of a bitch. Excuse me," En Jordana had said. He tried to agree with him. "L'Alsina is a son of a bitch." A son of a bitch, a son of a bitch. He could see him entering his office, silent and efficient. "The matter has been attended to, Senyor Joaquim." "I have reorganized the Sales Department, Senyor Joaquim." "I have plans for a better distribution of the Christmas bonuses." "We fired a girl who was causing disturbances in the Statistics Department." "The matter has been attended to, Senyor Joaquim." And he repeated to himself: he's a son of a bitch, a son of a bitch. He didn't understand it, and it disturbed him not to understand it, for he wanted to know what En Pere Jordana was thinking, what he was feeling, what he knew when he said that L'Alsina was a son of a bitch.

The faraway cry of an unknown animal perforated the night. He could not have said what kind of animal had screeched; he had never known anything about animals, plants, or country things. The cry was repeated, but longer this time. It seemed to him like the audible voice of all the things he knew nothing of. It was like a wail born in the heart of the night. It did not frighten him. On the contrary. He sat up in bed, the better to hear this powerful voice that was an invitation to contact, to friend-ship.

But the cry was not repeated. He rapidly absorbed the silence surrounding him. He drank it in, as if it were some stimulating drink.

"Perhaps," he thought, letting his head fall back onto the pillow, "En Pere Jordana has some ideas concerning me I had never imagined until now. Perhaps he says to his wife: 'Senyor Joaquim is a son of a bitch. . . .'"

His thoughts would not have concerned him a bit if he had been only a chauffeur—nothing had concerned him until now—if En Jordana had not carried him in his arms after the accident; if he had not watched over him, treated him and looked after him with peculiar affection, if he had not put his hand on his fore-head with a desire to calm him, if he had not been so ever-present. He would not have been concerned, perhaps, if he had not seen him stretched out in bed and seen their two arms alongside each other, his as defenseless and fragile as En Jordana's. Then, for a moment, he had felt that En Jordana and he were identical. That if their skins were identical, then so were the lives they sheltered.

It was as if he had caught a fever. The feeling of suffocation had passed, but the idea kept on going around inside his brain, unalterable, as if it had been converted into a crystal of blood.

The unknown animal again cried in the night, and it no longer seemed like the angry voice of all the things he knew nothing of. Now—it rang out for the fourth time—it seemed like something completely different, as if nature were ostensibly approving the small sense of certainty that was invading him, confirming the profound, mysterious oneness of living beings.

Suddenly he felt as if he had been asleep for a while. He felt a shudder of cold and pulled the sheet up to his nose. And a scene vividly presented itself to him: he was standing next to En Pere Jordana's bed, looking at him. En Jordana was sweating from all the alcohol he had drunk, his hair was falling over his forehead, his enormous eyebrows stood out, and one entire arm was outside the covers. He touched his icy hand. He bent his arm and put it back under the covers. Then En Jordana split into four, eight, sixteen, a hundred men all alike yet different, and all waiting inside the bed for him to put their arms under the covers. It was too much for him. There were always more arms to be covered up; he would never finish. He was perspiring and yet happy. Suddenly he thought that the only one he wanted to help was En Jordana, but he couldn't identify him among all those men. He did not stop until they were all covered. Then he noticed that his own arm was cold, and he went to bed.

He pulled the covers up over his nose. It seemed as if he had slept for a few moments. He tried in vain to make out whether he had dreamed it or experienced it. He went off to sleep for good without realizing it, but suffused with a warm sense of peace and with a strange feeling of satisfaction at having put all the arms under the covers.

The next day, when En Pere Jordana entered the room—the daylight was already slightly yellow from the sun—with the cup of milk in his hands, Senyor Joaquim remained immobile and watched his movements through half-closed eyes.

En Pere Jordana seemed perfectly serene. On each side of his nose there were slender, dark wrinkles that stretched out toward his cheeks, and there was a stubborn lock of hair at the back of his head. He thought that Senyor Joaquim was still sleeping; he adjusted the windows and started to leave.

"Jordana!"

He turned around and said, as unstridently as he could:

"Yes, Senyor Joaquim."

"It's a nice day, don't you think?"

"Exceptionally nice."

Senyor Joaquim announced:

"I'm going to get up."

"What about breakfast?"

"Afterward."

En Jordana opened the windows and left the room, for Senyor Joaquim was now capable of dressing himself. He rubbed his cheeks and realized that his beard had grown. He thought that while Senyor Joaquim was getting dressed he could shave.

He went out of the house, crossed the courtyard, and set up his shaving equipment on the stones around the irrigation pool. It really was a nice day. Not a bit of wind. The weak winter sun spread out on the earth like a breath, and after an hour the tepid earth began to exhale and return the warmth it had received. This amorous, joyful game would last until the early hours of the afternoon.

En Pere Jordana wet his face, but before putting on the soap, he decided to brush his teeth again, for his mouth was still full of the aftertaste of the liquor he had drunk the night before. Afterward he washed his neck, face, and forehead again, as if to rid them of a secretion he imagined was stuck to his skin.

When his face was covered with soap, the old woman crossed the courtyard. She was carrying an empty sack over her shoulder, and when she saw him she came over, walking with steps so tiny as to be scarcely noticeable beneath her long, full skirt. She seemed to be advancing on invisible little wheels, or as if she were mechanically operated.

"Did you like the liquor?" she asked.

"Yes," and En Jordana could not avoid having a bit of soap fall on his lips.

The old woman stared at him fixedly, with a strange intensity. Since for the moment she wasn't speaking, he picked up the razor and leaned toward the little mirror. This was the only moment of shaving he liked. When the blade cut in and removed the first patch of hair.

"Listen."

He turned around. The old woman sought out his eyes amid all the soap.

"Have you seen La Isidora?"

133

No, today he hadn't yet seen the girl with the ecstatic eyes.

But there was a peculiar insistence in the old woman's eyes.

"You haven't seen her?"

And En Pere realized that what she meant was *had he noticed her,* had he been aware of her presence during the four days they had been here. He made a long, slow stroke with the razor, and wiped off the excess soap with the blade. He then turned around and looked at the old woman:

"What about her?"

The old woman remained almost immobile. The empty sack was still on her shoulder, and her skirt reached the ground like a bell, or like one of those Nativity figurines they sell at a peseta and a half the dozen, but with her entire life compressed into her black eyes.

"La Isidora's timid, but she's a fine girl, the best in the whole region."

En Pere Jordana stared at her in surprise. The soap dried on his cheek.

"They're about to leave. Today, tomorrow. Soon. When the doctor from Tesera brings the car back. They'll leave because now they feel all right. They won't ever come back again." When she had wakened in the night, she had listened to the silence of the house, and this silence had seemed full of the presence of the two strangers, and she had felt that while they were here, with each ticktock of the ancient clock, with every drop of time, good fortune or prosperity would descend on the house.

"Take this, for now," the young man had told her soon after they had arrived, as he gave her five hundred-peseta bills. "Later on we'll take care of the rest." They had turned out to be quiet people, and they could have gone on living in the house forever without causing any inconvenience. Undoubtedly it wouldn't be long before they would give them five more bills. Compared with the strangers, the doctor from Tesera was a country man like them, and she had thought that he might also be interested in keeping them there—that he could help her keep them in the house. But she hadn't said anything to him.

Two days ago she had boiled three mint leaves for an hour in a little milk from a light-skinned goat, and then, after reciting a prayer, she had bathed them in blood from her own hand. The blood transmitted to them the strength of her desire. She put them under the old man's pillow, because he seemed to be the one in charge.

Something, however, had made her doubt the efficacy of this recourse. It was then that she had thought of La Isidora.

"The best girl in the whole region," she repeated, "and the most willing."

En Pere Jordana felt his cheeks grow hot under the soap. He had never had a single sensual thought about the girl. Perhaps the old witch had noticed that he looked at her with warmth and intensity. In fact he did feel an attraction to her, but it was an attraction that was not the result of normal stimulus, nor did it only spring from the fact that this small, silent creature was a girl. He had always contemplated her as he would a mystery, and he felt a strange, superficially unjustified, fraternal affection for her.

Now, in the placid morning air, he felt a violent wave of hatred toward the old woman. He turned back facing the irrigation pool and soaped his face again with rapid motions. He could hear the old woman drawing nearer, and a voice right behind him explaining:

"She wouldn't mind a bit."

It required a painful effort to contain himself, and he thought that if the old woman didn't leave soon he would not be able to control himself much longer. He put the razor down on the edge of the tank. "She wouldn't mind a bit." And in spite of this, he had always felt that the girl's happiness was natural and profound. Pure.

And suddenly he understood. He had never experienced such

rage and pity all at once. Why hadn't he guessed it before? The sweet, intense, ecstatic creature with the astonished eyes was an idiot. Had he seen father and daughter together for a moment he would have realized it.

The old woman thought that perhaps she had made a mistake, that it might have been better to make the proposition to the other stranger, the older one, the one who seemed to be in charge.

Senyor Joaquim stopped on the threshold of the house. He had not yet given up the protection of having a roof over his head. He looked at the sky—a blue sky that seemed very far away, very high, and polished with extraordinary patience, as if made of metal. And he quickly noticed En Jordana at the irrigation pool. He had finished shaving and was washing off the soap under his chin. He had rolled up the sleeves of his sweater to his elbow.

His first impulse was to call him, make him turn his head, and obtain an immediate physical approximation of the man who had not left his thoughts all night long. But he continued watching him as if hypnotized, following every movement of his nervous arms. He would have to shave too, even though his beard was blond and very thin. After four days his skin seemed covered by a layer of mist.

He approached the irrigation tank. It was in a dirty spot, with a strange odor rising from the earth or from the stagnant water. For a moment he thought he wouldn't have the courage to shave there. On the stone edge of the irrigation tank there were obscure lines, old spots, and unknown substances that had stuck to it. The corners and the inside of the tank—it was empty—had never been cleaned.

En Jordana heard him walking and turned around. There was a precise, shining drop of blood which had stopped halfway down his cheek.

He passed his hand over his lips, closed his eyes for a second, and said to Senyor Joaquim:

"Excuse me."

Senyor Joaquim looked at him without understanding.

"That's never happened to me before, I can't even explain it to myself. . . . The truth of the matter is that I'm not accustomed to drinking. . . ."

He had been wondering, from the moment he got up, whether it would be possible not to make the slightest allusion to the preceding night. He had decided not to say a word. He remembered hardly anything, and the only reminder of it was the aftertaste of the liquor. He did not know what he had said or what he had done, up to the moment when Senyor Joaquim had helped him to bed. Because of that he was horribly certain: Senyor Joaquim had helped him to bed.

And now he thought that this bitter taste in his mouth was not from the liquor, but material proof of profound discouragement. He told himself over and over again that the disaster was irreparable, that his lack of prudence had destroyed all his chances with Senyor Joaquim. He felt empty inside—what are you dreaming about, woman? What are you hoping for? For he too had got his hopes up and believed in this trip, that it would bring him money and children, and an illusion that stretched a bit every day like an elastic band, a faith in life and more peaceful sleep—and now all his vitality had been converted into this bitter saliva that kept forming in his mouth.

He had firmly intended not to say a word, to ignore the violence of the night. But when he saw Senyor Joaquim in front of him, he rubbed his newly shaven chin and said:

"I'm sorry; believe me, I don't know . . ."

Unconsciously he pulled off the scab on his cheek with his finger. As a result there formed another precise, shining drop of blood.

Senyor Joaquim had never got such a close look at a man, one so pathetic, ridiculous, fearful, and profoundly alive.

He put his hand on En Jordana's arm in a gesture of possession. He was a man accustomed to command, and the pressure of his fingers was the result of a new affection which, however, did not renounce ancient authority.

He said:

"Let's take a little walk, Jordana. We'll find a bit of sunlight and talk awhile."

All En Pere's blood had painfully gathered in his arm, beneath Senyor Joaquim's hand.

THIRTEEN

THERE WERE thick splotches of dust on the sides of the car. En Maurici drew over to the curb, put on the brakes, and, before opening the door, leaned back in the seat, relaxing his legs as much as possible. He did not understand why he was so tired.

While he went up in the elevator, he looked at himself in the mirror. There was a wrinkle on his jacket, next to the collar, as a result of driving for an hour without stopping. These wrinkles put him in a bad mood, even though he had done nothing to avoid them.

"Anything new at Terrassa?" asked his wife as she did her lace work next to the radio.

"What do you expect . . ." and he seemed to be saying that it was impossible for anything new to take place at Terrassa. He opened the little closet, took out a tall glass, and said: "A beer." He sat down. "En Martori has a strange mania of worrying when En Joaquim is away from Barcelona. But it's nothing, the factory runs itself. A hundred things were brought to my attention, a hundred problems; but they were all absurd details. Bah!"

A hieratic maid brought a bottle of Guinness on a tray.

"Where did you eat?" his wife asked, and her tatting shuttle went up and down like a butterfly.

En Maurici drank greedily and then looked at her, irritated.

"At Martori's house. He'd organized a party. When one of the directors comes up from Barcelona, the factory manager naturally has to invite him to his house. A party—the kind that's got up as if an elephant had been invited. He must have spent six months of his salary on it, but poor people haven't got the vaguest idea in the world how to go about it. And they oblige you to eat. . . ."

"Maurici, I forgot to tell you . . ."

He looked at her; there was one more drop of beer left in the glass.

"News about En Joaquim?"

"No. L'Artigues called and wants you to call him back."

At the last minute he decided to go, to erase the memory of the people he had seen and the fatigue of the trip.

"But if you don't like Schumann, Maurici . . ."

"It doesn't matter. I won't be listening to that junk anyhow."

("La Roser Massana will sing some Schumann *Lieder*. You *must* hear it. En Joan and En Benet are coming too. You promise me? Come on now, don't be a wet blanket.")

The car was still covered with dust and he went to wipe it off.

He thought: " 'La Roser Massana will sing some Schumann *Lieder*.' That's a fine idea!"

He had done well to come. From somewhere he could vaguely hear a piano and a voice singing. He refilled his glass with cognac and put another log in the fireplace.

"Look, that bastard's gone and bought Kafka's *Diary*."

He had never read anything of Kafka's, but he liked to rub the back of the book familiarly. All afternoon he had been forced to feel the new looms they had just installed, and he didn't know them either, nor did he feel tempted to find out how they worked.

He was satisfied with being able to take in with his eyes L'Artigues' entire library and, with each visit, to notice what changes had taken place.

While he was poking about among the books, En Benet was going through the records.

"What are you looking for?"

"L'Artigues told me the other day that he'd bought a sensational concerto by Béla Bartók."

("Faulkner, Hemingway, Caldwell, Steinbeck . . . oops, here's a Hemingway in the wrong place. . . .")

"Here it is!"

En Benet was holding a record in his hand.

"Are you going to put it on?"

"Why not?"

En Maurici went over to the door and listened: they were still playing the piano at the other end of the corridor, and every now and then there was a voice, like a timid moan.

"Put it on, go ahead!"

("Unamuno, Baroja, Azorín . . . This bastard's got everything. . . . I've read this one: *Confessions of a Small Philosopher*. It was like a soporific. . . .")

The Béla Bartók concerto had started. En Benet turned down the volume.

And those idiots in the living room putting up with La Roser Massana and poor old Schumann. . . .

They did not listen to the Béla Bartók concerto. They would not have been satisfied without the latest thing on their turntable, but they always forgot about it instantly. They did not have enough patience to listen to it.

"You look as if you're in a bad mood, Maurici."

"You don't have to be a genius. . . ."

He took out a book and sat down. He tapped his knee rhythmically with the back of the book.

"Do you know what it's like to spend a whole day, including dinner, with a factory manager? Of a factory that's yours and should therefore absorb your interest right down to the bone. And that's what happens to those people: they're interested in things right down to their bones. Whether with such and such a kind of loom you can do this, or with another kind you can do that. . . .

"Have a cigarette?" He held out the package. "I stopped for a moment inside the workers' entrance. Listen, there was no end to them. It was impressive. Old and young, boys and girls. Each person picked out his own card, put it in the time clock, and then put it back in its place. And more of them, and more and more, you understand? One after the other, and all of them sticking their cards in the clock and *clack,* and their time of arrival's registered on the card." He lit his cigarette. "It was terrifying to imagine that they all had a job to do in the factory and that I was paying them, and that they must think about me from time to time. They all had faces like chick-peas, the kind that . . . but the truth is that I couldn't calm down until I was back out on the street."

En Benet looked at him attentively. There were the confused strains of Béla Bartók. Their eyes met for an instant, and En Maurici continued:

"Your position's different. You're a doctor, and in order to make money you have to deal with your clients." He smoked. "But not me, not me. I make money without needing to meet anyone. And I'm glad, believe me."

"There's a person's interest in his job. . . ."

"Certainly, what you say certainly exists." He threw the cigarette in the fireplace. "But that's an emotion I don't possess. I don't give a damn about my job. Really. If I were interested in it, do you suppose I'd only stick my nose inside the office a little bit each day? I'd be like En Joaquim, my partner—you know who he is, don't you?" He warmed the glass of cognac in his hands. "I can sometimes imagine myself being interested in the business. You make so much this way, but on the other hand doing thus and such you increase it by so much . . . and then about provincial sales, and the travelling salesmen . . . That's all fine. I can close my eyes and make believe I know all about it, that I have the situation perfectly under control. And if right now they sent me a report on some aspect of the business, I'd read it and I'd get pleasure out of understanding it. I'd say: 'You see now, it's strange . . .'" He drank a bit of cognac. "But to touch it with my hands, you know what I mean? No. No. To have to deal with what's referred to as the upper echelon of employees and take notice of the machinery . . . If you have too much contact with the world of work it'll turn you into a blithering idiot. Contrast isn't possible. I found out that fifteen years ago Terrassa had thirty thousand inhabitants. Now it's got seventy-two thousand. The factory manager explained to me the mentality of these people. You can't even talk to them. I stepped on the foot of a worker who was on his way out, and I said 'Excuse me' without realizing it. He stopped dead in his tracks and looked at me, and asked: 'What did you say?' After two days people like that would have you accustomed never to saying 'Excuse me,' you understand? The only things they know about are points, work shifts, and overtime. . . ."

They stopped and listened for a moment. At the end of the corridor the singing had stopped and people were clapping.

"I wish En Joaquim would come back and run things whatever way he wants to. He's a bit of a simpleton whose only obsession is the business. That's why he doesn't mind it. In any case, mark my words, he's sloughed off the most tiresome, disagreeable work— seeing these people's faces and hearing their voices—onto the former cashier and made him a kind of assistant. En Joaquim can't listen to a man who stinks of garlic, you know." He took another drink. "Listen, you know those magnificent Romanesque churches they've got in Terrassa? Well, they've planted some cypresses and . . ."

"Wait, listen to this section . . ." and he turned up the volume, and the music of Béla Bartók crackled in the air, like an all-devouring bonfire.

En Piqué and En Velasco, on leaving the factory, went home together. It was a cold, still night. Hearing their own footsteps and voices in the black streets was a strange comfort.

"Off to sleep until tomorrow."

"Yes."

They walked fast, with their hands in their pockets and their heads bent over their chests, in order to feel the cold less.

"They say they might give me one of those new apartments in the houses they're building out there in Vallparadís," En Velasco explained.

"Really?"

"But until I've got the keys . . ."

"Then we won't be going the same way."

"Yes. . . ."

They went around the corner, and felt the icy wind from the mountains. En Piqué thought a moment and then suddenly proposed:

"What would you think about having a cognac before going off to bed? It's on me."

They'd never done it before. But why not now?

The little bar was painted a dark color. There were only two old tables, and the black and white marble on the counter was cracked.

"Two cognacs."

Until the alcohol had burned their tongues a bit, the bar didn't feel comfortable.

"Senyor Martori looked a little rattled today, didn't he?"

"What happened?"

"Didn't you see him go by with that tall, thin guy with the skinny face and the camel's-hair coat?"

"Yes."

"That was one of the directors who had come up from Barcelona. En Robert said someone had told him this guy was going to eat at Senyor Martori's house."

"Was that why he looked rattled?"

En Piqué rubbed his tongue against his palate.

"You tell me. Doesn't it bother you to have L'Estrems watching what you do? And he's only a section chief. Now imagine having the boss around. You've got to admit that would be a little tougher to handle than L'Estrems. And these bosses who live off somewhere else don't know anything about anything, and they want to know everything, and they ask so many questions it'd make you sick. I wouldn't have swapped jobs with Senyor Martori for anything today. He really had to sweat it out."

His glass had been filled so full that a bit of cognac had spilled over into the saucer. He picked up the glass with one hand and the saucer with the other, and, tipping it, he collected all the remaining brandy.

"I wouldn't have been in his shoes for anything, Velasco. Look, I know I've got to work and earn money. But I won't kill myself at it, and then when it's over stretch out my hand. Because no matter how hard I tried, they'd never give me a raise—they don't care how I manage to live, or how many kids I've got. They'd never come and ask me—they maybe don't even know I exist"— he drank. "I know all this. But then too, after a few years, you get to know how to fix things up with the section chief so he leaves you alone. Listen, Velasco—there's only one thing I know about the boss: he's my enemy and he's far away. I don't know if you get what I mean."

He took out his tobacco pouch, kept a few grains of tobacco for himself in the palm of his hand, and passed the pouch to his friend.

"Personally he's never done me any harm, but I'd still toss a bomb under his feet, you understand? That's the way things are, and I didn't make them that way. If there's one thing I believe, Velasco, it's that the bosses are on one side and we're on the other, and there's a burning line separating the two. Have you ever seen a worker put his hand on the boss's shoulder, Velasco? Or a boss ever put his hand on a worker's shoulder, eh? So there you are."

He lit the cigarette, which was too thick and gave off little sparks.

"That's why I say Senyor Martori's got an ugly job being near the boss. Trying to understand him and get along with him . . . Senyor Martori can't hate anybody—you call that living?"

144

En Velasco put on his beret, ready to go out. He smiled.

"Perhaps he's waiting for the day the boss puts his hand on his shoulder. . . ."

En Piqué let out a raucous laugh.

Out in the street it was a cold night, cold enough to make a man feel as if he were naked. They went up the street with their hands in their pockets.

"Listen, kid, I don't give a damn about all this. People say I should give a damn, right? Because it's my job and my life. Horseshit! Whether with such and such a kind of loom you can do this, or with another kind you can do that . . . Whether the boss thinks this and Senyor Martori thinks that, or whether me and them . . . it's a lot of garbage! I know who I am, and I know what I told you about the burning line. . . . Nobody ever crosses it, you understand? That's the way things are."

They went up the street with their hands in their pockets and their heads bent down on their chests, in order to feel less strongly the harshness of the wind.

FOURTEEN

Senyor joaquim put his hand on En Pere Jordana's shoulder and repeated:

"Let's take a walk in the sun."

En Jordana would have preferred not moving. From the moment he had got up he had thought that the best thing would be not to see Senyor Joaquim all day. This was impossible, of course, but he could not erase the memory of the night before. Had he dared, he would once again have said "Excuse me," but he felt dominated by the pressure of Senyor Joaquim's hand and by those eyes looking at him with strange intensity.

They went along the road with their heads raised, absorbing

with their lips, eyes, and every inch of skin the warm palpitation of the breeze.

"It's a nice day, isn't it?"

After walking some distance, when they had gone around the first bend in the road and the house had disappeared behind the trees, they experienced a feeling of being profoundly alive, as if they were breathing in rhythm with everything around them, as if they had suddenly become much lighter and were participating in the vast palpitation of the world.

But they soon stopped. The road began to rise up to the highway, and Senyor Joaquim found a long stone which could serve as a kind of bench. Here, in this setting, Senyor Joaquim seemed younger. The roundness of his features and his rosy complexion gave him an almost childish look. He was divested of the attributes indicating his social category and age; those elements, which, by comparison with others in the city, defined him, were lacking. In a certain sense, En Pere Jordana seemed older than he. En Jordana's nose was a bit too long, he had big ears, and, even after shaving, his chin still had a vague gray color, which was like the mark of an adult. Senyor Joaquim walked absolutely erect; En Pere Jordana with his shoulders bent. Senyor Joaquim seemed like a boy who had not yet become a man.

"Sit down, Jordana."

Two men sitting on the same stone, lost in the valley, small and strangely united.

"You know, I'm beginning to think I should take a couple of days' vacation every year. How many years has it been since I've taken one?" He made a mental calculation, and with the toe of his shoe he cleared the ground of weeds, pebbles, and dust until he had marked out a little area of naked earth. "When you come right down to it, I've never had a real vacation. One summer I had typhus, and a couple of years ago my mother-in-law died at Puigcerdà and we spent four or five days there. . . ."

He raised his eyes and looked at the branches of the trees, and

146

beyond them he saw the mountains and the sky which seemed to be illuminated from within.

"It's lovely, isn't it?"

He turned around, waiting for En Pere to agree. He smiled.

"How much vacation time do you get, Jordana?"

"Two weeks."

"Where did you spend it last summer?"

En Pere looked at him surprised. Why was he asking?

"In Barcelona, naturally. The trucking company that gives me work every Sunday has a lot of work in the summer, and they employ me every day."

It was strange. Strange and terrifying, Senyor Joaquim realized. He had looked at the mountains and at the sky, and everything had seemed so easy, agreeable, and familiar. Asking questions was painful if one had no idea of what the answers might be.

Why did he have no idea? With the toe of his shoe he cleared off the little patch of earth more carefully.

"Do you have any children, Jordana?"

"One boy."

En Pere took out his wallet, and out of the wallet he took a photograph he kept in the cellophane compartment. With a simple gesture he handed it to Senyor Joaquim, who took it with a certain anxiety.

It was a boy, in fact. A weak-looking boy, with black eyes and hair that had obviously been combed by force.

"How old is he?" he asked in order to say something.

"Seven."

He still didn't dare give it back. Why didn't he have photographs of his own children in his wallet? En Jordana knew that he had five children—he had mentioned it yesterday—but now he didn't ask about them.

"He's a good-looking boy," and he returned the photograph.

En Pere took it avidly. For a moment he had had the feeling that his son really was that piece of paper and that he was at the mercy of Senyor Joaquim's hands and will.

"Tell me, Jordana"—his foot had stopped clearing the earth; the tip of a cloud began to appear from behind the mountain— "are your parents alive?"

"No."

Senyor Joaquim looked at him intently.

"Neither are mine. It's strange. A man's parents are gone before he realizes it. They're always gone too soon. And the older you get, the more you feel the loss; I don't understand it. But you're still quite young; how old are you, forty?"

"Thirty-five," En Pere corrected quickly. He hadn't yet turned forty. He had always felt that something would happen before he turned forty.

He didn't know how to begin. Senyor Joaquim realized that he didn't know how to start a conversation that would interest him, and that En Jordana was looking at him worriedly, asking himself: "What's he talking to me about all this for?"

He did not know how to get a man to talk about himself without saying to him dryly and absurdly: "Tell me about yourself."

"What did your father do?"

"He was a mason."

"A mason . . ."

"Yes."

And En Jordana still would not talk about himself, because he could not understand that this was what he wanted.

But there must be some way, he thought, as he extended with his foot the area of ground he had smoothed out.

En Pere took the pack of cigarettes out of his pocket: it was all wrinkled. He put one between his lips, searched for his matches, and lit it.

"I tried smoking once," said Senyor Joaquim. "When I was twenty or twenty-two. The day of the big feast at Cardedeu and I won a pack target shooting. I haven't shot in a long time, but I used to be good at it. How about you?"

"Average, I guess. Probably not too good."

"I can still see the pack I got. Some brand they used to sell, I don't remember what it was called. It's probably been thirty years since I've thought about it. . . . I didn't even finish the first cigarette. My stomach or something; it didn't agree with me. My stomach's always been a bit . . ."

En Pere looked at him.

"Me too. I often get a kind of burning sensation . . . But I don't pay any attention to it."

"You too? You should be careful. One day, oop, and there . . ."

En Pere got a coughing fit; the cigarette smoke came out of his mouth in short bursts. Then there was total silence.

Senyor Joaquim felt grotesque. Why was he discussing all these things? It wasn't cigarettes or stomach troubles that interested him about En Jordana.

He could not remember ever having felt such torture. He was sitting on the same stone with this man, and they were extraordinarily united in the broad space of the valley. He had only to stretch out his hand to touch him on the shoulder.

He knew what he wanted from him, and it was painful not to know how to obtain it.

En Pere blew his nose slowly and noisily.

Why was he so clumsy, so incapable? There must be some way to find out the truth about a man without having to say: "Tell me about yourself."

They heard the motor of a car passing on the highway. The sound reached them muffled, as if wrapped in cloth, after passing the multiple barrier of plants and trees. . . .

"I suppose it won't be long before the doctor comes with the car," Senyor Joaquim commented with a trace of sorrow in his voice.

"Today or tomorrow," said En Pere, and he also said it in a somewhat complaining way that did not escape Senyor Joaquim, who was observing him in surprise.

"Do you find it too soon?" he guessed.

Then En Jordana saw the deeply curious look in Senyor Joaquim's eyes, and he understood that he was freely giving him permission to speak, that he wanted to listen. The air was not divided in hierarchical rectangles as in offices in the city; the air was the same for both of them, and there was no protocol or urgency, nor was there anything else to do but talk and listen. There was time to spare, it was being ceaselessly poured into their hands, and they could give it whatever form they wanted.

"Yes, it is too soon," he answered. "I wish it would never be time to go back."

Senyor Joaquim immediately understood that their closeness had started up like a flawless machine. He tried in vain to remember the word that had brought it on, the key word that had been equivalent to saying: "Tell me about yourself." And he did not know that it was not a word, but an attitude. That the torture of a man who, at a given moment, is in need of company cannot be hidden, and that En Jordana had seen it in him, transforming him, taking command, like a second nature, of his gestures, his silences, and the violent look in his eyes.

There arrives a moment in which someone's mere presence, in which simple physical contact consciously sustained, makes lack of understanding impossible. Indifference falls to pieces, and sometimes a sigh or a way of scratching one's head is to blame— hardly ever a specific word.

Then two men come face to face, and in their blood there arises, like a flower with an exacerbating aroma, either affection or antipathy.

With a deep, instinctive confidence, which would certainly frighten him when he thought about it later that night, En Pere Jordana started to explain animatedly, while a long, thin cloud grew and grew, and built a bridge between the two shores of the sky.

"I wish it would never come time to go back. This trip was a failure, and it'll really be one when we get back to Barcelona."

"That doesn't matter, Jordana. Not a bit. Our firms in the North can get along, for the time being, without my visit. We'll

150

send them the samples, and they'll be able to prepare for the coming season perfectly well. I would have liked to see these people, but that was nothing more than a personal desire. So . . ."

En Pere looked at his own hands, wide, square, and with gray spots on the skin.

"I wasn't thinking about our firms in the North, Senyor Joaquim, nor about the coming season, nor . . . I was thinking about myself and my affairs, and it makes me sad that this trip was cut short."

"But why, Jordana?"

En Pere was silent for a few seconds with his hands on his knees and his eyes fixed on the ground.

"I was confident that I'd prove useful on this trip, that I'd do a job for which I'd be congratulated and recompensed"—he looked at him. "No more, no less"—he smiled half bitterly and half amused. "Senyor Alsina, the office manager"—Senyor Joaquim also smiled, for he remembered that the night before En Jordana had said: "He's a son of a bitch," and probably didn't remember it now—"Senyor Alsina congratulated me on having been selected to accompany you, you understand? He more or less told me that after all these years, and taking into account my record with the firm, he had thought it only right to nominate me for this job, to give me this opportunity." He again looked at his hands, which seemed unable to come completely to rest on his knees. "And now I ask myself, what kind of job did I do? What kind of opportunity did I have?"

"Come, come."

"I wasn't able to control the car. Everything ended here."

"It wasn't your fault. That corner on the highway was like a skating rink."

En Pere Jordana didn't answer; he shrugged his shoulders a bit and Senyor Joaquim understood that he was saying: "Yes, but what difference does it make?"

"What kind of opportunity do you mean, Jordana?"

En Pere withdrew into himself. He was thinking about money

—and money was something he had learned never to discuss. At the last moment instinct made him keep silent. And he found it terribly simple, terribly grotesque, ridiculous, and absurd to be so obsessed by money. For he had not taken the job of driving with any desire to serve, he had not thought about the firm, nor had he felt the least bit of pleasure at the idea of sitting next to Senyor Joaquim.

Why did he take the job? It surprised him to realize that he had not really stopped to think about it until now. He hadn't even discussed it with his wife. What might have happened to him, if everything had gone as it should? He had subconsciously supposed that he would no longer be an assistant. . . . But then what could he be, what *else?* It was extraordinary: he could not find an answer, no horizon seemed to open up for him. . . .

But in spite of this, he had expected something very concrete: money, a fistful of extra money each month, and down deep he realized that he wanted to use it on something very concrete: to have his wife stop sewing buttons on shirts, to put in stronger bulbs, to have his child study, or . . .

"To have a little girl . . ."

He had said it out loud, even though Senyor Joaquim did not really understand him. But there was a look of hallucination in his eyes, and beneath his forehead an explosion of light previously held in, but which now made him go on talking, liberating himself:

"To have a girl, a little girl, before it's too late for La Maria. I have a feeling that expecting a second child would give you a new confidence in life, a sense of security. . . . I never felt so young as when I was about to become a father. And I think there's still time to become a father again. . . . The office is full of old men—I don't know if you realize it. I see them sitting around me, letting off a kind of gray mist that numbs you and paralyzes you. Like all old people, their lives only revolve around little things, and they limit their desires to wanting the maximum comfort and perfection within their daily routine. They think—and they know—that they've already done everything and that they'll always be the way they are. That's why they're old. Even little Manelet—you know him, don't you? He's growing so much I feel sorry for him; I gave him an old overcoat of mine, and even with him, even with En Manelet there's a shadow of old age behind the still waters of his eyes.

"You asked me about my father, and I told you he was a mason. But more than anything, he was an old man. I remember him as a hardened man, a man living in the world as if inside a rigid, unenterable circle. There came a moment when his life could only go on repeating itself; it could hold no more surprises for him.

"I thought that maybe I was still young, and could break this circle."

Senyor Joaquim was also resting his hands on his knees.

"Now I see what you meant by your opportunity, Jordana."

En Pere looked at him astonished. As if he had not intended to say a thing. As if he had not counted on Senyor Joaquim's presence. He took a deep breath. He would have said "Excuse me," if it had not been for the fact that Senyor Joaquim was looking at him so completely naturally that he felt obliged to continue.

"And my wife . . . you know how they are, women like my wife? The other day she got it into her head to make some curtains for the bedroom window. I understand—that's what women want, right? But the trouble is she never buys meat because there's never quite enough money; it's been five years since she's bought herself a new pair of shoes, and do you know that I've stopped going to soccer matches to save money . . . do you know that we're short of everything, but she felt we couldn't live one day longer without curtains in the bedroom. . . ."

Senyor Joaquim felt like asking him for an Ideal and lighting it up in order to get a feeling for En Pere Jordana's apartment—its odors, its dampness, and its bitter silence.

"Sure, they're very pretty, those curtains. Every night when we go to bed, she straightens them out to get me to look at them. But we always eat supper in a bad mood, do you understand? Every evening she presents me with some little, insuperable problem that has come up. The price of potatoes has gone up, or soap, or the kid's shoes have got holes in them, or she's got a toothache and will have to go to the dentist. Unimportant problems, right? But insuperable because every day you have to spend a bit more, but you can't earn a bit more every day. And I don't know why she talks to me about these things every night, because she knows there's nothing I can answer. Maybe she talks about them because she has to, just like she has to breathe, so she won't die of suffocation.

"On Saturdays she shows me the kid's report card from school. I have to sign it; if not, I wouldn't even want to look at it. It isn't that it's always bad, but that it drives me to despair to think that the kid could know more. I don't know if it's true, but I can't help thinking that at a good school, at the Jesuits' or some school like that, the kid would make more progress. And then I sign there under where it says *Father,* and I sign in a rage because I feel guilty, or like an idiot, or . . . bah!

"And now I think that maybe it was a good thing my wife made those goddamn curtains, and that she straightens them out every night to get me to look at them. . . . During the day I get mad when I think about them, but then when I see them something wells up inside my eyes and I wait a little longer before rolling over and going to sleep. . . ."

The sun had been slowly changing its position in the sky. Now it struck the patch of ground Senyor Joaquim's foot had cleared of stones and weeds, and one could see a line of ants, until then invisible, that stretched across it.

"I can't explain it any better," said En Pere, "or more logically; I don't know if you can imagine what it's like at home. . . . Sometimes I think that if I were a man who spent his time in cafés, things would be easier. I'd only be home at mealtimes and I'd avoid all these headaches. I'd say to myself: 'I do the best I can, right? It isn't my fault if I don't earn more.' But I'm not a man who spends his time in cafés. I never was. . . ."

154

And suddenly he thought about the liquor he'd drunk the night before and he looked at Senyor Joaquim, but he didn't have to say anything. Senyor Joaquim was not listening.

("It's strange how, while he's talking, I feel as if I can see his facial expression changing. But it doesn't change. It's that I've learned to imagine things, to see what's behind a man's face.

"He talks and talks, and each word is an insinuation, each sentence an evocation. Why is it that now I see this man as the protagonist of some story—that's it, a man with a story, with a way of being, a life—and other men, till now, have passed before me like expressionless puppets, scarcely more than blurred faces, forgotten instantly? Perhaps if I'd sat on a bench with each one of these ordinary men, perhaps if we'd been able to talk, I would have found out that each of them also had a story, a way of being and a life of his own.")

He looked at En Pere Jordana and listened as if, through him, he could get to know all the men who had passed before him. . . .

". . . but on the other hand I've always liked to dance. When I was young I never missed a dance. With my wife too . . . if you saw us now you wouldn't see what I mean, but we were the best dancers in the neighborhood. . . ."

("The best dancers in the neighborhood . . . an acquaintance in the neighborhood, a storekeeper from the neighborhood, a café, a crime in the neighborhood . . ." He had never belonged to a neighborhood, how strange. He had never used the phrase. It was always a friend in the Calle de Girona, a café on the Calle le Provença, or a store on the Calle del Bruc. . . .)

". . . and everyone wanted to go out with us because we had such a good time. When I was fifteen I had a bicycle, because I worked a long way from home. Then they organized a bicycle race at Poble Nou and I entered it. I came in third and they gave me twenty-five pesetas. Sometimes I think things would have been better if I'd become a cyclist. . . ."

(He'd had a bicycle too when he was fifteen. A bicycle that in

July he took to Cardedeu, and that in September he locked up again in the apartment in Barcelona. It had never occurred to him to ride it in Barcelona. There was an unspoken law that only poor people rode bicycles on the streets of Barcelona. Down deep, and without losing his own fear, he had always admired those boys of his age who flashed around like arrows between the cars and trucks. There was only one place where a child of good family could ride a bicycle without its being thought peculiar: at the upper end of the Diagonal. Because then it was obvious that the bicycle was being used for the only activity worthy of it, simply riding. . . .)

". . . and I also knew the names of all the racing drivers by heart. Now I've forgotten them . . ." he raised his eyes and looked up at the trees. "It's terrible."

"Sommer, Von Stuck . . ." said Senyor Joaquim.

"Von Stuck!" he repeated excitedly, as if it was the lost key to his youth. "Von Stuck! That race just before the war, at Montjuïc, that Nuvolari won. . . ."

"No," Senyor Joaquim smiled and looked straight into his eyes; "Caracciola won it, in a Mercedes."

En Pere looked back at him, but without seeing him, because he was thinking.

"Caracciola came in second. He gained ground at the end, but he didn't make it in time to catch up to Nuvolari."

"It was just the opposite," Senyor Joaquim smiled again; "it was a magnificent race. Caracciola won. Nuvolari was second."

En Pere hesitated.

"I don't think so, but . . . Who was third?"

The leaves on the trees were moving. There was a cold, timid breeze. The two men on the bench felt it a bit on their heads, and they searched around in their memories with extraordinary, unspoken joy. Who was third? They tried to recover some small spark from the fading light of the past, which now seemed to contain the hidden secret of happiness. . . .

"Third?" Senyor Joaquim thought out loud.

156

"I was still just a kid," said En Pere Jordana. "I'd got up on a rock or something, and was leaning on my father's shoulder, up above the whole race track. My father talked to me continually: 'Look, there goes Number Six. Look, there goes Number Fourteen.' I don't remember any more who Number Six and Number Fourteen were. I only remember the strange odor of my father's hair, which was right under my chin, and the cigarette smoke that rose in front of my eyes." He half closed his eyes as if the smoke were still irritating them. "It would be nice if my father were still alive . . . so I could ask him now who came in third. . . ."

("Strange. The same day, the same hour, this man and I were in the same place. Well, not exactly the same place. I had a seat in the stands. That must have been twenty years ago. . . . My father was there too, and he's also gone. I'm sure that Caracciola won, I was thirty at the time. . . . Strange: some man you meet completely by chance, a man you don't know, can have had the same emotion as you and have a similar memory; and this man could have no idea who you are, and think that he is the sole retainer of this reality which is already lost. . . .")

"My father," En Jordana explained, as he lit a cigarette, "died six years ago, when I wasn't a kid any more. And in spite of this, the twenty-four hours that he remained at home after dying were the most . . . the worst in my life. It felt, how shall I say? . . . as if I'd been crushed inside. Stupid, isn't it?"

He offered Senyor Joaquim a cigarette, forgetting he didn't smoke. Senyor Joaquim took it mechanically and played with it for a few moments with the tips of his fingers, and then—he didn't dare give it back—put it in his pocket.

("Crushed inside," he thought. His feelings had been similar. The worries connected with the business, the thousand occupations of his own life, all of which increased enormously with the death of his father, had masked this feeling of emptiness. But the feeling had been there. And how quickly this emptiness had vanished! He had forgotten the details which had seemed so unpleasant then, he had smothered everything in the comfortable reality of his own self. A man can't live empty. What would happen if one didn't block off these minute sorrows, which seem physically to open a little hole in one's chest, through which flows an invisible substance?)

"It was different with my mother . . . she died when I was very little, and even though people say I needed her, I don't remember her. It's better that way; it doesn't hurt."

("The memory of a father is painful . . . even the memory of a father like En Jordana's, whose hair gave off 'a strange odor' . . ." He thought that if his father and En Jordana's father had met one day, they would have turned away from each other with complete indifference. And now the sons sat on the same bench and, covered with the same tunic of sunlight, both listened to the pulsing of their blood with the same sensation of expectation, uneasiness, surprise, respect, desire, and a bit of fear: that is to say, they each recognized the immediate existence of the other. . . .)

Senyor Joaquim now understood how terrible it was to recognize the existence of people—it was equivalent to recognizing the fact that they had the same *reality* as we and . . . Once you started thinking about it, everything got so complicated and interrelated that there was no knowing where it would stop. It was wiser to stop at the first thought.

They got up, shook the dust off their trousers, and started back to the house. They walked in silence, with their heads lowered. The air was getting chillier by the moment, and on the sides of the road the humidity of the previous night had not yet evaporated. Delicate splotches of mist were forming a web over the valley, and the sun remained a yellow color and pleasant to look at, but it had lost its gentle, amiable warmth.

From far off they saw the girl with the staring eyes, the little idiot girl, Isidora, immobile on the threshold of the house. En Pere Jordana explained to Senyor Joaquim:

158

"I think I should tell you . . . the old woman offered me the girl, if you know what I mean. I guess the offer was also meant for you. . . ."

Senyor Joaquim stopped a moment and looked at En Jordana's impassive face, and then far away, the rather ungraceful, solitary figure in the doorway, like a little domestic animal.

People exist, he thought again, even though he had lived fifty years without realizing it, and the fact of their existence—and his too, that was the surprise—was something more complicated and painful than he had imagined.

When they entered the house, Senyor Joaquim fainted.

He didn't lose consciousness suddenly. He felt as if his head had begun to move *inside his head*. The sensation was difficult to explain and physically impossible, but terribly distressing. He was losing control of himself.

En Pere Jordana had at first grabbed his arm when he saw him spreading his legs too much and weaving back and forth. Senyor Joaquim got heavier by the second, and soon he could no longer hold him up with one hand. His legs were buckling, his eyes were half closed, and he was letting out muffled, confused, and unidentifiable syllables.

The girl had disappeared inside the house.

"It's all over, this is the end," thought En Jordana, as he took him into his room and laid him on the bed. "The end. Why was I so sure there wasn't any more danger? The doctor said the critical moment was past, but he's an ass." He looked at Senyor Joaquim, who was as white as a sheet, as white as death. He wished it were all a nightmare, but from somewhere there came the noise of geese honking—it was like a grotesque, merciless joke. "It's all over. Just when this man's life was most precious, most useful, most promising. Could the attack have come from my having disagreed with him about Caracciola . . . ? Ridiculous, things like this happen because they happen," and something deep inside him had been warning him for the past few days that everything would end badly, that things couldn't end any other way, that after all these years life would only permit him one adventure: that of failure, that of despair, that of cruelty. For it was malignantly cruel that this man should now turn to dust between his fingers.

Hadn't everything that he had ever looked at or touched with desire turned to dust?

The old woman entered the room. En Pere Jordana imagined that her eyes were challenging him: "Where's the person who's going to resolve all this?"

But the old woman advanced silently toward the window and seemed to open it more with an inaudible conjuration than with her hands. "He needs air," she said.

"Air! Nonsense!" thought En Jordana.

"He was in the sun too long, and he's still a bit weak. He's fainted."

En Pere felt she was accusing him. "Fainted. He's fainted. She thinks he'll come to." And suddenly he was invaded by a deep-seated excitement, and there was a part of him, like a powerful interior muscle, that was laughing with irresistible violence, while he gazed astonished at Senyor Joaquim's white face.

When Senyor Joaquim opened his eyes, the first thing he saw —like the other time, as always, it seemed—was En Pere Jordana's face leaning over him with an expression of intense emotion. This face was watching over him with maximum attention, and he could swear that it was transmitting to him a profound feeling of life.

With a feeling of confidence, he closed his eyes again.

Then there sifted through to his conscious mind, still a bit blurred, a feeling that it was also a face that was asking for something. . . .

That was asking . . .

What else had it done from the very first day, when watching over him, when bringing him breakfast, when emptying half a bottle of liquor, when speaking to him on the bench, and now?

En Joaquim Civit was what you call a good man. He felt like having a bit of a siesta. He was standing at the window—can't you see him—looking out on the clear, cold afternoon which turned every object—the branch of a tree, the far-off profile of a mountain, a bulky rock—into a delicate filigree.

En Joaquim Civit, before the glory and nakedness of the afternoon, seemed like a still better man. Had he not been, his contact with En Pere Jordana would have been absolutely sterile.

Look at him; wouldn't you say he was examining his conscience?

He has round cheeks, and he's a kindly man. I can assure you that all men—or almost all—are kindly, and even more so those who have been well brought up. You may doubt this, because they don't show it outwardly, they don't proclaim it in public—as poor people do—but that's because men who have been well brought up have also learned that it's not polite to shout—if you know what I mean—and that one should have a certain modesty about one's emotions.

If En Joaquim Civit interests us, it's because he's a good man.

When one of his children has a fever, he can't sleep. He now has five children, and he might have got accustomed to this, because he knows that even though children have fevers, nothing's ever really wrong with them. But it doesn't make any difference. He can't stand anything abnormal, and it pains him that the world should contain negative things.

And not only at home. If he comes across an accident in the street, he walks away quickly. Systematically. As a matter of principle. It's terrifying to think that a man could have died—perhaps he was just unlucky—for no reason at all, so stupidly. It's bad enough thinking about it without having to see it. And believe me, it isn't only that he hates the sight of blood, which he does like any decent man, but above all it seems to him that the poor fellow is worthy of pity, and that when it comes time for dinner he, En Joaquim Civit, will have no appetite. Isn't that kindness?

Surely now, alone in the room, bathed in the most pure and totally unsensual light, En Joaquim Civit is thinking about these things.

One of his maids broke her arm a year ago, when she fell getting off a streetcar. They took her to the hospital. En Joaquim made inquiries about the hospital, and on his saint's day donated twenty-five thousand pesetas to it.

The parish of The Immaculate Conception, at the end of the war, also received considerable help from En Joaquim Civit. One of the priests of the parish was a distant relative of his, and he alone could still remember now the real importance of the manufacturer's various contributions.

En Joaquim Civit was so sensitive about matters involving his emotions that he tried to avoid them. After many years of practice he had finally succeeded in building the necessary retaining walls around him, which permitted him to live tranquilly.

That was why, in this house, in this situation, which for him was not usual, he was vulnerable. There was a direct pressure from the things around him, the unexpectedly deep gaze of eyes, the most disquieting presence of a man. He felt a need for L'Alsina, the office manager . . . "who's a son of a bitch, excuse me."

Why couldn't he forget these words? He remembered them as if they were an accusation. An incomprehensible accusation.

"Excuse me," En Jordana had said. He knew that he hadn't asked to be excused because of the vulgar "son of a bitch," but because it applied in part to him . . . because by insulting L'Alsina, the office manager, he was also insulting him.

Then his head, which was leaning forward, touched the glass, and for a moment he felt as if his forehead had turned to glass and a chill went through his body.

He was undoubtedly thinking that in making L'Alsina office manager, he had set a diabolical trap for his own conscience.

162

L'Alsina was a son of a bitch, L'Alsina was capable of starting proceedings against a worker who fell asleep because he was forced to work at night too, L'Alsina was capable of treating people harshly, of looking at eyes filled with sorrow, of listening to fainting voices, of indulging in conscious cruelty.

The trap was obvious, and the truth terrifying: *he was L'Alsina.* Or perhaps he looked at it in another light: L'Alsina had agreed to take over all En Joaquim Civit's evil thoughts for five or six thousand pesetas a month. He remained free from guilt, free from cruelty. He had amputated the unworthy member, and he had no remorse. He knew nothing about what the office manager did.

Until suddenly he realized that he had amputated the malignant part not in order to kill it but, on the contrary, in order that it could live a freer existence, without destroying his own ability to be a good man.

The chill produced by contact with the icy window had passed. He took a deep breath—it was strange, his breath fogged the clear glass.

In the midst of this examination of his conscience, he could not avoid allowing comforting memories to enter his thoughts. When his brother-in-law's business had been about to fold, he had stuck his neck out for him. He didn't like his brother-in-law; he never had. He knew that lending him the money was, economically speaking, a mistake. But he had lent it to him. And he had never mentioned the matter again. . . .

The door opened. En Pere Jordana was surprised to see that Senyor Joaquim had not lain down to rest, and there was something impressive, something mysterious about a man who, facing a window, seemed to be witnessing a fascinating spectacle. . . . Beyond the window there was only the tranquil light and the filigree work of the tree branches.

And a strange shyness, a peculiar sense of delicacy, forced him to leave Senyor Joaquim alone.

Senyor Joaquim heard the noise of the door as it closed, but he heard it inside his own body, in a vague world, and he realized that a door, or that which he had been, was closing behind him forever, and would henceforth prevent him from returning to his usual refuge, his solitude.

He realized that he had crossed the barrier. For the first time in his life. A barrier which had been difficult to cross, but over which it was now impossible to return. This new region he had entered—the region of men, of pain, desire, and restlessness—had stuck to his hands as soon as he had touched it, like strong, greedy, swelling mud. His feet were rooted in this unknown land.

He could never again forget this new knowledge of the world. He believed in the dogma of the spiritual communion of saints, and he had never stopped to think about its necessary basis, the essential identity of all men.

It was a certainty that enriched him and tired him. It was a sad voice that was forever mixed together with his former peace, like dirty water—a muted voice, but one which would never again be silent.

At six in the afternoon, En Pere Jordana entered Senyor Joaquim's room and said:

"The doctor's come. The car's been fixed and he brought it with him."

And he bowed his head, as if to say: "Whenever you wish . . ."

FIFTEEN

En MAURICI put the car keys in his pocket, crossed the street, and pushed open the little door of the bar.

One could not enter this bar without descending, for just beyond the door there were three steps. It was strange how important these three steps were. This enforced descent was what made this bar different from an ordinary café, what made it different above all from the point of view of the atmosphere.

Going down those three steps was like participating in some mysterious complicity.

It was a small café, and its layout was the same as that of the pressing establishment next door. But the contrast could not have been greater. The pressing establishment had naked walls and a white light, and altogether—the clean laundry, the women's large hands, the old-fashioned irons, the wrinkles in the old woman's face and the shawl over her shoulders, the calendar of the Jorba Company on the wall—it gave off a fixed, familiar perfume of an epoch, a way of life, a specific moment in the city's past.

The café was the complete opposite. Everything there was deliberately imprecise and soft. With incredible perfection the owner had succeeded, in such a small space, in having nothing noticeable—nothing excessively noticeable.

The entire bar contained not one square centimeter of white. White had been killed—it was too pure and impudent a color— as much as possible. Along the wall above the bar stretched a slightly undulating rose-colored neon tube, and six inches above it another of a bluish-violet color. The resultant mixture was a weak, paralyzing light, which invited the heart to work more and more slowly—a light which favored obsessive ideas.

When he had first frequented this bar, En Maurici had suffered from feelings of exasperation such as he had never experienced in places with more strident, exciting atmospheres. He then understood that he was one of those people who reacted more violently to a maliciously prepared solitude of silent suffocation.

But he had already got over this. He was already more accustomed to the bar, and he sat on the banquette without a trace of nervous tension, without preoccupations, and with no other desire but that of being as comfortable as possible.

While he was taking off his overcoat, the bartender was already preparing his rum and water. Summer and winter. Sometimes he had a second drink, and then it was impossible to foresee what his whim would be. He was tempted by colors, and because of color he would decide on the most contradictory things: the mourning red of Campari, the cheerful yellow of Chartreuse, the sickly green of Pernod, and sometimes the diabolically ingenuous white of gin.

"It's hot in here," he said.

He had sat down to En Josep Martí, who was wearing a brightly colored vest and gold-rimmed glasses; he was a piano manufacturer.

En Josep Martí looked at him with a bemused look in his eyes.

"You woollen manufacturers are always too hot. . . ."

He was, moreover, almost completely bald, and he always looked at En Maurici like this—it was as if after he had passed his sixtieth birthday all his friends who were ten or fifteen years younger had been changed into children.

Next to En Josep Martí, in the corner of the banquette, La Carme was doing her nails with a tiny nail file. From time to time she would raise her eyes and look at En Josep Martí, En Maurici, or whoever was coming down the three steps. But without any special intensity.

"La Carmeta's never hot," said En Martí. "She's always got a sweater on. Right, Carmeta?"

En Martí always called her Carmeta. And such a familiar name seemed not to suit her too badly—strange though it may seem—in the impersonal bar which seemed outside any country or history; it was strange that it should suit so well this girl who was doing her nails simply and efficiently; who looked into people's eyes without passion, and who was proud of solving the crossword puzzles of the *Ciero*.

There was a great deal of sighing in this bar, perhaps because of the soft banquette, the pale light, and the feeling of being below street level.

"I hear the bottom's fallen out of the woollen industry," En Martí insisted, "and that at Terrassa, fifty per cent of the looms are idle."

"It's disastrous," En Maurici conceded, and then fell silent.

("If we can't export this year . . ." L'Alsina, the office manager, had said menacingly.)

But here and now in this little bar which was below the level of the street, below the level of the world, nothing had any importance, nothing in fact had life except this silence, this tenuous, slow breathing, this mercifully vague light.

L'Eduard Ribes, as he descended the three steps, always stopped for a second on the middle one and put his hands on the lapels of his overcoat. He seemed to be measuring the bar. He had a high forehead. It wrinkled and unwrinkled easily. He was a playwright—and he ran a haberdashery business.

"Not very lively in here today, eh what?"

He had broad shoulders, and he hurriedly took off his overcoat. He had said that the bar was not very lively uncomplainingly, rather with an amused inflection in his voice, for there was a secret wisdom which taught them that it was better when it wasn't lively.

He did not sit on the banquette. He sat on a chair on the other side of the table, facing La Carme, En Josep Martí, and En Maurici, as if to have them all within reach.

Then he began talking about various things—he interrupted himself only when the waiter brought his cognac and he said: "Fine, kid"—and his sustained loquacity never succeeded in completely absorbing the attention of the others. That dissolvent and narcotic substance which floated in the air of the bar was more powerful.

None of the three men who met there every evening could say that he had spent the night with La Carme. And not because La Carme was inaccessible.

Or maybe La Carme really was inaccessible for them, precisely because she was already too close to them, too familiar. Maybe once long ago they had really been with La Carme. But it had been forgotten. La Carmeta now meant something different to En Josep Martí, L'Eduard Ribes, and En Maurici.

From time to time some restless youth would descend the three steps, or some mature, petulant man, and, in her merely efficient way of doing her nails, they would find something frivolously artificial, and in her passionless eyes a spark of fever. Transient customers had too superficial an image of the bar. Possibly one has to look at things for a long time in order to see no more than what they contain, in order to accustom the vain eye to the truth.

La Carme lived off men's vanity—but she was cordially esteemed by those men who had lost their vanity and sought some kind of simple consolation below the level of the world.

In fact, each one of them was seeking a different kind of consolation.

Whoever distributes life had been too hard on En Maurici: he had been given a conscience, a slightly too lucid conscience. Not a conscience applied to the world one chooses for oneself, which is the normal kind of conscience. Everyone has this encouraging, complacent sort of conscience, which never requires a person to do more than he can. He had a conscience that was too vital and rebellious, which proposed standards in all spheres of life.

He looked down on En Joaquim, and at the same time, without ceasing to look down on him for a number of reasons—of temperament and intellect—he was capable of envying him. He knew that En Joaquim Civit had an accommodating conscience.

These were things it was better not to discuss—how could one discuss such things with En Joaquim? But it was not difficult to see what kind of conscience people had, provided they didn't suffer from the one irreparable piece of stupidity: that of imagining that there was only one kind of conscience.

168

En Joaquim Civit was a man who believed in God and believed in himself. He believed in his family, which he had fashioned according to his wishes—with five children he was trying to bring up to be angels. He believed in his work: in his moral rectitude and his competence. He believed in the established order, and in spite of being a peaceful man and perhaps sentimental, he believed there would always be wars and social inequality, for they were things inherent in human nature. . . .

While En Maurici filled his mouth with rum and water, he thought that it would be difficult to make a similar list of what he himself believed in.

He had no children, and he therefore could not believe in a family. (On the other hand, he had no desire to believe in one, but the void made him uneasy.) He did not believe in his work— what *was* his work? He had none, in fact, and desired none, but this was yet another void.

There were moments such as this, sunk in a banquette in the bar, when he thought he must be a man given over to hate, to the deepest sarcasm and total skepticism. But this wasn't the case. And this fact continually astonished him.

For he, who was almost useless as a person, a man whose will had been shattered, thought that the world could be made a better place; that peace, progress, and brotherhood were ideas perfectly compatible with human nature.

And every time he realized that he had this faith, this passionate faith, he felt a kind of bitter wave rising inside his chest—a bitterness which had become resistant to rum.

The door of the bar opened and from the street there entered a kind of snorting sound, intense and brief, which the door, upon closing again, snuffed out like someone stopping another's speech by putting a hand over his mouth.

A man with a pale face, a stiff gray hat, and a starched collar asked for a cognac and rested his trembling hands on the bar—

hands that awoke compassion, as if after sixty years they had not yet learned to move with assurance.

He looked out of the corner of his eye at the people in the bar; they probably weren't looking at him. He then took off his hat for a moment and rubbed his forehead and head with a handkerchief. He drank the cognac and, before leaving, he gave another look—which for a moment shone with desperation—at everything around him.

He went heavily up the three steps.

He opened the door and, because of his height, it seemed as if he would not fit through, but would be decapitated. He lowered his head, and both head and hat passed outside.

And then the *rrrr* from the street could be heard again—the noise of some piece of machinery—and the door closed behind the man, like a trap door snapping shut on his grave.

L'Eduard Ribes, the playwright who had the haberdashery business, took an electric razor out of his coat pocket. It was the latest, most perfect, and most expensive model in the world . . . and it had cost him hardly anything (considering how up-to-date and perfect it was). And of course he could always sell it.

The bartender came out from behind the bar to join in the discussion. The bartender had a mustache; he couldn't use such a machine. "That's why Americans don't like mustaches," commented En Josep Martí, the piano manufacturer. En Ribes pinched his own cheek: documental proof of its perfection. "There's nothing like a straight razor," En Martí affirmed. The discussion was already harmoniously orchestrated. Now its theme would continue to the end unaided, as in a divertimento.

Now that En Joaquim was returning—he had finally received a telegram: "Arriving Friday afternoon. Civit," which, even though it explained nothing, neither the incomprehensible silence of the past days nor above all the discontinuing of a trip which was to have lasted twelve days, had at least calmed people's worries—now that En Joaquim was returning he realized that he could not have stood for much longer the small amount of added work he had had these days: in reality a slight increase in responsibility.

He couldn't discuss this with En Joaquim either.

He had not spent three consecutive hours in the office since the day he had realized his faith in progress and the brotherhood of man. Now that he had seen the men in the big room, under the gray skylight, he had been able to verify the fact that, after three hours, they had made no progress whatsoever.

It was a stupid idea—how could they make any progress in three hours?—absurd, but it obsessed him; he wanted to draw some conclusion from it that would not be grotesque, a defensible conclusion.

"What do you shave with, Maurici?"

"A safety razor."

En Ribes took a close look at his cheek, with all the rigor of a scientific investigation.

"The skin's terribly irritated."

"The skin's irritated," said the echo inside Maurici. His mind was a blank, and this phrase roamed about inside him without finding obstacles: the skin's irritated, the skin's irritated.

There was something deeper within him, more sensitive and painful than skin, that was always irritated too. And he was sure that everyone had found some way to protect himself from irritating, painful contacts. Like En Joaquim. People who were invulnerable to doubt or uneasiness.

En Joaquim was capable of spending two hours in the office without being surprised by anything.

And then he remembered the grayish faces under the gray skylight—and he saw, very clearly, that what had impressed him was not the fact that they had made no progress in three hours, but that even the possibility of their making progress had not increased. . . .

He decided to listen to La Carme, and his head became filled with little logical, agreeable, precise phrases.

"You have to know French very well to understand it spoken on stage. . . . I get lost. It must have been a year ago—or maybe two?—that the 'Grenier' of Toulouse came. . . ."

"Whether you understand or not doesn't matter," said the playwright who ran a haberdashery business. "If we had actors as good as that . . ."

The little bar also gave off a strange perfume. The little bar, En Maurici realized, had the color, perfume, and unreality of a rose. The need for escape was here an incurable disease—too strong a temptation.

That was why they went there every day.

Tomorrow, when En Joaquim arrived, he could go to his house and have a long talk with him instead of coming here. He could talk with complete freedom, pour out all that was gnawing away inside him.

He was sure that En Joaquim would listen to him unperturbed. He counted on this imperturbability: he needed it. Standing before him would be enough to make his words lose their strength and urgency. En Joaquim's mere presence would calm him, because it would show him that there *were* men who could live in peace, who, even though they occasionally felt doubts about themselves, could overcome them just as one gets over grotesque childhood fears.

But in spite of the calming example that he knew En Joaquim could give him, he would not go and talk to him tomorrow when he arrived, but he would come, as he did every evening, to this little bar.

For En Joaquim was imperturbable—that was the way he was —but En Maurici was afraid of himself, of hearing his own voice. He was afraid of finally making concrete some ideas and emotions he had always tried to keep deliberately vague.

En Joaquim Civit was a man who demanded having problems

172

precisely presented. He would end up by resolving En Maurici's with a superior smile, with a Biblical quotation, or perhaps he would be content with alluding to some law, or contract, or . . . In exchange for presenting the problem, En Joaquim would give him a solution. The solution wouldn't do him a bit of good, and in exchange for that he would have fallen into the trap of formulating all his preoccupations, while at the moment—no more rum left—he did not know precisely what they were.

No, he didn't know.

He covered his forehead and eyes with his hands, and immediately asked for a dry martini.

Figuerola and Pradell, *artists,* entered the little bar.

They descended the three steps carefully, because they were carrying a painting in each hand.

En Pradell kept from getting cold by letting the dirt accumulate on his gabardine overcoat, and by letting the hair grow on his cheeks and the nape of his neck. He was the one who painted.

En Figuerola was wearing a green string tie, and he had round, mobile eyes. He was the one who talked.

They leaned the paintings, one next to the other, up against the bar, facing the customers. They were four landscapes filled with the same green as the string tie, with farmhouses, chickens in the foreground, a river, and trees yellow in the afternoon light.

En Ribes, the playwright who ran a haberdashery business, picked up a canvas and performed the one operation that most annoyed En Pradell and En Figuerola: he examined it with the light in back of it.

"Look at this," he said to his friends, "look how transparent it is. There's only a thin veil of paint."

And he laughed as if he had discovered the trap, as if they had tried to swindle him with the thickness of the color.

"How much do you want for it?" asked En Martí, the piano manufacturer.

En Figuerola, the artist who did the talking, rolled his eyes, altered the position of each picture so it would catch the light better, checked the position of his necktie, and said:

"Five hundred pesetas."

En Pradell, the artist who did the painting, leaned on the bar with his back to everyone and asked for a coffee.

A quarter of an hour later, En Maurici, for two hundred pesetas, bought the one with the chickens in the foreground, which was the one La Carmeta liked best.

Everyone said they couldn't believe that a man with his artistic taste should let himself be taken in like this.

But En Maurici insisted that the picture wasn't bad at all, that he even found that it contained a spontaneous charm, a kind of lyrical brushstroke, and a harmonious blending of color.

This was the right thing to say, he thought, and he felt reasonably satisfied with himself. For him two hundred pesetas was the price of one meal. For En Pradell and En Figuerola it was the price of forty meals.

This calculation impressed him.

He picked up the canvas and put it on La Carmeta's lap—who, when En Maurici got up to go, looked him in the eye with a long-forgotten intensity, in order to know whether he wanted her to leave with him.

En Pradell and En Figuerola, from the top step, before opening the street door, took one last look at the little bar.

The figures on the banquette were wrapped in a kind of blue- and rose-colored smoke or mist, a mist that was like bland cotton.

"Look, you'd think they were inside a little box. Don't they remind you, Pradell, of those little cardboard soldiers we had when we were kids, that we kept in cotton so they wouldn't break, or harm each other?"

"It'd be nice to be able to hide down in a rabbit warren like this. . . ."

Below the level of the world, below the level of consciousness.

SIXTEEN

As HE EMERGED from the subway exit he pulled up his overcoat collar, and had it not been for the darkness of the streets,
one would have noticed that the underside of the collar was of a
lighter color—the original color of the overcoat.

He cut rapidly around three or four corners. There were sections of the sidewalk waiting to be paved: a natural instinct or
years of practice told him not to put a foot down without care.
He sped up the rhythm of his walk on the uphill stretch, and he
finally took a turn to the left. Five steps farther on, and there was
the café.

One of the doorways he passed before entering the bar was
that of his own house. He did not stop or even slow down his
pace. He gave a glance: at the back of the patio shared by the three
houses, a weak light bulb attested to the shadows around it and a
quadrangular reflection, on the ground, of an invisible window.

He pushed open the door of the café.

"Hello, Ferran."

"Hello."

His table was in the back. The mason's assistant and the clerk
were already waiting for him; they always finished work earlier.
The locksmith was missing and, should he come at all, the old
mason's assistant.

Until he sat down at the table and said "Ah, shit!" En Ferran
did not feel completely free from the office, from the presence—
visible or invisible, it didn't make any difference—of Senyor
Alsina, the office manager, and from his own lack of interest in
what went on around him. Now that En Manolo of the café was
bringing him the coffee and *anís* and was spreading out on the
marble-topped table the green cloth, En Ferran felt like taking
a deep breath and talking in a loud voice.

The cards fell on the table like the leaves of a calendar, like
symbols of the minutes these men would now hold between their

fingertips—those free minutes they would pass back and forth so they could all enjoy them.

The truth of the matter was that everyone talked a bit too loud in this café. Everyone, at eight in the evening, felt the need to accredit his own existence. Unconsciously, they—the mason's assistant, the clerk, and the locksmith—were a bit astonished that they could really exist outside their work. They would be even more amazed if they could remember something they had by then forgotten: that their existence was anterior to their work—anterior and independent. That it was more natural to their human condition to be card players, idle and loudmouthed, than to be a mason's assistant, a clerk, or a locksmith by profession.

When En Ferran took off his old overcoat—why was it so hot in this café when there was no heating?—the mason's assistant gave him the news.

"Do you know En Salvador, who was going to work for the trolley company next month? Well, he lost a hand."

"What!"

"You heard me. It was smashed; a beam landed on it."

He took the unnecessary cards and shuffled with dexterity.

"You sure bring cheery news!"

"Whatever news there is. And just when he'd had some luck with the lottery."

"Ah, go on . . . !"

In this café things were as they were; they were presented, spoken, and thought of under a harsh light. It was a café exactly on a level with the street, and through the door there entered a continual draft, an incessant transfusion.

"Let's not wait; they'll come in a while."

They could play a couple of hands with just the three of them. It was the only table where people played poker, although even there somewhat secretively, for it was too refined a game for the coarse atmosphere of the café. En Ferran had been the innovator, and that was perhaps why the people who played *tuti* and *canari* glanced at him out of the corners of their eyes from time to time.

176

"I'm in a helluva mood too," said En Ferran, and he picked his five cards off the green cloth. "The office manager's got it in for me—I don't know why."

"How many?"

"Two."

Nothing much: two pair. But he decided to raise, just to see what would happen.

"What'd he do to you?" asked the mason's assistant.

"Nothing directly: luckily I don't see him much, and he doesn't consider me worth talking to. . . ."

"Three jacks."

"Tens full."

"Shit." He raised an eyebrow and pushed the cards toward the center of the table. "But he must think I'm stupider than the others or something. The boss took a trip up north and took along a chauffeur. He's already got one chauffeur, you see, but he left that one with his wife. . . . I thought maybe now I'd get a break. He went around the office looking for somebody who knew how to drive. He knows I can drive, but you can bet your life he never called on me."

"How many?"

"Three."

"But do you have a license?"

"No. But I've driven trucks for them when they had deliveries that couldn't wait."

"But without a license, Ferran . . ."

He gave him an angry look.

"I was good enough to do overtime, wasn't I? I *can* drive, can't I? Raise the pot!" and he turned in his chair.

"But that's different."

"You don't know him. He's got it in for me, that son of a . . ."

"Three tens."

"Two pair."

"Three jacks."

He picked up the cards and money aggressively.

"Didn't I tell you he was a son of a bitch?" as if his luck had proved him right.

He turned around a minute. Eight or ten marble-topped tables were covered with eight or ten green cloths, and on these green cloths badly shaven men with violent but contained emotions were trying to obtain from their card games—which they had unconsciously transposed to a higher plane—the justification of their existences, their failures and their difficulties.

"Everybody couldn't go; they had to choose someone."

"Yeah, sure, and what's more I can't complain about the guy they chose. . . ."

"So . . . ?"

"Listen"—he leaned forward and, after he had dealt, remained with his face only a few inches from that of the mason's helper— "what I mean is I've *got* to be myself, *myself,* you understand? Forget about the 'they had to choose someone' business. I don't want to know about it, and there's no reason why I should know about it. I only know that they didn't choose me, and they never will."

"How many?"

"None."

"Shit! You have all the luck."

Some people at another table began to shout. Two of the players had got up and were pounding their fists on the table. Somebody said *shhh* without too much authority. Everyone understood that people had to be allowed to shout—that by shouting one could live and breathe.

Finally someone interrupted them:

"Come on now, cut it out or you'll lose your appetite!"

And everyone laughed. It was a slightly nervous laughter, for they all knew they were lucky to be able to be in this café right now, while some of their friends would not leave work until nine, ten, or eleven o'clock. And they found the crack about

178

losing their appetite amusing, and they poured their last drops of coffee into their water glasses, so it would last longer.

The door of the café opened and an icy gust of wind entered.

A woman with two sweaters on, rabbitskin slippers, and a large purse was selling lottery tickets.

"Tomorrow's lottery," she said.

And it was strange how a bit of the icy air from outside accompanied this woman. It was stuck to the lottery tickets, which the men tried not to look at; above all, they didn't want to see the numbers on the tickets.

Her presence made them uncomfortable, and when finally the door closed behind the woman, everyone felt at ease again in the café, and the men once again raised their voices, which they had lowered without realizing it, and it wasn't long before they had regained the feeling that this was the only possible world—the only desirable world.

"How many?"

"One."

A nine. Just what he'd wanted: a nine.

The locksmith entered. He was wearing a thick, heavy hunting jacket that he had picked up during the war and which looked as if it would last forever.

He sat down silently. He did not want to say anything until they had finished the hand. Then, pointing to the newspaper folded up in his inside pocket, he said:

"It looks like they're thinking of passing a new law about rents and sublets."

"What's going to happen?"

"Nobody knows yet. There's some kind of project under discussion, but all that stuff always goes at a snail's pace."

"How many?"

"Three."

"We might as well start worrying right now. No good'll come of it."

"They want to clear up the subletting situation on the basis of so much per cent . . . like I said, nobody knows yet."

"It'd be better if they didn't start fiddling around."

"Tens full."

"Two pair."

"Aces full."

"And then En Gabriel and me'll get in another fight."

"En Gabriel?"

"Yeah, the people that live with us."

The locksmith motioned to En Manolo of the café to bring him the usual vermouth.

"Listen, you know the son of the old mason's assistant? Well, the court authorities went to his house."

"What'd he do?"

"He couldn't pay the installments on his radio—I don't know how many pesetas a month it was. But listen, the whole damned bunch of them came—the court secretary, the bailiff, everybody. And all of them writing things down, and talking about a law that says if you don't pay, and then the business of the seizure. . . ."

"What'd he want a radio for?"

"How many?"

"Two."

"Why shouldn't he want one?"

The door opened and another gust of cold air entered—and this constant transfusion between the street and the bar made it so that even the men inside could not submerge themselves in a privileged, friendly world, in a world of white- and rose-colored lights, below the level of life.

And on the other hand, if they were removed from the sphere of this harsh white light which gave to each thought, each color, each truth, its authentic, familiar shape, they would also not know how to live. Some completely selfless man, some very wise state, or some new religion would have to give them profound preparation.

"Three kings."

The only means of evasion within their reach was cards. But it wasn't a whole world. It was only an activity, without content, without possible valuation—that was why it did them no harm and why they enjoyed it and why it was healthy for them, like breathing with one's eyes closed under a broad sky.

And suddenly:

"Hey, Pop!"

En Ferran's son, from the door of the café.

"Mom says are you going to come and eat supper or what?"

SEVENTEEN

THE DOCTOR had left the car in front of the house.

In the middle of the patio, it looked like an enormous black insect, some monstrous species of beetle that had come down from the mountains.

The old woman was standing off at a distance trying to domesticate it with the mysterious power of her fixed gaze.

En Pere Jordana opened the door and got in behind the wheel. He turned the ignition key and the motor roared.

Some ducks quacked.

The motor roared louder, in spurts, and it sounded as if the car were about to take off like an airplane.

The doctor, taking advantage of a doctor's privileges, entered the house to have a drink and greedily pinch the cheeks of the young girl with the astonished eyes. Before, he had said to Senyor Joaquim: "They've fixed it perfectly, you'll see," and he had handed the bill to En Pere Jordana.

En Jordana released the brake and the car started to move forward. He skirted the edge of the patio and went up the road, in search of the highway.

And suddenly he felt alone, more alone than he had yet felt since leaving home. "The car again," he thought, and he felt betrayed, brought back to an epoch through which he had already lived; and the reality of the situation that presented itself to him so forcibly—he was the part-time chauffeur to a millionaire called Senyor Joaquim, and his obligations and rights were the explicit results of this relationship—was attempting to blur everything else, all the other thoughts and all the other relationships he had experienced and, above all, imagined.

While he was going down the road toward the main highway, he tried to identify the trees and rocks that had seen him pass by carrying Senyor Joaquim in his arms. He tried it with a greed that was almost sickly.

It was useless. And since the material evidence was lacking, he began to doubt if everything wasn't lacking, if everything hadn't been the product of his own imagination.

And in spite of this, it had not been an hour since he had had his last conversation with Senyor Joaquim. A conversation which had remained engraved on the most sensitive layer of the substance of which he was made.

A wrinkle had formed on Senyor Joaquim's brow, and something impalpable trembled beneath his eye—a bit of skin or perhaps a bit of his glance.

It was a wrinkle he had never seen on him.

"How do they strike you, these days we've spent here, Jordana?"

En Pere understood, naturally, that he wasn't referring to the weather, nor to the relaxation, to the pleasant relaxation, but to that indefinable thing which had risen between them, a kind of plant which had united them both beneath the same patch of shade.

"It doesn't seem as if we've talked much together. You must have known, Jordana, that I'm a man of few words. Right?"

He didn't smile familiarly. He was too preoccupied with his

own thoughts, and the wrinkle had remained as if fixed. Yes, he was a man of few words, and at the office he had never uttered more than eight or ten at a stretch, but now, in addition, he seemed to be having difficulty expressing himself.

"But I must say that these days have been the strangest I've . . . No, 'strange' is a meaningless word. . . . I don't know if you see it the way I do. . . ."

See what? And in spite of such imprecise expression, En Pere Jordana knew perfectly well that these days had been strange. It was a peculiar thing that when they were in the office and Senyor Joaquim's words were always precise, there was an irreparable distance between them. Now, in this house where any conversation floundered unavoidably, day after day, in the most pathetic vaguenesses, the contact between them had been deep and so close as to make them shudder.

"You, Jordana, carried me in your arms from the highway"— while he thought this, he looked at him through small eyes, stupidly. It had been a natural thing to do, something of no importance. So why did he have a secret fear of it? Why was it such an effort for him to translate something so simple into words?— abortive words painfully squeezing themselves out like lifeless blood. . . . And he wanted to know: "What else went on while you were carrying me, or what did you feel, and think . . . ?" He realized that he hadn't yet thanked him. "Does one have to thank a chauffeur for not letting one die all alone on the side of the road . . . ?" And he had an inescapable feeling that En Jordana still held him in his arms, that he would not let go of him.

He moved his lips without talking, and had he been a smoker he would have put a cigarette in his mouth.

"It isn't really that he's still got me in his arms. It's I that won't let go of him. . . ." It seemed as if they had changed roles. He felt En Jordana's proximity as a heavy burden, almost as if he were carrying him on his shoulder.

Couldn't one just close one's eyes?

He felt like stretching out his arms, putting his hands on En Jordana's chest, and pushing him away, far away, far enough away to break the sticky substance that joined them.

"It isn't strictly speaking a physical sensation. . . ." He also thought of the picture of the child with unkempt hair. "Something compels me to find out why the proximity of a man should weigh on me like something painfully oppressive—and the same thing compels me to put off finding this out as long as possible. . . ."

The silence, the stony stare, the sickness inside from the anguish—these were the fruits of the double compulsion, of wanting to know and not know.

En Pere Jordana, however, only thought that Senyor Joaquim had always been, in fact, a man of few words. But Senyor Joaquim's few words had been enough for En Pere Jordana to start up a small, intense conversation.

A conversation which, aided by the rhythmic functioning of the car motor, he now suddenly remembered, as if there had been no silences or hesitations.

"If the car functions properly, we'll be in Barcelona tomorrow evening, Jordana."

"We should leave here by midmorning then."

"Yes. Don't you want to return to Barcelona, Jordana?"

"Yes."

"What is it you miss most?"

"There's my wife . . . She probably doesn't know what's happened."

"Nobody knows what's happened."

"That's true."

"Even we scarcely know. . . ."

"You were right when you said these had been strange days. . . ."

"Have you ever lived in a place like this, Jordana?"

"Only in my mind. Sometimes I dream of a house like this, maybe because I come from a family of farmers."

"Oh!"

"I know that my wife would feel better if she could breathe this air, and wash clothes in the sun, and give names to four chickens. . . ."

"Is your wife sick?"

"No. But we've all got things that get on our nerves. . . . She'd be better off here."

"That's strange; this place makes me feel uneasy . . . Jordana."

"Yes."

"Jordana, perhaps down deep I was affected by the accident. Maybe I want to return home in order to rest."

"That's only natural."

"One day, after I've had a rest, when my head's a little clearer . . ."

"Did you take your temperature today?"

". . . and then we'll talk calmly about all this, Jordana, about . . . anyhow, we'll talk. . . ."

On the way back, En Pere stopped at the corner where they had crashed. He opened the door and got out of the car.

Standing on the highway, he felt a steady wind blowing past him, a wind which tirelessly drained the warmth from his face— a wind which isolated him uncomfortably from all the things around him.

This was the exact place.

Perhaps there was still a bit of blood on the earth—which now seemed like a different, darker earth.

And this was the rock, and this the tree. But no.

It was as if the harsh, unrelenting wind had taken everything away. Also the void and the shade of things which, for one intense moment, had been there. A wind that was like time.

When he was back on the smaller road and approaching the house, he thought that in spite of everything that moment had

185

existed and had produced new moments and new things, like a chain made up of infinite, unforeseeable links. . . .

He entered the house, for the wind was growing stronger.

The doctor was putting off leaving. . . . Senyor Joaquim had paid him everything; he owed him no more money. He only owed him a bit of understanding. One had to admit that he was neither likable nor knowledgeable, but who could foretell that he might not one day be both likable and knowledgeable? One had to recognize the misery of his present solitude.

That was why nobody turned his back on him when he put off leaving.

Senyor Joaquim offered him another glass of the old woman's brew, and they sat down near the kitchen fire. Senyor Joaquim had never before sat in this kitchen, and because he was now doing so, the old woman withdrew to a corner, as if she were nothing more than the stranger's shadow on the wall.

En Pere Jordana was not with them. He was going over the list of objects in his room that he wasn't to forget to put in his suitcase. He didn't need to have his tiny piece of luggage ready until the following day—there was plenty of time. But he had felt a need to be alone.

On the other hand, the four things spread out at the foot of the bed now had a very pronounced outline—they were like fragments of a mirror faithfully reflecting him.

His toothbrush, wrapped in a piece of paper which had become wrinkled and crushed from contact with water, caused him a strange sense of anguish. It was a toothbrush that had lost many bristles. It was strange that each day for three or four years he had picked it up without realizing that it was in a state of ruin. But in order to realize this, he had only to open Senyor Joaquim's suitcase the day of the accident. He had found nothing of the absurd things he had expected: bandages, disinfectants, cotton. There was nothing in the suitcase but small, ordinary objects: shirts, underdrawers, Eau de Cologne, pajamas . . . and a toothbrush. It was in its proper place inside a leather toilet case which also held a silver-plated cylinder with shaving soap, another one for the shaving brush, some manicure scissors, a mirror . . . When he had compared this sumptuous leather case with the damp paper in which his own things were wrapped, he had also tried to compare his face with Senyor Joaquim's. That morning he had shaved with a feeling of repressed violence. He had put a new blade in his razor and had pressed it energetically against his skin. But he hadn't been able to obtain Senyor Joaquim's look of rosy cleanliness. He had looked at himself in the mirror and seen that he had the same gray chin as ever, and the shadow under the cheekbones was like a stigma of his background.

And looking now at his half-ruined toothbrush he realized that, in spite of everything, it wouldn't be enough to throw it out and buy a new one—and buy a silver-plated razor and real Gillette blades—in order to cease to be a marked man.

He threw away the empty pack of cigarettes and picked up another. He crossed the hallway and, standing in the doorway of the house, he looked at the black car in the middle of the patio, like an annunciation of the night that was already settling down behind the mountains.

"If the car functions properly we'll be in Barcelona tomorrow evening," Senyor Joaquim had said.

He looked at the two great trees flanking the entrance to the farm, and at the irrigation tank, and at the four big wicker baskets in the corner, and at the slow procession of ducks off to the left, on the narrow path leading to the well, and at the light waning like a hand closing—and he smelled the odor not only of the earth, but of all the diverse things that had once been in the earth, and were now breathing it.

Barcelona was then a far-off reality, and its meaning difficult to fathom, in spite of its being so near, at nightfall. Tomorrow evening he would be there.

"And then we'll talk calmly about all this, Jordana . . ." He

had said it twice. With a strange confused look on his face, and
yet in a sonorous tone of voice.

He went out onto the patio and started to walk around it. As
he walked—and everyone, when walking, frees himself from his
surroundings—and rediscovered the physical and mental limits
of himself as a person, he became convinced that Senyor Joaquim
would in fact finally talk to him. That down deep returning to
Barcelona was a good thing, for in Barcelona everything that had
been under preparation here would finally materialize. In Barcelona, and in the office, Senyor Joaquim would once again find the
few precise words, but this time the words would be full of a
strength born of these days which En Pere Jordana realized had
been so favorable to him.

Some words that would have an economic value. Money's everything, En Jordana thought. Money makes it possible to rest at
night, to enjoy Sundays and the uninterrupted company of another child. A girl this time, who would restore to his wife a bit
of her youth.

En Pere Jordana did not think—he could not imagine—that
Senyor Joaquim's words could have another kind of value, and
even less a value superior to that of money. En Pere Jordana
thought that things had come to the point where it was only a
question of Senyor Joaquim's deciding if it would be three hundred, five hundred, or a thousand pesetas. En Pere Jordana did
not know—how could he know? what preparation had he had for
loftier hopes? for how many years now have men like him believed
that, as hard as they try to remove it, a shadow like a stigma will
always separate them from men like Senyor Joaquim?—En Pere
did not know that Senyor Joaquim, for the first time in his life,
had a more serious problem on his hands than that of increasing
someone's salary.

After the doctor left—he had come in the car and was returning in the idiot's cart, once again entering the cloud of dust which

was his life—Senyor Joaquim did not move from his seat in the dark kitchen. A strange lethargy had come over him.

In his dream En Maurici was very tall, and he, En Joaquim, was continually trying to come up to his height. He stood on his toes—at the same time trying to conceal the fact that he was doing so. They were in a room that was familiar to him, even though he could not identify it with any specific room he knew.

En Maurici's hands were full of little colored objects, which could have been coins, poker cards, or chicken bones. He was playing with them, making them move rapidly between his fingers. En Joaquim followed these evolutions with hypnotic fixity, and he would have liked to break this spell because he knew he was in front of En Maurici for another purpose, something important and urgent.

He had the feeling that days and years passed; that he would never break the spell.

When En Maurici began to speak, the anguish suddenly ceased. His voice made everything logical, easy, and normal.

"How do you feel now?"

"Fine."

"In any case, you'd better have a general checkup. My brother-in-law's a friend of En Pedro Pons."

"It isn't necessary. Something spectacular, but basically unimportant . . ."

Basically unimportant? Basically unimportant?

It tired him to be always on tiptoe, trying to be on a level with En Maurici.

"It was good for you to have a vacation. Doing nothing, thinking of nothing . . ."

"It wasn't exactly a vacation," he protested. "And I was thinking . . ."

En Maurici grew slightly taller—just as he had finally succeeded in being really on a level with him. "I was thinking," he repeated, but strangely enough En Maurici was slipping away and couldn't hear him.

He made an effort to entice him back.

"I've seen new things, Maurici. Let me explain."

"You've found out how farmers live, eh?"

"Yes."

"What a primitive existence!"

"Yes."

"And picturesque."

"Yes."

"The misery of those families lost up there in the mountains."

"Yes. But I've discovered other things, Maurici. Things which made an absurd impression on me. Let me explain."

And then the little colored objects again started moving rapidly between En Maurici's fingers. He was smiling, and En Joaquim felt as if his head was being emptied.

And then there came a moment in which all the mist of the dream vanished. He woke up sitting in the low chair, surrounded by the darkness of the kitchen, and he realized that it wouldn't be easy to talk. Not easy at all, but in spite of this he had to find some way of doing so.

Then he imagined the scene with admirable clarity.

It took place in En Maurici's living room. The Venetian lamp, the little Gothic triptych, the vase with the green magnolia branch. When he sat down on the sofa, he sank way down in it, and from that moment on Senyor Joaquim could talk only in hushed tones. There was always some book—on a little table, on the mantelpiece, or even occupying an armchair—looking as if it had just been put down. An artificial naturalness of which En Joaquim Civit had never been suspicious—he really believed that En Maurici (that was the kind of fellow he was) was reading them.

In the living room, naturally, there were only two people: En Maurici and himself. In appearance, everything was as it always was. As at other times when they had been there to exchange impressions or resolve some minor problem. En Maurici had poured himself some Carpano—he had a mania for it—and En Joaquim, who couldn't stand anything bitter, had taken nothing but a half-glass of soda water. But he wouldn't even taste it.

"Here was the front door, you understand? There was the kitchen. A terribly dark kitchen. You could never tell if the old woman was there or not."

"Strange that the kitchen wasn't a part of the entrance hall itself, as in most farmhouses in the region . . ."

En Joaquim Civit shrugged his shoulders, uninterested. He had no idea why the house was the way it was. He had been talking for quite a while now, with the sole intent of accumulating information, observations, and details. He realized that he could discuss this situation as much as he wanted, but he would never succeed in transferring his uneasiness to En Maurici.

"And over there was a pile of hazelnuts; you'd step on them without meaning to and they would give off an intense, dry odor."

Over there, now, there was a little rug that was supposed to be Persian and handmade, and worth a fortune. Why, thought En Joaquim Civit, wasn't his voice as sure as he would have liked? As he spoke, he contemplated the huge reproduction of a Picasso painting, the Chinese bibelot, and the collection of silver ash trays, and he felt as if he were recounting a dream, that his story sounded as if it had been invented, that this was the only reality. When he spoke of the *accident,* it felt as if he were trying to deceive En Maurici. When he said *Pere Jordana* he could not make intelligible the real dimensions of the authentic Pere Jordana.

To the point that En Maurici had once made a mistake and referred to him as *Pere Jansana.*

En Joaquim decided to take just a little bit of Carpano.

"I can assure you that if I'd had to trust the people who lived there, I would have been lost. The man was like an animal; he couldn't articulate one word. His wife was the closest thing to a witch you could possibly imagine. ('This drink really is bitter, but it doesn't seem too strong. . . .') Luckily, En Jordana acted like a kind of bodyguard. It amuses me to think about it now: he took over to the point where the old woman didn't dare approach my bed any more, and she hid away her concoctions and her receptacles."

"Too bad he's just an employee. . . ."

En Joaquim looked at him a moment and squeezed the glass between his fingers.

"He's an employee, Maurici, who picked me up off the ground, stopped my hemorrhaging, carried me on his shoulder. . . ."

He took another shot of Carpano.

"Let me tell you something. For me, now, En Jordana's no longer just an employee."

"That's only natural. You feel grateful."

It was too easy a word, too worn with use. En Joaquim watched the movement of the liquid inside the glass, and said nothing.

"I suppose you intend to give him some kind of reward."

"That isn't the problem."

"No, obviously not."

He hadn't expressed himself well, thought En Joaquim. He should have said: "That isn't the *most important* problem."

"Are you getting to like the Carpano?" asked En Maurici admiringly.

He didn't know if he liked it, strangely enough, even though he had taken a second glass.

"I wonder if all employees are like this Jordana fellow."

"More or less, I should guess they are."

"I've had little to do with people, you know. I'm not like you. And these days I was forced to live with—I don't know if you'd call that living with—but I was in the company of a man whom I didn't know at all . . . Don't you have the heating turned up too much, Maurici? At first, it gave me a certain feeling of distress. . . . As I said before, I'm not like you."

He was about to say: "Look, after all these years I'm not even completely at ease with you. . . . I still haven't been able to make your company something completely relaxing for me. . . ." Why should this be?

"People like that," En Maurici commented, "sometimes seem

192

to have no idea whatsoever of what it means to be discreet. . . ."

"I can assure you he didn't bother me. He's not the talkative type."

He drank a little, and he seemed thoughtful.

"In fact, if I try to recall what we talked about during those days, all that comes to mind are inanities. Then I realize to what degree his mere presence was a weight, so that it should result in this."

En Maurici looked at him with curiosity.

"Result in what?"

Another wave of heat within the house. Perhaps it wasn't all due to the heating. Perhaps it was the Carpano. . . . But the Carpano was helping him, and he continued to squeeze the glass between his fingers with an obstinacy which formerly he would have been at a loss to explain.

"It's strange, Joaquim. It isn't just now; yesterday in the office you seemed a bit peculiar. Changed. You seem preoccupied with something. . . ."

He put his hand affectionately on his knee. Deep down he had always considered En Joaquim as a child. He was proud of knowing him through and through. He was easy to understand. If on the one hand he had always admired him for being all of a piece, he had also, for the same reason, considered him inferior, benevolently inferior.

Now, however, he looked at him with intensified affection. And, for the first time, with deep interest. He insisted:

"What was it that happened?"

"This man"—En Joaquim felt his pockets nervously—"this man has a wife . . . ('That sentence doesn't sound good') and a child ('Why worry about how it sounds? It's a question of talking, not of interrupting oneself'), and I guess everyone's got a wife and child, but when you find out ('Is the Carpano good or isn't it?') what a wife and child really is, and who's involved ('What's that?') . . ."

In his coat pocket he had come across a little soft, cylindrical object. . . . How did this cigarette get in his pocket?

"Have you started smoking too?" En Maurici asked admiringly.

En Joaquim looked in complete surprise at the cigarette between his fingers.

"Put it down, I'll get you a better one."

While En Maurici got up to look for the green box of Abdullahs, En Joaquim regained the image of their first walk down the paths of the lost valley, beneath the distant sky. Far off they could hear the quacking of ducks, and there arose the tenuous odor of sun-baked earth, when En Pere Jordana offered him the cigarette and he, without realizing it, accepted it. . . .

"No, I'll smoke this one."

He would smoke this one. One of the twenty cigarettes En Pere Jordana smoked every day. He wasn't accustomed to it; he got too near the match and half of the cigarette was gray from the smoke.

His mouth immediately filled with thick saliva. He couldn't, for the moment, make up his mind to swallow it, until he had the feeling he was choking.

"Don't insist on going on with it," En Maurici said smilingly.

Yes, he would insist on going on. Fearfully. Hesitantly. He would go on until he could make En Maurici understand. Probably in the end, without making any effort, En Maurici would explain and give precise definition to his uneasiness. Surely his problem wasn't original. There must be some label to define it— he realized that his problem and his uneasiness were of more general proportions, that they affected everyone. En Maurici would undoubtedly know the formula that would resolve the question.

The only difficulty—outside of the world of business, he had always been inept—the only terrible difficulty, for him, was the presentation.

194

"Do you know what this Jordana's ambition is? To have a daughter."

"He doesn't have one?"

"No, he's got a son."

En Maurici moved one hand agilely.

"One of each. That's only natural."

One of each. That's only natural. He could say it cheerfully, without frowning. One of each: that's lovely and natural.

"You could do him a good turn. You could give him a raise, couldn't you?"

"That's already occurred to me."

It had already occurred to him, yes, but still, from the moment he had made this decision, he could not fathom whether or not En Pere Jordana was expecting something more, whether or not this was *all* he expected. For not once, in the days they were together, had he said anything to clarify this point. He had not, even unconsciously, put forward any claim. It was not difficult to believe that at that precise moment, sitting with his wife and child in a dining room that was growing darker by the minute, En Pere Jordana was much more tranquil at heart than he. This was what paralyzed him, what most distressed him. No one had forced upon him this feeling of uneasiness. There was no struggle, no demand, no external enemy denying him his former peace of mind. His uneasiness was nothing more than a tiny, incandescent point of light moving about within him. Between the Persian rug, the Gothic triptych, and the lovely magnolia branch, he incomprehensibly—he felt it unconsciously—was an inept revolutionary apprentice.

"But do you know what happened? I had the feeling En Pere Jordana was asking me permission to have a child. Do you understand?"

Why wasn't En Maurici laughing now? He always gave everything a malicious twist.

"Obviously, I'll give him a raise. But that isn't as easy as you think. What about the others?"

"What others?"

"All of them. All the Jordanas in the office."

He had already smoked half the cigarette. It was supposed to be the worst brand of cigarette in Spain. Wasn't there some danger of its producing cancer of the lip?

"Are you afraid they'll protest?"

"No. But why should En Jordana get special consideration? Haven't you ever thought about all the others who've never had the opportunity to ask me permission to have a child?"

He put down his cigarette.

"I wanted to know if En Jordana was just particularly unfortunate; that was why I asked you before if all the employees were like him. I understand now that he's just a man like any other. Then I ask myself what meaning there would be to giving him a raise of four hundred pesetas because I know he needs it . . . when I realize that all the others need it as well."

"You're losing your sense of perspective, Joaquim. If you better his position, it would be because he's rendered you a service."

For an instant, En Joaquim looked at him timidly. But the Carpano—he finally knew he didn't like it—helped him.

"No, Maurici. If I were to better his position, as you put it, it wouldn't be because he's rendered me a service, but simply because his position is capable of being bettered. He's a man who has desires I can now understand."

He had a vague idea, floating about in his feverish brain, that he was repeating the scene with En Jordana and the old woman's brew: he could only speak clearly with his mind blurred.

"He's a man like me."

"I don't think so."

En Maurici, without looking at him, diluted his vermouth with a spurt of soda water.

"All right, not like me. In fact, we don't resemble each other a bit. I don't know if I'm making myself clear. What I meant was that he *could* be a man like me, and that he could be a bit more like me if *I* desired it."

196

From the street came the piercing wail of a fire engine, and time stood still in the living room—it was as if thought had been nailed to the wall by a stiletto.

"So there's something more to be done than just raising the salary of a man called Pere Jordana. Don't you think so?"

En Maurici tugged at his mustache obstinately.

"Well, don't you think so?"

En Maurici rubbed his cheek.

"Then there's a lot to be done," he admitted. "First of all you must ask yourself how far you're willing to go."

"And if I told you," said En Joaquim after a silence, "that I didn't know, and that it was precisely to clear up this point that I wanted to talk to you?"

Then En Maurici once again put his hand affectionately on En Joaquim's knee.

"Look, talking won't get us anywhere. The only remedy is to work and do things. The only remedy is to make up your mind to give in to the disease, do you understand? Begin anywhere; that isn't the most difficult part. Give En Jordana a raise. Fine. Then get somebody else; he doesn't have to be a technician or an economist. Somebody who's got a clear head. Explain things to him, laying all your cards on the table. That you earn, each month, eighty or ninety times more than En Jordana—or En Mateu, L'Hernández, or whoever you want. That you have five children and he has one. That you've built yourself a house at Viladrau and that he's fixed up a broken windowpane with Scotch tape. That every Sunday you have a pound of almond brittle sent up from Llibre i Serra, and he spends his Sundays bouncing around in the cab of a truck. And above all explain to him that you're what's known as a kind person. That you believe that a man should have a lot of children, live in a pleasant house, and rest on Sundays. And then let him go ahead."

He pointed to the bottle. "Do you want some more?"

En Joaquim refused with a shake of his head.

"It strikes me that if you do it like that, the solution is extraordinarily easy. But believe me: give someone else the responsibility; don't try to do it yourself. You can't do it with any feelings of personal emotion or direct charity. It'll fail."

En Maurici's lips were pursed into a peculiar line, and he went on:

"For En Jordana it wouldn't help him to expect some sudden, daily self-denial on your part, and for you it would be a constant preoccupation. The other solution is much easier and surer. Take advantage of this first lucid moment, and alter the situation from top to bottom, once and for all. It isn't as exciting, but it will give more results."

En Maurici got up from the sofa and took a long pipe out of a tobacco box he had brought from London.

En Joaquim's eyes were fixed on the rug, and his soft, rosy hands were resting on his knees like two flames.

Amid the silence there arose a mixed odor of wood and tobacco.

"As for me"—En Maurici talked with his back turned, while he poked around inside the pipe with a metal cleaner—"if you want to know my feelings on the subject, I couldn't care less one way or the other. You've known me for a long time. . . . Nothing that you've done till now has ever interested me. . . ."

When he turned around, En Joaquim saw that the edges of his eyes and mouth were covered with tiny wrinkles.

"Extraordinary things could happen, Quim. Or maybe I've just got a terrible imagination. You could change the lives (and the thoughts and feelings) of a handful of people. I can't imagine how it will all end. Perhaps then we'll finally know if you were right, if we are all equal. Maybe your name will be in the papers. Maybe, for the sake of your children, your wife will have you judged legally incompetent because of your prodigality"—and he twisted his mouth in a strange way—"or perhaps they'll make you a saint. . . ."

In spite of what he was saying, what a profound impulse, what a terrible feeling of temptation, what a timeless sincerity was making him tremble from head to foot and changing him into a man of impressive animation, a man emerging from the depths of time, when he said the simple, worn-out phrase:

"I'll take care of it myself."

And with an outstretched hand he invited En Joaquim to rise to his height.

EIGHTEEN

In the corridor Senyor Alsina, the office manager, met L'Ignasi, the clerk, who seemed to be coming from the bathroom. He would never be able to understand what went on with these people who had to go to the bathroom every hour. He had not used the office facilities for perhaps a year, perhaps two. . . . He never forgot to move his bowels in the morning, while the water for his shower was heating up.

But it was obvious that these people led less ordered lives. This Ignasi's hair was not combed in any normal way, and it was as black as sin.

When L'Ignasi plastered himself up against the wall to let Senyor Alsina pass by freely, along with the privileged layer of air that surrounded him, the office manager remembered that this man had been living through a drama.

"How's your child?"

For a moment L'Ignasi semeed to unstick himself from the wall and acquire a certain volume.

"Almost cured, Senyor Alsina. The doctor told me that the chloromycetin saved him."

"On with your work, then. . . ."

L'Ignasi slid rapidly past and, like a beetle, tried to do so unnoticed by means of running along the angle between floor and wall. And Senyor Alsina's glance followed him as if it were attempting to be a broom.

It would have been a shame, he thought, if this man's child had died. And he undoubtedly would have died if L'Ignasi, instead of working for a firm like this which advanced him two thousand pesetas for chloromycetin . . .

He wondered if he had given the memorandum to En Riera, the cashier. He went back to his office: there it was on the desk. Deduct a hundred pesetas a month from his salary.

The light entering from the overhead window was insufficient, and the electric lights had to be turned on. In the outside world it was now noon. On the streets, every now and then, a man carrying a package or dragging a cart would look up at the sky and—in spite of the clouds and gray cold, it was noon—take some part in the fleeting exultation of the world.

The shoeshine boy, seated on his little box, looked at the legs of the girls passing by—this year they were wearing their overcoats long. The trolley inspector, waiting at the stop, relit his cigar, right now at exactly noon, even though he did not know it. A dog barked from a fourth-floor balcony because a noisy truck had passed by—and, fraudulently hanging on to the back of the truck, was a boy with a cigarette butt in his mouth, swinging his legs and singing *"Santa Marta, Santa Marta tiene tren. . . ."*

It was noon in the city, and it was even more noticeably so on the other side of the mountains, far off, where the fruits that hung from trees, at that hour, were full of music like little bells, there where everything exists in an air of freedom and where some nameless dogs were walking down paths of flowering dust. . . .

Since the light entering from the overhead window was insufficient, it was necessary to turn on the electric lights in the office.

En Manelet looked at En Vila's hands, and then at the buttons on his sweater, and little by little he raised his eyes—En Vila's necktie, his mouth, his mustache—until he met the eyes of the man in front of him, on the other side of the desk.

Every time he made a mistake, his blood seemed to heat up and he felt as if his taut chest were about to explode. Since the day En Pere Jordana had left—since the day he had been replaced by En Vila—he often made mistakes. There was nothing to justify these errors, for he did exactly the same work in front of En Vila as he had done in front of En Jordana.

But he was afraid. Little Manelet, who was growing so much that winter, was afraid that En Jordana would not come back and sit on the other side of the desk. He imagined his life as being tightly bound to that of En Pere, and only beside him could he make progress. That was why this friendly man's absence distressed him. He was worried that while he was away, while he could not stretch out a hand to him, En Jordana would be altered into something different and superior, something he could not recover. Something evolving alone while he went on growing alone, uselessly, and making mistakes.

En Vila, who was gazing at him penetratingly, guessed that he had made another mistake. En Vila was cleverer than En Pere Jordana—and En Manelet was already at an age where one begins to notice these things. But on the other hand, one couldn't say that En Vila treated him badly, nor did he comment on his errors. But his eyes and voice had a kind of hardness, and it was a hardness that wasn't directed especially to En Manelet, but was something more general, like the look of a man accustomed to seeing dead people.

"He's not very smart," En Vila thought, looking at the boy, "and he doesn't trust himself for anything. It's ridiculous that he doesn't yet know how to do his job with any degree of confidence. But then why should he be smart? It's only natural that he should be just a kid like the others, and you can only hope he doesn't have too much bad luck; that he doesn't get sick, that no one in his family gets sick, or that he doesn't fall in love too soon. . . ."

No, this Vila wasn't like En Pere Jordana, En Manelet thought. En Vila had a frank, open look, but it was unsympathetic—because he thought that everything around him had inescapable limits and an interior death; but what did he expect? In contrast to En Jordana, whose eyes had a slightly perturbed quality, and who wanted to have a boy just like this intelligent, sensitive, hard-working, tall, and marvellous boy who was growing so much that winter . . . but why, after all?

The cashier let two minutes pass by after the silent hand of Senyor Alsina, the office manager, had deposited on his desk the memorandum concerning how much was to be deducted from L'Ignasi's salary every month.

After the two minutes had passed, he pushed his chair back a bit, parsimoniously took out his tobacco pouch, and said to L'Antoni, the assistant cashier:

"The Spy probably won't be back for another half-hour. Let's have a smoke."

They called Senyor Alsina, the office manager, the *Spy* because he walked soundlessly, stuck his nose into everything, and then reported his findings to the boss. They also called him *One-Arm*, but that was just to be mean, because in fact he was missing only the tip of one finger.

"What's this about a raise in salaries?" said L'Antoni, passing his fingers through his hair.

"A lot of hot air, that's what. Listen, don't you already earn more than any raise they can possibly give you? So?"

The cashier couldn't accept the fact that L'Antoni, the assistant, dressed as well as he, not to say better. L'Antoni always wore expensive white shirts with wide, pointed collars, and he always bought the latest-style shoes. It made him unhappy that this should be done by the man who sat at the desk next to his and was, in fact, under him—even though, many Sundays, they went to the soccer matches together.

L'Antoni was a bachelor. But did that explain everything? L'Antoni had a mother and two brothers, and even though these brothers had done well and supported their mother, how was it that he had no obligations, nor the common sense to put aside a certain sum? He knew well enough what he earned: twelve hundred pesetas a month. He always smoked blond tobacco and exhibited a variety of neckties that was exasperating. He could have sworn that he spent the twelve hundred pesetas, every last one of them, on himself . . . and he was an assistant cashier.

The cashier didn't understand it. But no matter what one said, it was unpardonable, and he took it as a personal offense. He recognized his right to do whatever he wanted with his money—everyone was free to make his own choice in such matters—except that he felt it was wrong to throw it in people's faces. And every time he looked at him and saw his necktie, his shirt, and his shoes, he felt as if his face were being rubbed in the money.

There should be a law against it. He himself bought neckties only at Christmas and on Sant Lluïs. There should be a law against men like L'Antoni being assistant cashiers—a man whose job was rather on the modest side shouldn't be allowed to go around looking like a millionaire.

Because, in the long run, this had had an unfortunate result: Senyor Alsina, the office manager, considered that L'Antoni, who was better dressed than he himself or anyone else, was the most capable employee in the entire firm, and the one with the most brilliant future, and he thought this for no other reason than because he went around dressed like a mannequin; the vice of squandering was mistaken as a virtue of dignity. And, in a certain sense, L'Antoni was an accusation against all of them: he was the proof that their wages were sufficient, not only to live on, but *for dressing up.* . . .

The cashier squashed his cigarette out in the ash tray, and once again bent over his books. As he picked up the old-fashioned green fountain pen with which he could write such thin, slender figures, he said: "Don't you ever think about getting married, Antoni?"

L'Antoni laughed.

"What made you think of that?"

The cashier, down deep, would have liked to see L'Antoni get married, to see what would happen. And he thought that on the calendars that the management passed out all over the office, instead of the views of Switzerland or reproductions from the Prado Museum, there should be, so as to make things clear to everyone, some drawings with the price of eggs, potatoes, olive oil, and gas.

The day contained five minutes that passed extraordinarily slowly. They were the five minutes before one o'clock.

Everyone, without knowing why, tried to make less noise. As if each person's noise could now disturb the precious task of time, which it was best not to interrupt.

Finally the bell rang brusquely, and it seemed to have rung when the general desire had already become irresistible. Then started the running—the running that would not stop until, two hours later, these men would return precipitously to their places at these same desks. These men found peace only here—here where they renounced the onerous burden of being men, where they acted like useful machines which, although technically antiquated, were still insuperably economical.

L'Esteve and L'Isidre left together and ran to the stop of the No. 58 bus which would take them to Corts.

"Do you know that En Jordana's coming back this evening?"

"Yes?"

"Yes. La Francisca told me that they gave her the telegram over the phone."

"What did it say?"

"Nothing; just that they were arriving."

"And nobody knows what the hell went on?"

"I don't think even One-Arm knows."

"He must be about to flip his lid."

"Who?"

"One-Arm. He always knows everything."

"But let me tell you, I don't understand this business of being five days without any news from them."

"It isn't like Senyor Joaquim."

"If it goes on any longer they'll raise the roof around here."

"You think so?"

"Judge for yourself. Haven't you noticed One-Arm getting more and more nervous every day? Acting like he's so important, and then in the end . . ."

"And Senyor Maurici . . ."

"Oh, him!"

"Senyor Joaquim's the only one that counts, the rest don't matter."

"Something must have happened."

"En Jordana'll tell us."

"Get in."

The No. 58 had come early. Now if they had luck with the traffic lights, he would have time to eat his tangerine sitting at the table.

"Look, I've always thought that a lot of the things that go on . . ."

"What?"

"The business of scrimping on the Christmas bonuses, and deducting the advances right away from your salary . . . you know what I mean. Take En Mascaró: you weren't here then and you don't know, but during the war he was head of the Comité, yes, that's right, of the Comité, and you know what he said to old Senyor Joaquim, you know, the one that died? He said: 'You're still the boss, you know. Nothing's changed around here'—just like that."

"Step to the front of the bus please; plenty of room up front."

"That's not bad, eh what? It's not everybody who'd do a thing like that."

"There's nobody kinder than En Mascaró. . . ."

"Well then, last September En Mascaró said to One-Arm: 'On Thursday it'll be twenty-five years that I've worked for the firm.' Twenty-five years, you realize what that means?"

"He must be getting along. . . ."

"Yes. But listen: you know what One-Arm answered?"

"What?"

"He said: 'Good Lord, how time flies!' Just like that. 'How time flies!' And 'Go jump in the lake.' "

"He's a son of a bitch."

"Sure."

"And he must know that En Mascaró . . ."

"You said it! And that's what I was getting to: I'll bet you anything that Senyor Joaquim doesn't know anything about this. It's only natural that it wouldn't occur to him whether En Mascaró's worked for the firm for twenty-five years or not."

"Senyor Joaquim's got so much to think about . . ."

"You said it. That's what I mean when I said if he knew about what was going on . . . things would be different. You can be sure of that."

NINETEEN

WHEN THE IDIOT saw En Pere Jordana crossing the patio and carrying the suitcases out to the car, he scratched his head. This was his way of saying good-by.

In any case he had made a special point of being there when they left, instead of going into the woods as he did every morning. His presence—his mere presence—was to be taken as an instinctive proof of respect, or perhaps it was only a matter of irresistible curiosity.

It looked as if it were going to rain again.

The old witch had offered them the little jug of her liquor, for the road. She imagined the expedition to a region she had never seen as being an extraordinarily long adventure. They refused the liquor, but they couldn't avoid allowing the happy outcome of their trip to be entrusted to four leaves of a mysterious plant which were mixed with four handfuls of white rabbit fur and then burned rapidly.

Nothing, however, was so distressing as accepting the parting look of the girl with the ecstatic eyes. It was a look that pained one precisely because it was without purpose, because it was tragically inexpressive. Leaving this girl was as difficult as leaving a drowning man.

"You haven't forgotten anything, Jordana?"

No, he hadn't forgotten anything. But he went back to make sure, for if they forgot something they would never come back to get it.

And suddenly he had the feeling that in fact he had left something behind in this house—something which had become invisible and which he could no longer recover.

When he went back out onto the patio, the first bit of breeze brought him a dry odor of hazelnuts which pulsated against his skin.

"We aren't going to have very good weather," said Senyor Joaquim as he pulled his scarf up over the nape of his neck.

"We might have some rain, but at least it isn't cold."

Why did these final moments seem to take so long? The air still held the first light of day, and Senyor Joaquim as well as En Pere Jordana moved about in the patio at a slow, rural tempo, as if their blood and thoughts had acquired the deep rhythm of the valley.

Finally everything was ready and En Pere opened the car door for Senyor Joaquim. It was a ritual act, which remained artificial and plastic, as if from some ridiculous ballet, amid the dust of the patio.

The motor began to throb, and it was quickly answered by the ducks—and it was as if these cries were the voice expressing the confused exaltation of the old woman, the idiot, and the girl. It gave them a strange sense of anguish to leave while the ducks were quacking; it was like betraying or squashing something.

And suddenly things lost their stability. From the window of the car they could see each object begin to be displaced: the house, the irrigation tank, the cart in the corner, the idiot with a lock of hair hanging down over his forehead, the old woman, black and bell-shaped, and the girl—now for the first time he realized that she was thin, very thin—and the trees and the well, everything was being uprooted, wavering, progressively losing its volume and ending by looking like a decal stuck to the window.

While they were on the dirt road, all this still formed a part of the landscape, but when the car came out onto the highway, Senyor Joaquim and En Jordana felt that they had entered the mainstream of their return, the path that led forcibly to the end.

"You aren't smoking, Jordana?"

"Yes, Senyor."

En Pere Jordana had not yet had time to think whether or not he would smoke. During all these days he had smoked in front of Senyor Joaquim without giving a thought as to whether or not he should. But now that he was behind the wheel, and Senyor Joaquim had spoken, he remembered that on the trip out, in the same situation, smoking had always been something implicitly against the rule, a secret rebellion.

"You aren't smoking, Jordana?" had been an invitation to smoke. He picked out an Ideal with his fingertips and put it between his lips. "Something's happened," he thought, "between the trip out and the trip back." Something which made him expel the smoke forcibly and hold the steering wheel with vast confidence.

"Don't push it too hard, Jordana," said Senyor Joaquim, smiling.

Out of the corner of his eye he saw the familiar image of Senyor Joaquim's round, pale hands resting on his stomach, and occasionally they would disentwine and re-entwine in a different way. These hands were very different from his own, but now he knew them well for he had taken their pulse.

Senyor Joaquim took a deep breath.

"Do you feel all right?" asked En Jordana.

"Fine. I was just thinking that today we'd be in Barcelona."

Now they were travelling along an unending straight stretch and slowly gaining speed.

"I won't forget it , Jordana."

Faster. The straight stretch they were devouring kept on being renewed at the other end. En Pere Jordana redoubled his attention. "I won't forget it, Jordana, I won't forget it, Jordana, I won't forget it."

"Don't push it too hard," Senyor Joaquim repeated.

Did he mean something else by the phrase *don't push it,* En Pere thought for a moment. But it kept on sounding, twisted in through the heart of the motor, and he couldn't silence it. "I won't forget it, Jordana, I won't forget it, I won't forget it. . . ."

There wouldn't be time to forget it. Barcelona was near, and he, as he pressed on the accelerator, was drawing nearer to it every minute. Barcelona, where there were the papers, the payrolls, the file cards, the cashiers, and the money. Senyor Joaquim would be there to see it all soon.

"It doesn't look like rain."

Surely, at another time, he would have said: "It's going to rain."

Senyor Joaquim was looking distractedly out the window. He would not be able to forget it, that much was certain. There were supposed to be people who were suddenly converted, who received grace and for whom everything became clear. It had been the reverse for him. He had also had a kind of intuition, he had *known* that behind this man there was a world of unknown things, but this new light, instead of bringing him peace of mind, had brought him preoccupations.

First of all he had to discuss it with En Maurici. And he was afraid of En Maurici. In the solitude of the dark kitchen he had perceived En Maurici's reaction with extraordinary precision. For quite a while now he had known that En Maurici was an unusual sort of person. The sort who, in everything he did, had always gone much further than himself. In matters of artistic taste, of gastric demands, and of women. And he had a presentiment that now also En Maurici would go further than he. Further, not to bring him peace of mind, but rather to bring him preoccupations. He would go to a point where he himself would be unable to follow—as he had been unable to follow him in his taste for Picasso.

He rubbed his finger against the windshield and drew some straight lines which were slowly erased by the fogging glass.

And he knew that if he didn't discuss it he would never be able to resolve anything; for he would never be able to forget.

It was pretty watching the lines being erased. . . .

And he would not be able to.

The smoke from En Pere Jordana's cigarette struck him in the face. He coughed.

Why did it have to be he who had the revelation? Why couldn't it have been En Coma Devesa, En Puig Sala, En Farré, or any of the manufacturers whom he saw every month or two to discuss taxes, social legislation, and exports?

And then he realized that everything was the result of chance. It was chance that En Pere Jordana was blowing smoke in his face, that En Pere Jordana was there next to him, had carried him over his shoulder, had cleaned his wounds and watched over him at night. In reality revelation was nothing more than contact.

Surely all men were surrounded with a kind of glue, and it was dangerous to get too near them. It was a thin layer of glue with infinite elasticity; it permitted one to draw away, but it could never be broken.

En Pere thought about his obsession again. Having something happen before he turned forty. Having more money, more children.

Money was everything.

He might even get two thousand pesetas. Every month, one

after the other. Two thousand! The kid's school, a steak from time to time, some nylon socks. This was one of his dreams: to have some nylon socks, which wouldn't tear and wouldn't have to be darned.

You were right, Maria. This was our opportunity. Hiding a hundred pesetas away in the closet for years, just in case.

He opened and shut his eyes several times, and then finally rubbed them with the palm of his hand.

Everything had been so easy, everything was now so clear!

"I won't forget it, Jordana."

A great man, that Senyor Joaquim.

"This is a fine stretch of road, isn't it?"

La Maria would ask him: "Tell me what happened, Pere." And when he finished explaining, she would say: "Are you absolutely sure he'll keep it in mind?"

"Take my word for it. I took good care of him, and not with any ulterior motive, if you know what I mean. What could I do except take care of him? And he said: 'I won't forget it, Jordana.' Just like that."

"All right, but who knows what he meant when he said he wouldn't forget it?"

"What do you think? It can't mean anything else but a raise, can it?"

"No, obviously it can't mean anything else. . . ."

"Don't worry. It's a sure thing!"

Yes, it's a sure thing. Wasn't that what he wanted?

And suddenly he realized what he was doing and threw away the cigarette he was almost finished with anyhow.

"Excuse me. Did the smoke bother you, Senyor Joaquim?"

Senyor Joaquim turned around and looked at him, and En Pere Jordana could have sworn that his eyes were filled with an opaque, mysterious cloud of smoke.

"We could make Lleida in time for lunch, Senyor Joaquim, even though it might be a bit late."

"Yes."

"That way we could take it easier this afternoon."

"Yes."

You could see he was happy, thought En Joaquim Civit. You only had to get him a little wound up and En Jordana would start in talking.

He was happy, and *he* was the *cause* of it. Strange. Then on the other hand, why should he worry about a man who was happy?

He had also worried one day, however, about the dog they had to have put away because of old age—although it still wagged its tail when it saw him. He had also worried about the children from the orphan asylum—even though they used to go down the street singing.

And then he understood the painfulness and gravity of his problem: he was, at the same time, equal and superior to En Pere Jordana. He *knew* the dog was going to die, he *knew* the condition of the children, and he *knew* what sort of person En Jordana was capable of becoming—something which En Jordana himself did not know.

It pained him to *know* his own superiority—because it made him responsible.

"It's a pretty village, isn't it, Senyor Joaquim?"

A little village with its four houses facing the highway open-mouthed. Two women talking in a doorway turned to watch them pass.

On the other hand, Senyor Joaquim thought, if he had to worry about everyone . . . These two women, for example. Why shouldn't he worry as much about these two women, or all the inhabitants of the village, as he did about En Jordana, or En Vila, or En Manelet, or any of the other employees in the office?

He could have been that old man who, at the other end of the village, was weaving a basket larger than himself. . . .

To worry about everyone, because everyone contained a bit of oneself, because all men were equal, and yet, he did not know why, *not* equal . . .

En Jordana looked at him a moment.

Was Senyor Joaquim really feeling well?

But if all men were to preoccupy him, there were only a few with whom he had to be occupied: those near him. He had to begin with those who participated most in his own life.

But how, when, in what way?

La Lluïsa wanted to go to Italy this spring.

It was only natural for her to want to go to Italy. Her cousin Remei had gone there last year, and you couldn't talk to her five minutes without having her mention the Duomo of Milan, the Signoria of Florence or the *delicious* coastline near La Spezia. . . . It was only natural for La Lluïsa to want to see it too, and moreover it was quite feasible; there was no impediment to their going to Italy this spring.

But in spite of this . . . Was it possible that from now on, every time he started to spend fifteen or twenty thousand pesetas, he would think of En Jordana, or En Vila, or En Manelet, even if just for a moment? Was it possible that he would think of them as an obstacle?

His conscience had always been at ease. Yes, he'd had some evil thoughts and that sort of thing, but that was only natural. But it had never occurred to him when he went to confession—he confessed at Easter, on the Feast of the Assumption in August, and he then took advantage of the following day, which was his saint's day, to take communion, and at mass on Christmas Eve—it had never occurred to him to wonder whether he could spend ten or fifteen thousand pesetas to go to Italy, or to buy some paintings, or perhaps to install a swimming pool in the house at Cardedeu.

It was grotesque to imagine that all this could have some relation to morality. The most demanding confessors would limit themselves to saying rapidly: "I suppose you have fulfilled your obligations as a husband, as the father of a family, and as the director of a concern . . ." He could have brought in records and documents as evidence. . . .

Perhaps, in fact, he didn't feel completely well. He seemed possessed by a disagreeable sense of confusion, and thoughts came and went without his being able to control them sufficiently.

He had a deep feeling that something was hatching within him, and that the symptoms, including his present feeling of vagueness, were all significant.

"Where would you like to eat, Senyor Joaquim?" En Pere Jordana asked as they entered Lleida.

"Let's see if we can find some nice place. . . ."

Had it been up to him to choose, En Jordana would have picked La Manduca, but he didn't dare suggest it to Senyor Joaquim. They left the car in the Plaza de España and headed for the beginning of the Calle Mayor. Beneath the colonnade, En Pere looked for a restaurant that Senyor Joaquim might like. And he had few qualms about pushing open a door, for in the narrow street the cold cut like a sword.

It was their last meal together. They both used similar napkins, were served by the same waiter who was equally pleasant to both of them, and drank from the same bottle of wine. That night Senyor Joaquim would dine at one end of his long table, and the six light bulbs lit up among the twenty-four of the large crystal chandelier would give out on the walls and on his face a thousand little reflections, as if he were eating beneath a private night sky.

En Pere Jordana would eat with incomprehensible appetite, wiping the bottom of his soup plate clean of olive oil, and La Maria's gaze would pass in wonder from En Pere's indefatigable fingers to his lips, which would go on uttering words between pieces of bread, and from his lips to his eyes, illuminated by a joy more intense than the yellow light from the naked light bulb.

214

Now they were eating together for the last time, and more than together, they were eating face to face.

One could only hear the little noises produced by En Pere when he put his fork down on the plate, when he clumsily bumped one glass against the other, or when he made any one of those slight movements characteristic of a man eating with absolute freedom of mind. Senyor Joaquim, on the other hand, having been better brought up, made no noise—and moreover was silent; he said not a word.

"It's a shame La Maria couldn't have come along on this trip," En Pere thought. There was something—a joyous light or an intoxicating odor—rising from the napkins to his face and giving him irresistible animation. "It's a shame." But this summer they would take a trip. He, La Maria, and the child. If only an excursion along the coast. The first year of their marriage, before they had the child, every now and then on a Sunday they would go swimming at Badalona. How much time had passed since then! And something more than time: those desires, joys, and satisfactions which little by little were lost beneath the continual, implacable assault of passing hours.

"I think the doctor was right, Senyor Joaquim. Basically we were very lucky; it was a miracle that we came out of it all right."

Strangely enough, he scarcely listened to Senyor Joaquim's answer. He could not imagine that they might not agree: it was all so obvious!

"What luck we had!"

("If this fellow continues to feel so happy," thought En Joaquim Civit, "there'll come a moment when I won't be able to stand it.")

For En Joaquim Civit had realized that, in fact, this man had no reason to be really happy. If this man could be *really* happy, he would now feel as tranquil as he had a week before.

And while he listened to him talk and watched him eat, his own thoughts were in a state of total confusion. He realized that his worries and scruples seemed to increase in a vacuum, nourishing themselves only on him, devouring him, without En Jordana's having the slightest cognizance of this fact.

Later, in Barcelona, would it have to be he, he alone, who would decide that it was necessary to do everything possible to bring about greater contact with the men, to impose the idea of basic equality, and to better the lot of his employees not only in a purely economic way?

When it came time for coffee and Senyor Joaquim had ordered two cognacs, he twirled the little glass between his fingers and said, slowly: "Jordana . . . There's something we have to discuss."

En Pere's hand trembled on the table, as if it wished to take flight in order to protect his defenseless eyes or mouth, but in the end it did not dare.

"Jordana . . . What would you think of two thousand five hundred a month?"

En Jordana looked up at him, picked up his glass, and drank. Senyor Joaquim pushed his chair back and got up.

He would have liked to know what En Pere Jordana was thinking—he had muttered an inaudible phrase, undoubtedly "thank you." He would have liked to know if his only reaction was gratitude.

("Maria," thought En Pere, "Maria, it's a sure thing now! What we were hoping for—what we needed. This really was our chance, you were right. And it didn't come too late. Another child, and the steaks, and the kid's school, and the nylon socks.")

Senyor Joaquim watched him put on his overcoat with the gesture of someone protecting himself, of someone who, in a certain sense, had decided to take no interest in what went on around him, for something within him sufficed.

How could it be that money should be so important as to suffice for him, that the solution should be so easy, grotesque, and disproportionate?

En Joaquim Civit was thinking of all the other employees.

216

These two thousand five hundred pesetas that En Jordana received purely as a token of gratitude, he had not given out of gratitude. It was a decision he had taken knowing perfectly well that it bound him to innumerable future decisions.

Why did En Jordana disengage his own situation from that of the other En Jordanas?

When En Pere Jordana opened the car door for him, En Joaquim Civit thought that it was not the result of egoism, but of ignorance.

In any case he sank back into the seat with a feeling of deep fatigue—something he had eaten was proving difficult to digest.

TWENTY

They passed the Bruc hills surrounded by a thick mist. En Pere Jordana was driving with infinite care: there was no use taking risks now that there was so much to lose. When he approached a corner, he almost brought the car to a standstill.

As they entered Martorell, they passed a truck half turned over on the side of the road, with the wooden back all broken.

"It's bad weather to be driving in," said En Pere. "And these truckdrivers go like madmen."

Senyor Joaquim wasn't afraid. En Jordana had turned out to be very prudent—extraordinarily prudent in all ways. In a certain sense, it was this very Jordana who, for a few hours now, had been infecting him with the sense of prudence which was slowly overcoming him.

He tried to take advantage of these last minutes of solitude in order to evaluate his future actions. Within an hour he would see En Maurici. He would see him and would have to talk to him. Within an hour he would once again enter a vertiginous world, a world which demanded constant activity and gave one responsibilities without one's realizing it.

This was the lesson he had received from his vacation.

Later there would no longer be any opportunity for reflection.

When they passed through a village he would not have known but for En Jordana's announcing joyfully "Pallejà!" he looked in wonder at all the closed doors and the deserted streets. And so near Barcelona! This abandoned village, he thought, must also have its problems, and it occurred to him that such sullenness was nothing more than discretion, a deep-seated shyness before the strangers who were constantly passing through and looking at their faces. Discretion, prudence, and cowardice: the three sensations struggling within him.

And everything had seemed so clear back there in the mountains! It had then seemed as if the only possible solution were to burst out talking. He had imagined a conversation with En Maurici, perfectly logical and sensible. It had seemed completely sensible to him.

He looked at En Pere Jordana out of the corner of his eye for a moment. En Jordana had obviously changed. There, he had talked about his wife, his child, and his poverty. They had exchanged memories of their parents. En Jordana had never, in fact, complained, but in each gesture, in each word, and above all in his mere presence, there was something profoundly pathetic. He could no longer identify this man grasping the steering wheel with the Jordana who drank a bit too much liquor. . . . This Pere was so serene, calm, and contented that Senyor Joaquim began to think that maybe his worries had been excessive and that En Jordana had had a bit of fever that had fortunately passed.

Perhaps he was just playing with all these ideas in order to achieve the same state of serenity and silence. Within an hour he would see En Maurici, and then what should he say, what should he do?

"He'll know the solution; he's an unusual man, intelligent and humane (this he had never denied). He'll dispel my doubts and give me a valid answer," he thought once again. He squeezed his elbows in against his ribs and contracted his legs. It was cold inside the car.

"And La Lluïsa . . . La Lluïsa, if she knows I'm coming, has probably left her bridge session. A fine woman, La Lluïsa. But how could one present her with a problem that . . . all at once, like this . . . ?

"She might say: 'What's the problem? That problem was taken care of years ago.' "

He also thought it had been resolved. He had always thought so. And it was precisely for this reason that he should fear nothing.

"We're almost there, Senyor Joaquim."

No, they weren't there yet. No use exaggerating. They had just passed Esplugues and they were heading for the Diagonal.

("Must think about it a bit more. These last few days have been very strange.")

"They're almost over now, these days which have been so strange—right, Jordana?"

"Yes, Senyor. They're almost over."

Obviously. Now the moment was coming when he would have to get his bearings again. The accident would be a thing of the past—and with it all the uneasiness it brought, and the house lost in the valley and the mysterious people and the unaccustomed climate.

To get one's bearings, think clearly ("for this uneasiness had undeniable value, and the problem is really interesting, really transcendental, in both emotional and social terms") and finally make a decision, later on, cautiously. Later on. There was no hurry.

"It's a pretty sight, isn't it?"

The city lights were starting to go on. From the top of the Diagonal, the car descended with increasing speed, with a definite feeling of decision.

"One of these days I'll get rid of this headache," he thought.

For it was a headache. And Senyor Joaquim did not yet know

that a man who suffered from it for a single day could never be completely cured of it. There were people, however, who became accustomed to it, and if they managed to do so long enough, it became like those irritating sounds one no longer hears and finally forgets about.

"It's happening again; ridiculous": every time he went rapidly downhill in a car, his ears became blocked and he didn't hear a thing.

He suddenly realized that En Pere Jordana was moving his lips. Had he said something? It would be annoying if just at this moment he had said something really important.

Out on the sidewalk, at the door of the office, there was a clerk keeping an eye out for them, and he went in to announce their arrival.

En Pere Jordana did a meticulous job of parking the car. He got out and opened Senyor Joaquim's door.

En Maurici and L'Alsina, the office manager, came out to greet them.

"What happened?" asked En Maurici. "Such a long time without hearing from you, and now . . ."

"An accident?" guessed L'Alsina, pointing to the new red paint covering the damaged parts of the car.

Senyor Joaquim smiled reassuringly.

"Yes, a minor accident, *of no importance.*"

En Pere Jordana had set both suitcases down on the ground. En Maurici looked at the two men who had just arrived and were standing next to each other, and he tried to notice some trace of what had happened.

"If you're in as good shape as you were when you left . . . If nothing's happened . . ."

Senyor Joaquim made a gesture with his hands as if to say: "See for yourself."

A trolley passed, making a din as if it were demolishing some invisible building, nothing of which remained in the silence that followed.

Then Senyor Maurici pointed to the enormous suitcase containing the samples and commanded En Pere Jordana:

"Don't leave it there on the ground. Take it into the office."

For a hundredth of a second, Senyor Joaquim bowed his head and waited.

"We can't talk here in the street," he thought. And besides, was it really necessary? He still didn't see things clearly enough. Maybe someday . . . But . . .

En Pere Jordana didn't hesitate. En Pere Jordana bent down from the waist—like someone bowing to an indisputable power —and joyfully picked up the sample case. He went into the office, and when everyone looked at him from behind a desk, there fell on his forehead, like a gray sacrament, like a bit of tremulous ash, the last rays of the day coming through the skylight.